Unstrung

by

Cynthia Morrow

TELEMACHUS PRESS

Cover Designed by Telemachus Press, LLC

Cover Art:
Additional cover images used from photos taken by the author.

Published by Telemachus Press, LLC
http://www.telemachuspress.com

Visit the author website:
http://www.cynthiamorrowmysteries.com

ISBN: 978-1-940745-19-0 (eBook)
ISBN: 978-1-940745-20-6 (Paperback)

Version 2013.12.16

Printed in the United States of America

10 9 8 7 6 5 4 3 2 1

What Readers Are Saying About
The Blanchard House Mysteries

With the dexterity of a trained musician and an ear attuned to human frailty, Morrow has orchestrated a delightful mix of music and mayhem. Her combination of witty dialogue, tight plot line, and characters real enough to invite over for coffee leaves readers of the first Blanchard House Mystery eagerly awaiting an encore!

Elaine Woods, author and
producer of OpenMic/Local Voices for radio

Cynthia Morrow captures the essence of the musician's life. Her wit and intelligence, coupled with a thorough knowledge of music, makes for a captivating and rollicking fun read.

Jack Cousin, Los Angeles Philharmonic

Morrow has subtitled this book, "A Blanchard House Mystery." If she's hinting at the possibility of this becoming a series, it's reason to rejoice. She has created engaging characters, a wonderful setting, and most importantly, the chops to deliver a grade-A read. Encore!

Blue Ink Review, April 2013

But the best part for me was the guided tour into the world of professional musicians ... a world where the right instrument is worth killing for. Don't be put off by the prologue, read on—when this writer hits her stride in Chapter One she will entertain you no end.

Lisa Murphy, Bookshelves: Mystery/Thriller

Cynthia Morrow has created a cast of intriguing characters who bring the world of music and mystery to life between the covers of her books.

Cecylia Arzewski, Former Concertmaster
of Atlanta Symphony

Murder and music harmonize seamlessly in this latest mystery from Cynthia Morrow.

Mary Daheim

To Gary. Merry Christmas.

Unstrung

PROLOGUE

Los Angeles, California, 1961

THE UNRELENTING HEAT of a late August afternoon shimmered on the concrete pavement in oily waves,
the same illusory curves that danced on the sunbaked
hood of the sleek blue Cadillac Biarritz convertible as it
slowly cruised the residential streets of Hollywood.
Tinted windows and dark wraparound glasses hid the
driver from the stares of appraising pedestrians as he
carefully scanned both sides of the street. He turned right
onto Franklin Avenue and continued for a few blocks,
idling in front of one decrepit building after another,
eventually easing the car left, up into Beachwood
Canyon. Enormous white letters spelling
HOLLYWOOD now loomed directly ahead, beckoning
him up into the tree-shaded hills and away from the
bustle of the increasingly sordid business district below.

A small "For Rent" sign had been discreetly placed in a second-floor window on the opposite side of the pleasant boulevard. Tall stands of bird of paradise plants and bursts of deep crimson bougainvillea hugged the walls of a white stucco Spanish-style building. It had been designed and lavishly executed in the twenties, a boom time for the burgeoning movie business. The hills of Hollywood were dotted with a surprising number of these exotic buildings, built for a growing population of motion-picture stars and newly wealthy film moguls, elegant Spanish villas with wrought-iron balconies and long casement windows or the occasional Moorish minaret. Beachwood Canyon had been the movie industry's first playground, retaining even now the echoes of its exotic past.

Ralph glanced up from his reading, the repeated clacking of cheap plastic bracelets on his wife's bony wrists wearing on his delicate nerves. He watched her push aside the floral-print draperies covering the long windows of the apartment manager's first-floor suite. Doris, a fortyish bottle blonde, was squinting directly into the afternoon sun, seemingly transfixed by something or other that was probably none of her business— or so he thought.

"Hey, Ralph, get a load a this," she called over her shoulder. "That's one swell car parkin' out front, a brand new Caddy, a convertible too, with that fancy kinda grill you like so much. The top's up. Can't imagine why in this heat, 'less it's got air-conditioning. Oh, *c'mere*! You gotta see what's gettin' out of it. I think this guy's a movie star or somethin'. He sure is gorgeous enough."

"Ah, that's just your Trenton talkin' again," her husband, a shriveled and balding fifty-something, told her, returning to his magazine.

"Why can't you just admit you're jealous, Ralph? Just 'cause no one'd ever look twice at you—"

"You been readin' too many a them trashy magazines, Doris. You're always thinkin' that some broad ahead a you in the supermarket is Zsa Zsa or Lucy or somebody else she ain't. They're all just wannabes out here—that's all. Fakes. Everybody in LA is tryin' ta look like they're somebody, but they ain't." He pulled himself up reluctantly from his seat at the kitchen table when the doorbell rang.

Before him stood a tall, well-proportioned man in his mid-thirties, for once as truly impressive a visitor as his wife had described, elegantly turned out in cream linen slacks, bone Italian loafers, and a short-sleeved yellow boucle shirt that was casually open at the neck. There was something familiar about this guy, perhaps a certain resemblance to Gary Cooper. Yeah, that was it, Gary Cooper.

Ralph held the door open and invited the stranger in, feeling insignificant and just a tad resentful of this much younger man whose air of self-assurance bordered on arrogance. The manager glanced quickly at his wife, noting with some annoyance that Doris had hastily pulled out the bobby pins that had been holding some screw curls in place around her forehead. Now he could see that she was alternately involved in smoothing out her tight pencil skirt, an act that necessitated the flashing of her long blood-red nails and multi-hued bracelets, and clearing a place for the potential renter next to her on the sofa by brushing aside some fan magazines and a half-eaten package of sandwich cookies.

Ralph was relieved when the visitor ignored Doris and remained standing just inside the doorway.

"I'd like to rent the apartment if it's available to-day," the younger man said, a lingering trace of the East Coast in his voice. "How large is it? Is it furnished, and how much do you want for it?"

"You sound like you're from New York. We're from Jersey ourselves."

The stranger checked his watch.

"You're not much for small talk, are ya, mister? Well, that's okay by me. I'm not all that social myself. Doris is always tellin' me I should chat it up more when we go someplace, but I always say, 'Why bother? Who cares what I have to say?'" Ralph took a breath and looked up hopefully at his potential renter. No encouragement was forthcoming. "So let's get down ta business. Here's the deal. The apartment comes furnished, all very classy. The owner had one a them swishy decorators come in and spiff it all up. He was a pip, he was!" Ralph looked up into the lenses of his visitor's dark glasses, seeing himself ridiculously distorted in each lens.

The potential renter looked around the apartment and sighed impatiently. Ralph drew a breath and went on at a faster pace, eager to get through his duties and return to the car magazine he'd been obliged to leave at the kitchen table.

"Lessee. Ya got new Venetian blinds in the bedroom, just one bedroom, an' drapes in the livin' room. Supposed ta look Mediterranean if ya like that kinda thing. Doris, she thinks it's just swell, but I dunno. Seems kinda phony if ya ask me." Doris shot him a deadly look, but he ignored her.

"We're talkin' two hunnert an' fifty smackers a month, first and last, an' a hunnert fer yer cleanin' deposit. A six-month lease. No pets. Well, maybe a canary. Who'd know? No paintin' the walls or makin' holes, either. I'm supposed ta ask for references, too. So, ya still interested? Ya wanna see it?"

"Not really. It sounds perfect. Can I have it today? And about those references," the younger man said, stepping farther into the living room and pulling a substantial roll of bills from the hip pocket of his perfectly

v

creased linen slacks, "I have them right here." As the manager and his wife exchanged knowing looks, he deliberately counted out a stack of hundred-dollar bills and laid them face up on the coffee table in front of them. "That should take care of the first six months and the deposits."

"I should say so!" Doris piped up. "We got a coupla keys we can hand over right away, haven't we, Ralph? The original and a spare. I'll just go get 'em," she said, raising her skirt a few inches above her knees as she stood up, giving her new tenant a sly smile and a good look at her backside as she sashayed down the hallway toward a peg-board full of keys. "If you need anything, honey, and I mean anything at all, you just let me know. Ralph gets up pretty early and goes to bed around nine, but I'm up 'til all hours."

Ralph started to protest but was cut off by his wife's return and the handing over of the keys. He watched the way she placed them carefully in the stranger's upturned hand, her fingertips gently brushing his palm.

"Don't worry about the formalities, either. Just call me Doris. I'd be more than happy ta help ya fill out all the paperwork later today if ya wanna move your stuff in right now."

"I'll just bet you would," Ralph mumbled under his breath.

"Thanks, that would be great," the man said, turning abruptly and heading to his car.

As the door closed behind him, the manager snarled, "That's just swell, Doris. Who the hell does he think he is? The Lone Ranger? We don't even know the guy's name."

"Just count the bills, honey. We'll get his name later. I think he's gonna work out just fine."

***

The backseat of the Cadillac was crammed with valises, shoeboxes, and custom-tailored suits still on their wooden hangers. The convertible had been a surprise birthday present the last week of June, something he'd only dreamed of owning, air-conditioning, power windows, a sterling example of her generosity—or so he'd believed at the time. This afternoon, speeding along the Arroyo Seco Parkway away from his life with her and everything he'd ever held dear, it suddenly came to him with blinding clarity that the car had been meant as so much more than that. It was her parting gift as well. This morning, she'd been firm about the immediacy of his leaving, and he understood for the first time the full magnitude of her intention and his own powerlessness in the face of it. It had been a long time since he'd allowed anything to stand in his way. He was a concertmaster, a powerful player in the Hollywood studios, and yet he could see clearly now that he was no match for the woman he loved, nor could he save her.

He unlocked the passenger side, gingerly touching the sun-seared metal of the handle, yanking it just hard enough to make the heavy door swing open and wedge itself into the grass alongside the curb, releasing at once a wall of intense heat and the achingly sensual smell of her favorite summer perfume. He pushed aside a pile of his heaviest coats and carefully removed several shaped, alligator-leather violin cases and a small framed painting that had been resting facedown beneath the winter clothing on the front seat. Everything else was allowed to remain just as it was, locked once again inside the convertible's oven-like interior.

He made his way purposefully through the arched entrance to a well-maintained, Spanish-style courtyard crowded with bougainvillea, wildly blooming roses, jasmine, and honeysuckle. He walked quickly past a splashing fountain and up the tiled staircase that led to the massive wooden door of his new residence, resting the violin cases and the painting on the bristled welcome mat. The key moved smoothly in the well-oiled lock, he noted with some satisfaction, surely a good sign.

Cool air from inside roughly plastered walls surged outward as he stepped across the threshold. He found the drastic change in temperature oddly soothing. The heavy door shut firmly behind him. Only the deep resonance of its closing permeated the tomblike silence of his new apartment. He headed directly down the spacious hallway to the bedroom, never turning his head. His hands, which had been generally steady until now, began to exhibit a slight tremor as he gently set the violin cases on the bed, opening them one by one to lovingly check on his beloved instruments. He'd hated leaving them in the car for even a short while in the summer heat, but they seemed to be none the worse for it. Carefully placing the violins back in their cases, he set them on the polished wooden floor and pushed them gently beneath the bed with a well-shod foot. Next, he held the small painting at arm's length, squinting to somehow see it differently, letting his fingers move gently across its surface, finally propping it unsteadily on top of a tall bureau opposite the bed and against the stark white of the wall, carefully angling its gilded frame so he might observe it clearly even while he was lying down.

He stepped into the bathroom and flushed the toilet several times to make sure it worked properly. Only then did he lower himself onto the edge of the bed and remove his shoes. Fully clothed, he stretched out on top of the floral damask spread and matching bolster, eyes wide open, staring dully at parallel strips of light and shadow reflected narrowly through the Venetian blinds onto the smooth plaster ceiling above him. Eventually, he slept.

Two days later, he emerged into the courtyard, emptied his car of all his worldly goods, arranged them neatly in the small closet and the chest of drawers, and signed a lease.

All truths are easy to understand once they are discovered; the point is to discover them.
—Galileo Galilei

Chapter 1

WHILE MY EX-HUSBAND, Dennis Littleton, and I were still together and masquerading as the perfect Hollywood couple, we were invited to a swank dinner party based on a game titled "How to Host a Murder." My ex gargled stiff double scotches all night and topped off the evening by vomiting in our host's new koi pond. I, on the other hand, solved the virtual "murder" before we'd even tasted the hors d'oeuvres, which were curried cheese balls, if memory serves. It didn't seem fair that *I* was the one accused of ruining the evening for everyone. Needless to say, we were never invited back.

Shortly thereafter, things changed. I got dumped and took back my maiden name, Althea Stewart. Dennis got the house in Malibu and a rich new wife. Since then, I've avoided parties whenever possible; however, it's been years now since that hideous debacle, and I figured the statute of limitations was running out. Besides, I finally had something to celebrate.

Nobel Prize winners and poet laureates are probably charming company at cocktail parties and such, but
if you're in the market for really good eaters, it's
professional musicians all the way. That's why my best
friend, Grace, and I invited a bunch of them. We'd just
spent weeks planning a lavish Christmas tea, all for the
satisfaction of seeing our cherished musical friends and
colleagues eating their heads off and generally giving
your average plague of locusts a considerable run for
their money. This was our way of announcing our
recent purchase of Blanchard House, a rambling old
mansion in Kirkland, Washington. It was also a launch
party for our newest venture, a private music school, a
shared dream of ours ever since we'd met in LA almost
twenty years before, two sexy, young, Hollywood
studio musicians laying down string tracks for disco
records. We're still considered pretty sexy, just not as
young.

Anyway, the plan entailed me torturing the young on
violin and viola, with Grace doing the same on cello and
possibly voice. For the past month, we'd anguished over
the guest list, the decorations, and of course, the food,
making sure that everything was as close to perfect as we
could make it. Althea Stewart and Grace Sullivan had
their hard-earned reputations as formidable hostesses to
uphold, and we were determined to pull off this latest
shindig in grand style. Instead, it seems that we were un-
knowingly creating our own version of the same ghoul-

ish parlor game that had been haunting me since my former life in LA. Believe me, hosting a real murder isn't as much fun as you might think.

At precisely five o'clock on that fateful Sunday afternoon in December, the doorbell chimed its melodious Westminster Cathedral greeting, and in poured a crowd of rain-soaked guests who had obviously arrived *en masse* at Blanchard House long before the appointed time. This unison entrance might have seemed eerie to others, but Grace and I were used to such highly predictable behavior by now. Classical musicians are punctual to a fault. We have to be. There are always so many people counting on us to be in the right place all together and on time, instruments tuned and ready to play, that we may easily be the most reliable group of professionals in the world. Studio hours and concert hall rental times are measured in hundreds of dollars per minute, so tardiness is never an option. I was pretty sure that most of our guests had been sitting in their cars, shivering and checking their cell phones for at least fifteen minutes, waiting until the exact time of the invitation to step onto the porch and ring the doorbell.

We'd managed to invite a number of local music teachers and freelance musicians to round out the guest list, one composed primarily of former colleagues, escapees from the LA studios from which Grace and I had happily fled, as well as a few Seattle Symphony members and their spouses.

Two young and aspiring violists, Tor Nordquist and his fiancée, Amy Lindal, led the parade across the threshold. They stepped inside briskly and shook themselves out, getting water all over the oriental carpet. Tor let out a soft whistle as he admired the grand staircase directly to the right of the entryway, which was draped with fresh fir swags and red velvet bows. All my friend Grace's efforts, I assured them. My dogs, Winnie and Bert, responded to that whistle immediately and dashed over to inspect the couple and sniff their outstretched hands.

Tor, tall and slim, appeared to tower over his short, plump girlfriend. Amy's pale blonde hair and blue eyes clearly bespoke her Nordic heritage. Both wore those knitted Norwegian hats with tassels and hanging earflaps that you see all over Seattle. The woolen, braided ties hung loose and bobbed when Amy spoke.

"This is the most elegant house I've ever seen, Althea! I hope you don't mind my asking, but how can you afford to heat it? It's tough just keeping our little rental house warm these days." Amy made a definite point, one that was constantly on my mind. We hadn't experienced our first power bill yet but were holding our collective breath. We also seemed to be going through our newly delivered cords of wood at an alarming rate.

"We'll probably start breaking up the kitchen chairs first and then move on to the coffee table and the smaller bookcases. You know the old joke about the difference between violas and violins," I said.

"Yup. Violas burn longer, but I think you should start with a cello or two just to be sure."

"Spoken like a true violist. Honestly, Amy, I have no idea what the utility bills are going to be every month if the weather stays this cold. I shudder to think."

Still, Grace and I were both beaming with pride as Andrew and Marilyn Litzky, appearing appropriately festive in brightly felted woolen scarves and gloves, stepped through the door and oohed and aahed at the carved balustrade and the inlaid oak floors. *As long as no one leans on one of those picturesque railings too hard, we'll be just fine,* I thought. Andrew was in the first violin section of the Seattle Symphony, and Marilyn was a well-respected oboist who frequently played for the ballet and opera. I'd known them both in LA since before they were even dating. They'd been a beautiful pair back then, young and in love, lots of curly hair, his sandy blonde, hers a deep chestnut. To an outside observer, it looked as if marriage agreed with them.

"My mother is here visiting, so we left Amelia with her. I hope you don't mind us not bringing her along," Marilyn said, referring to Amelia, their adorable and always welcome toddler. I'd rather been looking forward to playing the fairy godmother role, but apparently, it wouldn't be tonight. "Last time we looked in on them, my mother was sitting on the floor cross-legged, building castles with the wooden blocks, and Amelia was knocking them over and screeching with glee."

"Yes, I believe that particular game has always been a big hit with the younger set," I said and nodded.

"The last time my mother sat on the ground was during her brief stint as a Girl Scout when she was a pimply adolescent, and even then she hated it. But dignity apparently counts for nothing when it comes to her first and only grandchild. I don't think those two even know we're missing."

"I just wanted Marilyn all to myself for one night." Andrew Litzky put an arm around his wife and pulled her closer. "My mother-in-law's been here for a couple of weeks already." He turned to face Marilyn and pushed a stray curl out of her eyes. "I know you love her, honey, and I like her. I really do. But we needed a break! At least, I do." Andrew took his wife's puffy down coat and hung it up along with his ski parka on the bentwood coatrack near the door. They left their wet boots in the hall, headed into the living room in their stockinged feet, and were soon talking and laughing with other colleagues from the Seattle music scene.

Bert and Winnie, who were intent on doing their doggie jobs as official greeters, dutifully sniffed each new arrival and then padded into the living room to sit in front of the fireplace. Lydia, the calico, was sizing up the crowd, looking for the one person there who might have a distinct aversion to cats. She would undoubtedly stalk her unsuspecting prey until she could manage to snuggle herself into her victim's lap, purring melodiously and giving it her seductive all. Many a cat-hater has been charmed by Lydia's methods, and it's always satisfying to see her work her feline magic. As I watched her sidle up to a macho-looking trombonist, rubbing herself around his ankles and staring up at him adoringly, I realized that this evening would be no exception. The poor man would undoubtedly be flattered by such lavish attention and eventually wind up the evening by telling anyone willing to listen how much he finds himself admiring this particular cat, although he's never been a big fan of the species in general. It happens all the time. Many a lonely woman could learn a few tricks from observing Lydia in action and copying her surefire approach.

"What a stunning Christmas tree! There's nothing like a real fir tree, is there? And I haven't seen antique glass ornaments like this in years! It smells absolutely delicious in here." Delilah Cantwell inhaled deeply with her well-developed singer's lungs, puffing out her magnificent double-D chest and smiling as she gazed around the room. Strategically placed jars of fragrant candles were exuding wafts of cinnamon and bayberry all over the house, so there was plenty of sniffing to keep her busy. Delilah, a Junoesque mezzo soprano, was wearing the regulation Seattle party regalia, no makeup, a dark, shapeless, woolen sweater over a long, rumpled, peasant skirt, heavy tights, and Birkenstocks. I'd bet anything that there was a fabulous figure hiding under all that, but it was a well-kept secret. James Cantwell, her tall, lanky baritone of a husband, was rakishly attired in long cargo shorts, dark woolen socks, and hiking sandals.

Grace and I had obviously wasted hours on hair and makeup for this crowd, I mused. Grace looked like something out of *Town & Country* magazine, lovely in a flowing paisley skirt and a soft cardigan over an ivory silk blouse. With her honey-brown hair piled becomingly on top of her head, she might have given any English duchess a run for her money. I'd pulled on a cashmere turtleneck sweater and long tartan skirt in honor of the season. At the last minute, I'd added a Christmas brooch with matching earrings, and now I felt overdressed at my own party. You just can't win.

"James and I wondered who'd buy good old Blanchard House. It was on the market a long time. We're so relieved that it was you two and not some greedy developers," Delilah Cantwell said, peering into the kitchen and admiring the well-preserved, original tile on the counters and backsplash. "They'd have knocked the place down or turned it into tiny upscale condos with granite counters and sleek, designer kitchens. If I see another hunk of polished granite on anything other than a tombstone, I think I'll scream! It's become the latest must-have item for Kirkland real estate. Every house on the market within fifty miles apparently has exactly the same kitchen. You'd think no one could cook a meal without a huge slab of polished granite and stainless steel appliances."

"You have no idea how happy we are to have you ladies in the neighborhood, Althea," James Cantwell said, interrupting his wife's rant, "and not just because you've saved Blanchard House from the wrecking ball. We've really needed string teachers desperately on the east side for some time now, especially viola and cello. I'm betting that you and Grace will soon find yourselves with more students than you can handle."

Delilah and James Cantwell both sang professionally in the area and taught orchestra and chorus at our local high school. They'd been after me to volunteer as a string coach one afternoon a week, and I was thinking about it. They handed me a warm bottle of Chilean Riesling along with a cellophane-wrapped bouquet of wilting supermarket flowers and proceeded to find a seat in the living room.

"Humph!" That all-too-familiar throat clearing of Marvin Pratt immediately set my teeth on edge. "Who would have thought you girls would be foolish enough to take on an enormous project like this? It's falling apart, you know. What a disaster! Fortunately, I have the phone numbers of several excellent building contractors you might be interested in consulting. We did an extensive remodel at our house on Queen Anne last year, and it turned out rather well, if I must say so myself. It wasn't inexpensive, of course. Nothing top-notch ever is, but the results were well worth it, weren't they, Annabelle? Feel free to use my name when you talk to those contractors.

It will carry some real weight, I can assure you!" Marvin Pratt, former concertmaster of just about everything in LA, had arrived. He was blithely unaware of the comedic effect of that pronouncement coming from a man anyone would have to categorize as morbidly obese.

I struggled to stifle a laugh but only managed to turn it into a hacking cough. Annabelle Gardener Pratt, his long-suffering wife and an extraordinary violinist in her own right, hung back as Marv waddled in before her, taking up most of our hallway. He shrugged his enormous girth out of a black overcoat and cashmere scarf and tossed them at me, crushing the flowers I was still holding, not that those pathetic dyed carnations and bedraggled daisies didn't deserve a good crushing and then some, but I cringed nonetheless. Marv appeared to have gained even more weight than the last time I'd seen him, which hardly seemed possible. *It must be quite a strain on his heart*, I thought to myself, *if he indeed had one, to be carrying that much extra poundage.*

"Come, darling," he beckoned to his wife. "Let's get something to eat. You might want to grab us some seats over by the fireplace while I fill some plates. It's probably warmer there. It's drafty as anything in this old ruin, isn't it?"

Annabelle Pratt ignored him. She looked handsome, if thinner and more fragile than I'd ever seen her. Her classic Chanel suit hung limply on her petite frame. All the usual sparkle was missing from her amber eyes.

Nevertheless, she was elegantly turned out, her makeup perfect, if a bit more heavy-handedly applied than usual, every hair of her now-graying chignon artfully arranged.

"It's so kind of you to invite us, Althea, darling." Annabelle leaned over to air-kiss my cheek. "We hardly ever get out anymore, except to restaurants and the symphony. We heard Hilary Hahn play at Benaroya Hall last month. Did you go? No? A pity. She was marvelous, and of course, Marv insisted on going backstage afterward. He always enjoys giving up-and-coming young violin soloists the benefit of his expertise, you know," she said without a trace of irony. *She must really love the guy*, I thought to myself. Annabelle handed me a large box of chocolates decorated with silver foil and the requisite holiday bow, and a bottle of chilled and very expensive champagne. She hadn't forgotten my weakness for chocolates and, even though she herself has always been deathly allergic to them, she'd been kind enough to bring me a huge holiday box of See's Candies with Nuts and Chews, my absolute favorites. She extended her small, jeweled hand to Grace and gave her a gentle smile and another air kiss.

"I see you couldn't take it anymore," she murmured close to Grace's ear but loud enough for me to overhear. "You're very brave, and I know it wasn't easy, but I admire you for making the break."

"It was all Althea's doing really," Grace answered somewhat gaily. "She found this wonderful old house and twisted my arm until I promised to leave LA."

"Oh, I didn't mean that, my dear, although moving up here must have been quite a big step too. I meant leaving Rolfe. I'll bet you were relieved that you had the foresight to keep your maiden name. Grace Sullivan suits you perfectly, you know. You could never have been happy as Grace Kirchner. It sounds so terribly 'Swiss,' if you know what I mean. Brava!"

Poor Grace was temporarily stunned into immobility, looking like the work of a first-rate taxidermist. Annabelle, meanwhile, moved as smoothly as a Yankee clipper ship under full sail into the living room, gracefully passing through the sea of guests, leaving Grace to suck in her cheeks as she pondered this breathtaking pronouncement. I watched Marv guide his wife rather solicitously to a small English wing chair close to a warm, crackling fire. Bert and Winnie were soon putting their heads in Annabelle's lap while she petted them, looked deeply into their eyes, and told them in no uncertain terms what good dogs they were and how much she'd missed them.

"Humph! I see you got Rolfe's black leather Eames chair, Grace. I'm surprised he let it go." Marv, having accomplished his husbandly duty, had been padding slowly around the living room, visibly assessing the value of every possession in our new home, a sandwich in each of his meaty hands. Now he was standing intimidatingly close to Grace, observing her from his greater height as if she were a helplessly pinned insect under his microscope.

"He didn't want to let it go, Marv, believe me, but it wasn't his to keep. That chair belonged to my father. I brought it with me into the marriage," Grace said, sticking her chin up to look squarely into his jowly face.

"What a shame! Poor Rolfe always loved that chair. And I see you got some of his oils, too. Mmm. This salmon is really delicious. Annabelle, *Bellissima*, come try the salmon! There's lots here that isn't chocolate. Come taste these little lemony things!" Marv called across the room, turning briefly away from his smoldering hostess.

Grace's eyes were flashing dangerously, but she took a deep breath and pulled herself together. "No, Marv, I hate to correct you, but those paintings were always mine. I purchased them in New York before I ever met Rolfe."

"Humph. Hard to fathom, a girl like you buying such sophisticated artwork. Wouldn't have credited it. Always liked Rolfe, you know. Decent cellist. Darned good accountant too, I don't mind telling you. The man has saved me a fortune with the IRS over the years. He used to bring me back the most delicious cheesecakes from Junior's whenever he went to New York. I can still taste them." Marv sighed, licking his lips. He pushed his way past me and into the dining room to refill his plate at the buffet table.

It was easy to imagine Rolfe Kirchner, a slim but prematurely balding accountant, in his three-piece, pinstripe suit, holding a neatly string-tied bakery box on his lap all the way from JFK to LAX in order to deliver a special treat to Marv Pratt in exchange for a few choice studio dates. I wondered what he'd brought home for Grace from these little East Coast junkets, and knowing Rolfe, it was a pretty sure bet the answer was "nothing." She was only his wife, after all, not a music contractor.

I reminded myself that it was my obligation as a hostess to be gracious. I forced myself to pour a fragrant cup of hot tea, and brought it reluctantly to where Marv had finally found a seat large enough to accommodate his bulk. To be perfectly honest, I was secretly hoping he'd choke. Fat chance. On what might almost be described as his lap, he balanced two fragile and antique china plates overflowing with delicate pastries, scones, and tea sandwiches. Somehow, he managed to sip at the cup of hot tea, alternately stuffing and slurping without pausing to breathe or murmur a grateful "thank you." *Years of practice at being a boor*, I mused.

Marilyn Litzky's unmistakable laugh caught my attention. I watched her toss long, dark curls this way and that as she giggled over something James Cantwell had just said to the small group assembled near the window. Andrew Litzky handed his pretty wife a plate of tea sandwiches, and she smiled up fondly at him.

It soon became painfully obvious that Andrew and Marilyn were keeping well away from the Pratts. They'd certainly both known Marv and Annabelle during their years as struggling musicians in LA but had pointedly avoided saying so much as a hello to either of them or even making eye contact. I seemed to recall hearing about a problem between Andrew and Marv, an altercation of some sort that had occurred many years before, but couldn't remember any details. I was fairly certain, however, that Andrew had studied violin with Marv Pratt when Marv had been on the faculty at one of the larger universities in LA and Andrew was still an undergraduate student. It had to have been a long time ago before Andrew took his successful Seattle Symphony audition and before the Litzkys moved up here permanently.

Fortunately, Marilyn and Andrew were far too well behaved to make the other guests privy to their discomfort, but I was in that state of hyperawareness that comes to all experienced hostesses. Anyone could clearly see that the Litzkys were making a point of admiring the house and chatting amiably with all the other guests, putting in that bit of extra effort to show that they were having a good time, but I wasn't fooled one bit. Grace and I weren't alone, I realized, in wondering why we'd bothered to invite a royal pain like Marv Pratt to our little holiday soiree.

Tor and Amy wandered around the house with their teacups in hand, discussing the English cottage style of architecture, the various moldings, and the vintage wallpapers and reading aloud the titles of my psychology books in the library. Grace collects teapots. I collect textbooks on schizophrenia and developmental disorders. Go figure.

A number of the symphony musicians never left the buffet table, and more than a few people returned for a second slice of my rum-soaked Italian cream cake. As a group, they appeared well fed and happy. Everyone did, in fact, look better by candlelight just as Grace had predicted before she set about making Blanchard House into the kind of cheery firetrap that would certainly send any visiting fire marshal into apoplectic fits with her keen determination to cover every possible surface with flickering tapers, scented columns, and tea lights. Every fireplace was working overtime, busily throwing out sparks and making dangerous crackling noises, each one giving its all to keep our guests cozy and warm. Blanchard House looked beautiful. Perhaps our little party would be a memorable one after all.

At the time, I couldn't have predicted just how memorable.

Chapter 2

A NUMBER OF our guests demanded a house tour, so Grace and I dutifully led the group from attic to ground floor through the rear stairs and then back up the main staircase. We'd knowingly saved the best for last, throwing open the doors of the ballroom and flicking on the chandelier. We'd had an electrician rewire this antique gem and hang it properly, covering its new brass chain with a dark red velvet sleeve in the process. Its elegant teardrop crystals had been carefully hand-washed and rehung, and the entire chandelier was then garlanded with boughs of evergreens for the occasion, a full day's work for both of us, but worth every minute. The kaleidoscopic effect of golden light in the mirrored panels made the guests gasp in appreciation. Andrew Litzky began the applause, and soon, even Grace and I were clapping and grinning at the sight of her magnificent Grotrian grand piano in the middle of that glorious room.

"What a lovely, intimate recital hall you've got here!" Amy said. "It reminds me of those gilded baroque salons we saw in Vienna last summer, doesn't it, Tor? Wouldn't poor old Mozart just love it! It's perfect for chamber music. I know this is going to sound kind of forward, but do you think I could give my viola recital here next April?"

Amy Lindal's request couldn't have pleased us more. This was a space that cried out for music, and we wanted our friends to feel free to enjoy it and bring it to life.

"Humph!" Marv cleared his throat incessantly these days. I wondered if he'd developed a chronic throat irritation or a tic, or if this was merely some sort of attention-getting device. Whatever it was, it was annoying as hell. "Who do you think will come out to Kirkland to hear you play?" he asked Amy offhandedly. "There's no culture on the east side to speak of. You've got to book a hall in Seattle proper. Anyhow, no one's really interested in a viola recital. You're not exactly Yuri Bashmet, you know."

Amy looked as if she'd been slapped, and Tor moved protectively to her side, shooting Marv Pratt a look reserved for poisonous snakes and professional music critics.

"What about the Kirkland Performing Arts Center?" countered Delilah Cantwell. She was on the Arts Center's board and sounded pretty miffed. "Lynn Harrell

played a fabulous program there just last year, a Haydn
Cello Concerto with Sinfonia Northwest. He was marvelous, and we sold out months in advance. In fact,
we've had any number of major artists on our concert
series!"

"There's no secret to getting a full house for a viola
recital on the east side, Marv," I said through clenched
teeth. "First, you hold a car raffle. Then you hand out
free pizza and beer. After the encore, if there is one, you
offer the rubes a round of bingo and door prizes and
maybe a few strippers." My voice was becoming steelier
by the minute, and no one was laughing.

"I'd come," Annabelle Pratt spoke up softly, "even
without the strippers." She moved to stand in front of her
husband and looked directly at Amy. "It would be a great
pleasure to come to this beautiful house and enjoy a salon
concert, especially yours," she said, putting her hand
gently on the shoulder of the hapless young violist.
Annabelle turned to me and smiled brightly. "I used to
drive all the way to Malibu to hear your violin and viola
duo whenever you and Dennis played a concert at the
Beach Club, Althea. Do you remember? It was wonderful!
Sometimes an unusual venue can make the music that
much more alive to the listeners, don't you agree? I think
this ballroom would provide a lovely period setting for
your recital, my dear." As usual, Annabelle had intervened
and attempted to repair the damage Marv always seemed
to leave in his wake. I, for one, was grateful. So was Amy.

"I remember that you always came to hear us play, Annabelle, and I always appreciated it. I know Dennis did too," I said.

"Humph! Annabelle's always gone out of her way to be supportive of others, no matter how uninspired the performance or the performers. Whatever became of him, your ex-husband? Does he still play the violin?" Marv's half-full sherry glass sloshed precariously in one hand while he waved a sandwich in the air with the other. "He was nothing special as a violinist, I always thought. Annabelle, you always admired his playing, but I never understood why." The assembled company stood there in horrified silence, helpless bystanders watching a train wreck occurring in slow motion.

"You're talking about the gentleman to whom I was married for twelve years," I said, despite my best intentions to ignore Marv's repeated barbs. "Dennis was a damned fine violinist, Marv, or at least he used to be before he started self-destructing." I could feel myself growing angrier by the minute. Please, I prayed, biting my lip, let him stop right there.

"Oh, come now," Marv said in his most condescendingly nasal tone of voice, temporarily halting the trajectory of sandwich to mouth as he warmed to his subject. "Dennis Littleton was nothing special as a fiddle player, very average. I wouldn't give you two cents for his technique or his interpretation of anything even before he became a lush."

Now I was furious, and even the presence of our astonished guests couldn't make me hold back the rage I'd been suppressing for years. "He used to play beautifully, and you know it better than anyone, Marv. I have a recording of Dennis playing the Franck Sonata when he was only twenty years old that still makes me weep. It's so poignant and lovely. He played the Lalo 'Symphonie Espagnole' for me just before he went and played it for you and your toadying orchestra committee, his very last attempt at an audition. It was fabulous, and you dismissed him as if he were a high school student."

Grace put her hand on my arm, but I shrugged it off angrily, pursuing Marv as he continued to stroll around the piano.

"He even went to you for a coaching afterward to try to figure out what he could do better, but you told him he had no hope of ever getting anywhere on the violin and should give it up."

"And I was right, wasn't I?" Marv smirked. "He just wasn't up to it."

"You made sure he never had a chance. You destroyed his career and his hopes every chance you got. You made snide comments about his playing at sessions in front of everybody. You put him in the last chair on record dates whenever you couldn't just plain keep him off the job. You were the final straw, the reason Dennis began to drink every night, the reason he put away his violin and abandoned our marriage, and I will never, ever let you say one more hateful thing about that man!"

As soon as the words were out of my mouth, waves of shame began washing over me, and my knees shook with released adrenaline. I could feel hot tears welling up but couldn't stop them from spilling down my cheeks. Annabelle was pale and trembling.

"You don't know the first thing about it, Althea," Marv sniffed, clearly unruffled by my outburst. "I just didn't like his playing. How could I promote such a lesser talent? He was a pleasant enough fellow, I suppose, and quite good-looking before he started drinking heavily, just not much of a violinist in my book. It was nothing personal, nothing at all." He slowly looked up at the chandelier, calmly inspected the condition of the gilded mirrors, took a sip of his sherry, and waddled back down the grand staircase, undoubtedly in the direction of the buffet table.

My momentary sense of shame was replaced by blinding hatred. I'm afraid that if I'd had an ax in my hands at that moment, I'd have unhesitatingly used it on him. The rest of the company continued to stand there, frozen in an embarrassed and rather astonished tableau, too stunned to resume their conversations, and as yet unwilling to be the first to follow Marv downstairs.

"Am I too late for the party?" a gruff voice called heartily from the doorway. "I hope not. Merry Christmas, everybody! Gosh, you all look shell-shocked. Am I interrupting something? By the way, Thea, I just saw the most hideous type of vermin you can imagine sniffing around your beautiful buffet table down there. Or was that our old friend Marv Pratt picking over the spread, and without any adult supervision? Someone should go down there and shoo him away before he contaminates everything."

There stood a grinning Conrad Bailey, my oldest friend and peerless concert pianist even at seventy-something, wearing his usual plaid shirt, jeans, Birkenstocks, and gray woolen cap, scraggly beard and all. I threw my arms around him and gave him a huge hug, my tears wetting his shirt as I buried my face against his scratchy shoulder.

"You *are* the party, Conrad! Thank you so much for coming," I said. "How was the ferry ride from Whidbey Island?"

"Wet. Plenty wet. I missed the first ferry by minutes and had to sit waiting in the rain for another hour. Good thing I had my trusty Alfred Brendel Beethoven CDs with me, eh?" He held me out at arm's length and realized that I'd been crying. "There, there, Thea. You're making me even wetter." Conrad patted me as if I were a tiny child. "Here. Have a hankie. You'll get all blotchy and ruin your makeup. You look so pretty all dressed up and everything. You don't want to spoil it, now do you? Don't you worry. If something's wrong, we'll fix it!"

I accepted his hankie gratefully and gave an enormous blow.

"And are my old eyes deceiving me," Conrad said over my shoulder, "or is this the lovely Grace Evangeline Sullivan? How are ya, Grace E., my beautiful girl?"

"You're the only person in the world who still calls me that, Conrad, and I wish you'd stop it! You know how I despise my middle name!" Grace pretended to scowl before she gave him a huge grin and a peck on the cheek.

"Sorry, old girl. I was just so glad to learn that Thea dragged you up here that I forgot myself. Have you finally given up playing musical chairs with the studio mafia? Won't you miss all that paranoia, all that backstabbing? On second thought, we'll always have Marv Pratt up here to give us a whiff of the real Hollywood," he said.

Yessiree, Conrad was in prime form, and he cheerfully greeted each guest as he moved around the ballroom. He alternately kissed and hugged the Litzkys and asked after little Amelia. Conrad moved on, shaking hands with various musicians he knew, and it seemed that he knew everybody, occasionally laughing or patting an arm as he went. He stopped dead in his tracks, though, when he got to Annabelle Pratt. His manner became gravely formal. "Good evening, Annabelle. I hope you're well."

"Do you?" she replied stiffly. "I can't imagine why." Annabelle turned on her heel and headed for the stairs.

This was so uncharacteristic that I found myself staring after her. *She must be miffed because of Conrad's comments about her husband,* I thought. Oh, well, what was a little more tension on a night like this? It already felt as if *Who's Afraid of Virginia Woolf?* had just been reenacted in our very own home, Marvin Pratt and yours truly in the starring roles.

"Let's all go downstairs to the living room by the fire and have some sherry," I croaked. "We have some lovely petits fours from a new French bakery that just opened across from the library, and I can brew up some coffee and some decaf if anyone wants it," Grace chimed in, herding people down the stairs and toward the buffet table in the dining room.

I caught my reflection in the hall mirror and winced at the red-eyed, puffy mess that stared back. Some women look hauntingly lovely when they cry. I'm not one of them. Conrad, meanwhile, couldn't resist trying Grace's piano and tossed off, "It's Beginning to Look a Lot Like Christmas" in alternating meters, following it up with some witty desecrations of a few other seasonal ditties.

Downstairs, we were all surprised to see that there was anything left of the pastries after Marv got through raiding the table for the umpteenth time. I busied myself pouring generous sherries for everyone while trying to regain my composure. Andrew Litzky eventually came up and put his arm around my shoulder, steering me

gently but firmly to where Marilyn sat on one end of the
sofa, well away from Marv. Were those waves of com-
passion radiating toward me from our guests, or had I
merely embarrassed myself and everyone else?

So this is what they mean by "tea and sympathy," I
thought. Marv Pratt had done it again. Why had I allowed my feelings for Annabelle to override my common sense? Wasn't the definition of insanity "doing the
same thing over and over again and expecting a different
outcome?" Was I insane to have invited Marv Pratt anywhere near decent people? Or perhaps I'd just needed a
sharp reminder as to why I'd been glad to leave LA in
the first place.

The company watched in genuine astonishment as
Marv strolled back to the tea table yet again for a final
round of goodies, proceeding to fill several napkins with
little sandwiches and tea cakes for the ride home.

"What a greedy, obnoxious pig! That man needs
killing," Grace hissed in my ear.

Too soon, it would become apparent that someone
agreed with her.

Chapter 3

"WELL, THAT WAS the worst party we've ever given—in fact, the only bad party we've ever given—and it's pretty much all my fault," I said dejectedly as Grace and I sat in the kitchen, sipping Irish whiskey and water while picking at the remains of the tea sandwiches.

"Don't be ridiculous, Althea. The food was fabulous! People seemed to really admire Blanchard House. Lydia made a new conquest of that hunky trombone player, and Winnie and Bert were a big hit with everyone."

"I know," I said. "The animals behaved perfectly. I, on the other hand—"

"Stop beating yourself up," Grace said, topping off my drink. "Personally, I enjoyed watching you give Marv Pratt the business. He deserved it. It's about time somebody told off that obnoxious know-it-all."

"Yeah, but did it have to be me?"

"Of course it did," she said, giving me a toothy smile. "You're really good at it."

"Gee, thanks," I said.

"Look at it this way, honey," Grace said. "What happened here last night will make you a living legend in the music biz. People will be begging for an invitation to our parties, heck, even our garage sales, hoping to hear you verbally disembowel an annoying guest or two. You'll be famous!"

Grace bounced up from her seat, purposely placed a foot on the chair, folded one arm over her knee and the other behind her back, Bob Fosse-style, while she belted out, "He had it coming! He had it coming," from the musical *Chicago*. It was easy to see why she'd been a successful singer in New York before she'd headed out to Hollywood to play the cello. She really should be back onstage. No, I mean it. She really should.

I halfheartedly threw a shrimp salad sandwich across the table at her.

"Oh, c'mon … laugh, Thea. You were right to take him on, even if it was in defense of the idiot who broke your heart. Marv Pratt's always been a horrible bully. Now he's just an older bully. Age doesn't excuse bad behavior, does it?"

"Not really, but I was determined to be nice to Marv for Annabelle's sake. I should have known where the evening was headed when he kept extolling the virtues of your ex-husband. At least you maintained your dignity and didn't go all psycho on him. No, you left that particular honor to me."

"I was barely controlling myself ... believe me," Grace said. "This wasn't your fault, Thea, and I'm sure no one thinks any less of you for losing your temper with him. We were all itching to slap him. He had no idea what dangerous ground he was on—that's all. It never occurred to him that you might still have feelings for Dennis."

Grace was right. I hadn't even realized myself just how deep those feelings were.

"In a way, though, Marv was just being Marv, wasn't he?" I said. "He's an innate critic. He holds strong opinions about everything—music, instruments, wine, and certainly violinists. Marv's a collector of the very best money can buy, and he needs to let everyone know it."

"Right!" Grace said, taking another sip of whiskey and screwing up her face. Grace is no drinker by anyone's standards, but she tries. "And let's not forget that when you're a studio concertmaster, everyone in town auditions for you at some point in their careers. Judging people's playing becomes second nature after a while. It would be easy for anyone, let alone a narcissist like Marv, to slip into abusing that power."

"You're absolutely right, Grace," I said. "I'm sure it also made for more than a little paranoia on his part when he was a concertmaster. In Marv's world, players have always been separated into two camps, either with him as part of his sycophantic little band or against him."

"Marvin Pratt always made sure he destroyed the careers of anyone he imagined was a threat to his position in the studios or in the chamber orchestra. I can't imagine what he had against Dennis, though," Grace said. "I remember Dennis as being rather unassuming and almost lethally cheerful at work. Everyone liked him, and I always thought he was one heck of a good violinist."

"Don't you think that's rather the point?" I asked. "A young, handsome, popular guy who played excellent violin must have seemed pretty threatening to Marv. I know that Annabelle always praised Dennis's playing, and it probably set Marv against him even more."

Grace looked up from her drink. "Did you know that I envied you being married to Dennis in those days? Yup, I did. He seemed like a genuinely nice guy and a lot different from Rolfe. Of course, Rolfe made anybody look good by comparison."

"Dennis wasn't such a nice guy once he started drinking," I said. "You know how it is. You convince yourself that the person you love will wake up one day and choose you instead of the bottle. It sure didn't happen that way with Dennis and me though, did it?"

"He didn't want a musician for a wife, Thea. He wanted a drinking buddy."

"Believe me, Grace, I even tried to be that, too, but I'm no good after two drinks. I fall asleep."

I could still picture Dennis pouring himself one stiff scotch after another, becoming louder and more insensitive as the evening wore on. It remained in my memory as a clear vision of a fine violinist committing professional and social suicide glass by glass.

"Sometimes I find myself wondering if he's happy now or if he even remembers what life was like when we were together. Everyone said we were the perfect couple—everyone except his mother, that is. God, how that woman detested me."

"I never could understand why she insisted on wearing those boxy tweed suits with crepe-soled English walking shoes," she said. "All she needed was a monocle." Grace was right. Ruth Littleton would have been at home in any English village, striking fear into the hearts of local orphans and church committee members. She'd been handsome in an aristocratic sort of way but cold as gun metal in January.

"A few months after Dennis and I bought the house in Malibu, the rusty spring on our heavy garage door gave way. The thing coldcocked me, broke my cheekbone, and gave me a black eye that lasted for a month," I said.

Grace shuddered. "I'm so sorry. That must have really hurt."

"It did," I said. "Anyway, when my mother-in-law heard the news, she actually giggled and said, 'Well, at least you don't have to worry about it *marring your*

beauty!" Wasn't that sweet of her? You know the absolute best part of the divorce? I'll never have to see Ruth
Littleton ever again!"

We raised our glasses in a mock toast to beastly
former mother-in-laws everywhere.

"I can't help wondering how Mama Littleton gets
along with Dennis's new wife, Simone," Grace said.

"I keep hearing that the woman drinks like a fish, so
maybe she's found a way to deal with the mean old bat
that doesn't involve gun play." *Lots and lots of martinis
might just do the trick*, I mused.

"I've met Simone, you know," Grace said, "She's
good-looking, streaked blonde hair, very tan, but she
comes off as being a little tense if you ask me. She's no
Althea Stewart."

"But then ... who is?" I laughed in spite of myself.

We both turned toward the kitchen windows at the
sound of a car pulling up to the entrance, crunching over
the newly spread gravel. Had someone forgotten a coat
or a purse? It was after nine o'clock, and the guests had
mercifully gone almost an hour before. Understandably,
the Pratts had been among the first to head for the door,
Marv stuffing a few more sandwiches into a napkin before taking his unceremonious leave. Annabelle had
taken my hand in her own fragile ones, thanked me for
the party, and air-kissed both my cheeks before she followed Marv out to the car. I hadn't felt especially de-
serving of those tender gestures, however Annabelle had

always been unfailingly kind to me, and this evening had proven to be no exception.

I threw open the front door before Conrad Bailey even had a chance to knock or ring the doorbell. He grinned sheepishly from under his dripping wool cap and bushy brows.

"The traffic's backed up all the way to the 405 in both directions," he said. "There must've been an accident. I've been sitting in my car with the engine running for the last forty minutes, and I'm afraid I'll run out of gas before I get to the ferry. I made a U-turn into someone's driveway as soon as I could and hightailed it back."

"Why don't you wait it out here?" I said. "They usually clear these things up in a few hours."

The rain had picked up, and the wind was howling ominously, filling our nostrils with the scent of the fresh pine wreath on our door and the huge Douglas firs that ringed the property. Conrad was dripping wet, clad only in his plaid woolen shirt rather than a warm winter coat. Even through my turtleneck sweater, long woolen skirt, and heavy tights, I could feel the piercing cold of the raging December storm. I pulled him inside as quickly as I could and shut the heavy door behind him.

"We do have a guest room or three, you know," I said. "Would you consider staying the night and driving back in the morning? Unless, of course, you have a hot date. I'll get you a nice dry robe, okay? Come in the kitchen, and we'll pour you a drink or make you something warm."

"I don't need a robe, Althea. I'm a wash 'n' wear kinda guy. I don't drink anymore, either. It interferes with my meds. You get to a certain age, and you don't get to do much of anything anymore, including having hot dates. Got some herb tea?"

"Of course. How about some leftover sandwiches?" I said.

"I don't know about that. Did Marv Pratt happen to touch them? He was pawing the food every time I looked up, and I wouldn't want to inadvertently eat anything he's had his grubby little mitts on." Conrad might have been joking, but then again, he might not.

"So Gracie, or should I say Grace," he corrected himself as he ambled toward the warmth of the kitchen, "I never got to congratulate you at the party. Seemed wrong to do it then at your nice get-together, but I want you to know that I'm really happy for you. Leaving that jerk Rolfe was the best thing you could've done for yourself."

"Do you really think so?" Grace asked, looking up from busily twisting her napkin until her fingers turned white. "You're not the first person tonight who's said pretty much the same thing. And here I thought I was such a good actress that no one could tell anything was wrong, but apparently, I was mistaken." Tears gathered in the corners of her eyes, and one slid down her cheek almost to her chin.

Poor Grace. At least she'd been the one who made the break though, I told myself. I thought back on all of my own self-inflicted mental torture, beginning with the stunning realization that Dennis was really leaving me, and lasting for over a year. It didn't solve a thing, but I did manage to lose almost twenty pounds, giving me that lean, concentration camp look so coveted by the fashion industry. Don't worry. I put it all back on with a few extra pounds to spare.

"Rolfe's temper began to frighten me," Grace said, looking up at Conrad and me. "Once he started banging the furniture around, I really got scared. Everything seemed to be escalating, and I didn't want the next object he slammed around to be me."

"I had no idea," I said.

"Of course not. I should have done it years before." She dabbed at her eyes with what was left of the twisted napkin. "Did you know he tried to take my cello as well as my piano in the divorce settlement? I've had that cello since I was twelve years old! It was a gift from my father, and, out of the blue, Rolfe and his attorney began demanding that I should sell it and give him half the money. Ugh!"

Conrad and I looked at each other with barely concealed disgust. Nothing is more vile to a musician than the thought of someone taking away a professional's instrument, which is, after all, a musician's voice as well as the means to making a living.

"Allow me to raise a toast, ladies. Here's to Althea Stewart and Grace Sullivan," Conrad said, lifting his steaming teacup, "brave lasses both. And to Blanchard House. May your new venture bring you health, wealth, and happiness."

"To Blanchard House!" we chorused before we scarfed down whatever remained of the party leftovers.

Chapter 4

THE NEXT MORNING brought the most welcome sight in all of Western Washington, a cloudless day. The storm had moved on overnight. Sharp winter sunlight reflected dazzlingly off the surface of Lake Washington and beamed directly through the casement windows of Blanchard House. Our kitchen looked as inviting as one of those impossibly perfect photos you find in decorating magazines, giving us a glimpse of what our beloved home might reveal itself to be when summer finally arrived.

Conrad was already up. We could hear him singing a rousing, if somewhat off-color, sea shanty in his bath. Grace was reading *The Seattle Times* and sipping tea.

The jarring ring of the wall telephone made us both jump. I was closest to it, so I grabbed it before the second ring.

"Good morning," said a brisk but intriguing male voice, very Sean Connery, the kind of voice I've always dreamed of hearing on the other end of my telephone line. "This is Detective Harry Demetrious of the Kirkland Police Department. May I please speak with Althea Stewart?"

I assured him brightly that he was doing just that. I instantly decided to donate generously to the local policeman's ball based solely on the husky quality of the voice on the other end of my line.

"Ms. Stewart, I'm sorry to have to tell you this, but there's been a serious accident. It occurred last night a little before nine. I'm afraid the vehicle's passenger, a Mrs. Annabelle Pratt, has been seriously injured. She gave us your name this morning as a contact and family member." My romantic fantasy instantly dissolved with those terrible words.

"How is she?" I asked. "Is she going to be all right? What about Marv?"

There was a brief pause.

"Unfortunately, the driver was pronounced dead at the scene."

"Oh, my God!" The breath whooshed out of me, and my head began to pound. "What happened?"

"As far as we know, the driver lost control of the vehicle and crossed three lanes of traffic, plowing into the center divider. It was extremely bad weather last night, with poor visibility. It appears that he may have had a seizure of some sort or a heart attack. The cause of death hasn't been determined at this point, but we'll know more after the autopsy."

I felt suddenly light-headed and took a deep breath.

"The *autopsy*? You're doing an autopsy?" I was stunned.

"I'm afraid our Medical Examiner insists on an autopsy in cases of accidental death, and the insurance companies are quite insistent as well."

It made sense, I supposed, to determine if the deceased had been intoxicated or under the influence of drugs. That would probably affect the liability of the insurer.

"Marv and Annabelle were both here with us at our house until around 8:30 last night," I said. "Marv had a sherry or two during the course of the evening but hardly enough to make him intoxicated, especially considering his size and how much food he consumed. He gobbled his food but sipped his drinks. My God, I just can't believe he's dead! What can I do for Annabelle?"

"Well, there's nothing much you can do right now other than check in on Mrs. Pratt in intensive care over at Evergreen Hospital. I would imagine she's still in shock. She doesn't seem to recall anything about the accident itself or the minutes leading up to it. That's fairly normal for victims of severe trauma, though. At this point, the hospital is admitting only the immediate family. Yours is the only name she gave us, so I assume you're her next of kin."

I found myself mumbling incoherently. Although I certainly wasn't a blood relation of Annabelle's, that didn't stop me from wanting to be there for her now. If I had to stretch the truth and pretend kinship to sit by her bedside, I wouldn't hesitate for a minute. After all, I reasoned, she just might not have any living family members, none that I'd ever heard of anyway, and she'd already given the police and the hospital my name.

"I appreciate your calling me, detective. I'll be over to the hospital as soon as I get dressed."

"I'm sorry, Ms. Stewart." He did sound genuinely sorry, too, that husky, sympathetic, incredibly sexy voice of his calming me momentarily, washing over me like a gentle wave on a Hawaiian beach. *Police training is a lot better than it used to be*, I thought to myself. Did the Kirkland Police Department pay for vocal coaching as well? This guy was good.

"We may have to get in touch with you and your fellow partygoers a little later on to go over a few details after the autopsy report comes in, if that's all right," he said.

And if it wasn't?

"Certainly, officer." I gave him my cell phone number as well as our address.

"What was that all about? It didn't sound good." Grace had stopped sipping her tea and reading the paper in order to catch my end of the conversation. I had to sit down at the table to steady myself before I could stop shaking long enough to relay the news.

"Marv's dead, Grace! He lost control of the car. Maybe had a seizure or a heart attack. He was an awful man, but no one deserves to die like that—no one. It's horrible." I couldn't suppress the chill that ran like a current through my entire body.

Grace looked ashen. "What about Annabelle?" she asked.

"All the officer could tell me is that she's in intensive care. At least she was temporarily coherent enough to give them my name. I'm headed over there in a few minutes to see her. Can you give Conrad breakfast and ask him to stay until I get back? I think we may need him for moral support."

I hurried upstairs and threw on some warm clothes. It occurred to me that this might have been the accident that tied up the freeway last night and kept Conrad Bailey from returning home to Whidbey Island. The unbidden thought entered my head that the Pratts' misfortune might have been my unintentional gain. I more than enjoyed having Conrad here in Blanchard House. I felt safe and protected for the first time since Dennis had left. How selfish of me to even think that way at a time like this; however, there it was, that perverse thought, and no matter how I tried to push it away, it kept coming back.

Chapter 5

I FELT SORRY and just a tad guilty about involving
Grace in all this. After all, I was the one who invited her
up here only a few months before for what was supposed
to be a brief visit.

As soon as I'd picked her up at Sea-Tac airport one
rainy October morning, I'd dragged her to a coffee shop
in downtown Kirkland for a little chat.

"You and I both know that the recording business is
dying a miserable death," I'd told her. "Look at the
dwindling number of heavily orchestrated film scores
and weekly TV dramas that string players used to be able
to count on. Now all a film composer needs to score an
entire movie is a laptop and a couple of synthesizers.
Face it, Grace, the Hollywood we knew and loved
doesn't really exist anymore. When was the last time you
had a record date or scored a major motion picture?"

Grace nodded miserably as I ranted.

"Can you honestly say that you're making a decent living playing low-budget musicals in Orange County?" I asked.

"Well, not right now—" she said.

"And how many miles do you drive every year, lugging your cello so you can play pops concerts with third-tier community orchestras all over Southern California for practically no money?" I asked

"You don't really want to know," Grace said.

"And what do you spend on gas each month?"

I could tell from her repeated wincing that I was hitting her pretty accurately where it hurt, especially with gas prices soaring ever upward, but I was saving the biggest swat for the end. "And how about your love life, honey? Are there any narcissists left in LA that you haven't been out with at least once?"

Now this probably wasn't fair, but I wasn't playing fair. I only play to win. Unfortunately for her, Grace had provided me with plenty of ammunition in that department. Her dating disasters were the stuff of legend.

"Althea, stop. You're being cruel, and you know it. I haven't had anything resembling a date in months. In fact, I've hardly gone anywhere at all except back and forth to rehearsals with second-rate orchestras out in the boonies."

"Right," I said. "And who do musicians ever meet but other musicians? Just the other day, it dawned on me that we must be the most incestuous group in the world, especially string players. Every couple we know seems to have wound up together by default."

It's true, I thought. *We'd both been married to fellow string players, and look how well that had turned out.*

"I actually did meet a very attractive man, a '*normie,*' at a dinner party my attorney gave last month," she went on. "He seemed kind of sweet at first, good-looking, the right age, divorced, a residential designer in Santa Monica, but then he announced over dessert to anyone who happened to be listening that he's just doing design work until he can get his acting career going. *And* he just happened to hear that our hostess's brother-in-law is a casting director, *and* he just happened to have his head shots with him out in the car in case she wouldn't mind passing them along—" Grace trailed off, head drooping dejectedly toward her latte. On one hand, I hated to see her so despondent, but on the other, this latest foray into the shallow dating pool known as LA was helping me build my case.

Grace had told me about some real creeps over the last year, but it would have been unkind to bring them up. Let's see. There was the too-handsome-to-be-true plastic surgeon who was a walking advertisement for his own work, a control freak who yearned to "fix" every little thing about every woman he met, including the already beautiful Grace, to make them more "perfect." Who could forget the aging screenwriter who paraded himself around town dressed up like Harrison Ford in

Raiders of the Lost Ark and actually lived in a cramped North Hollywood apartment with a collection of lizards that made the entire floor of his building stink like the reptile house of a zoo? And what about that incredibly cheap character actor who was still renting a small room in his former Laurel Canyon house from his ex-wife who, according to him, was still interested in an occasional "threesome?" Then there was the guy who'd been a regular on *Star Trek* episodes for almost ten years playing a Romulan, a man who suggested that Grace make a bunch of extra sandwiches to bring along on their picnic so he wouldn't have to make his own lunches that week. Oh, yeah, LA may be home to the rich and famous, but it also attracts the weird and the smarmy in vast numbers. By now, according to Grace, she'd met and dated at least half of them.

I wiped off my latte mustache. "Look, I'm not suggesting that the Seattle area is bursting at the seams with sensitive, emotionally available men, although there must be at least two or three, but the odds are definitely in your favor the more miles you put between yourself and Hollywood. There are lots of real, interesting people here."

Grace looked around at an entire coffee shop full of mostly male computer nerds concentrating on their various electronic gadgets. She didn't look convinced.

"First of all," I said, "the economy isn't driven by movie studios. In Kirkland, it's all about Microsoft and dot-coms and Boeing engineers. And did you know that Seattle is the most literate city in America? You can hardly get a seat in a public library."

"Big whoop," Grace said.

"Big whoop, indeed," I said. "Concerts here are actually attended by knowledgeable people who come to listen to the music, not just to show off their wardrobes. Most people in Seattle don't even have 'wardrobes,' and folks up here are so ... so decent!" I waved my arm, indicating the rumpled, slightly damp, but noticeably well-behaved clientele sitting all around us. Grace's head again swiveled in their general direction, but the rest of her appeared unmoved.

"The first few years after I moved up here I kept waiting for that famous *other shoe* to drop," I went on. "It never did. I'd heard all that blather that you probably have too, stuff about native Washingtonians hating Californians, but the people I've met here have been nothing but kind to me. My music students are adorable, and so wholesome that they could have stepped right out of an old 1950s episode of *Leave It to Beaver* or *Ozzie and Harriet*."

Okay, at this point, I admit that I probably sounded like a crazed cheerleader for the Great Pacific Northwest; however, this had truly been my experience so far, and I'd been residing here happily for almost three years. I carefully neglected to tell Grace that I hadn't actually gone out on a date with anyone since I had arrived. Oh, a number of men had mumbled something about meeting for coffee, which is considered a "hot date" in Seattle, but I just hadn't had much interest in finding a relationship since my divorce. Now *that* was the real reason I had to get as far away from LA as possible.

"So what am I supposed to do up here to make a living?" Grace asked, slowly sipping her latte. "Forty-one is already way too old to audition for the symphony, even if they had a cello opening, which they currently don't." She was right about that. Symphony orchestras have very little interest in hiring players over a certain age because it means that the orchestra will wind up paying out for their retirement without having first worked them to death through their twenties and thirties.

"There's always freelancing, you know, the opera, the ballet, chamber orchestras, or we could start another string quartet," I said. "We've been pretty successful doing that in LA, haven't we? You're an amazing soprano, too, but I don't know if you have any interest in going back to singing. I seem to remember that you've always talked about teaching, though." I might have added that Grace Sullivan is one of the most stunning women you're likely to meet. Sometimes that's an asset in the job market, and sometimes it's not. You can never be sure. At this moment, she was staring into her lap with those luminous sea-green eyes, all ringed with impossibly long lashes, and I had to admit that even sopping wet she looked fabulous. Long tendrils of damp golden brown hair were curling around her face becomingly, and the smoky-hued crystal earrings dangling to her chin line set off her eyes perfectly. Think Julie Christie but with a whole lot of Lucille Ball thrown in. Women have been known to hate her on sight, but she is so genuine and always willing to laugh at herself that they ultimately forgive her. Well, most of them do, anyway.

We'd met when we were both young and idealistic musicians a few years out of prestigious East Coast music conservatories. Grace had majored in cello and voice. I was a violinist and violist. She'd gone on to acting and singing in musical theater in New York, and I'd done my time in a few symphonies and even Las Vegas show bands before we both settled into studio work as elite Hollywood string players. We've recorded the scores of countless films and television shows over the years. Our all-woman string quartet was in demand year-round, providing romantic music for hundreds of weddings at hotels and country clubs in Beverly Hills and Bel Air. Consequently, we each have a closetful of fabulous black gowns which we, year after year, attempt to convince the IRS are "uniforms." Well, they're not exactly street clothes, now, are they? Can you imagine us pushing our carts through Safeway in those long, flashy getups? At any rate, Grace and I have shared great music, bad conductors, and nasty divorces, and we have watched Hollywood rather quickly trade its glamour for the easy money to be made producing reality television.

I still play violin and viola every day, but not for MGM or Paramount. Musician friends who'd moved up here from LA long before I had kept suggesting that I think about teaching a few kids on the east side, and although I protested that I was a performer only, they persisted. To this day, I'm glad that they kept at it because their nagging pushed me to try something I believed I'd hate. I was so wrong. Becoming a private violin and viola instructor brought wonderful young people into my life and utilized every ounce of my talents and experience. It felt right from the very first lesson and has become my new favorite thing.

Everything about me has become more relaxed up here. My signature chic French haircut has long since grown out into shoulder-length auburn waves, more often than not piled up in a twist or a hair clip. A turtleneck sweater and jeans have become my Seattle uniform, but always with really good jewelry and perfectly applied eye makeup. Some things I will never give up, even if they mark me as an outsider. Still, at forty, I happily traded in my stilettos for UGG boots. Three years later, my feet are still thanking me.

"I have a proposition for you, Grace," I said as she took a final and rather noisy slurp of her nonfat latte. "It may sound a little insane at first, but hear me out. How would you like to completely change your life?"

Grace Evangeline Sullivan leveled those startlingly green eyes at me and ever-so-sweetly whispered, "If this is a pitch for Amway, Althea, I swear I'm going to kill you."

Chapter 6

ANNABELLE LAY PERFECTLY still, tiny and pale as a child in her enormous hospital bed. There was no sign of her rose-colored suit, just a washed-out floral cotton gown. Her gray hair was loose and seemed to float on the pillow. Tubes were sticking out of her every-where. She had an incredible shiner, casts covering both arms and wrists, and there were still speckles of blood. *Perhaps even Marv's blood on her face and neck*, I thought with revulsion.

I lied. I assured the hospital staff that I was a member of her immediate family. I also informed them that I was sure that she and Marv had the best insurance money could buy through the Musician's Union Health and Welfare Plan, but I could tell them very little after that.

"Yes, she said that she had a daughter, Ms. Stewart. I assume you're her daughter. Is that right?"

"Mhmm," I lied again, feeling completely flustered by this strange new role. Annabelle had no children so far as I knew. What if she really did have a daughter, one who eventually appeared at her bedside? I'd look like an idiot, and a dishonest idiot at that. On the other hand, perhaps Annabelle felt closer to me than I'd realized. The more likely scenario was that I was the only person whose name came immediately to her mind because she'd just been at my house and she was very much in shock after the crash.

"I'm terribly sorry about your father," a tall, middle-aged nurse said, looking deeply into my eyes and smiling sympathetically.

"Wha ... what?"

"Oh, I beg your pardon. I just assumed it was your father in the car. It's hard to know sometimes—" she said, looking away in obvious embarrassment. I just stood there, for the moment completely witless, having forgotten the small detail that were Annabelle my mother, Marv might have been my father. I pulled myself together enough to nod in the affirmative.

"No, no. Don't apologize. He was my stepfather. I didn't mean to imply—It's all been quite a shock," I said.

"Believe me ... I understand. We see a lot of it in the ICU. Your mother's been through a severe trauma, but at least she survived. She apparently wasn't wearing her seatbelt. The air bags deployed, but she must have been bracing herself against the dashboard before the impact. Both arms and wrists have stress fractures. The air bags saved her life without a doubt, but we're pretty sure they also caused the broken ribs and arms. You must be aware that in a woman of her age and with her preexisting medical condition, any sort of bodily trauma is going to be more damaging than it would be for a younger, healthier person."

"What condition?" I asked the nurse as the youngish male doctor who was attending Annabelle stepped into the room at that moment and grabbed her chart from the foot of the bed. He looked momentarily taken aback by my question.

"I assumed you were aware of the state of your mother's general health," he said, turning to me briefly. "Unfortunately, every hospital in the country has very strict rules concerning patient confidentiality these days, and unless we have the express permission of the patient, we can't really discuss any preexisting medical conditions the patient might have, even with family members. I'm sure you understand. Your mother will probably tell you all about it when she's able to talk. Right now, we have her intubated to keep her airways clear."

I walked over to the side of Annabelle's bed and gently touched her fingertips. She didn't stir or open her eyes. The medications had completely and mercifully put her under for the time being.

"Does she know Marv's gone?"

"We can't be sure what she knows. She may have been aware of something at the time of the accident, but I

doubt that she could have assessed the nature of his injuries or whether he was breathing. Everything probably
happened quickly and rather violently. We won't bring it
up with her unless she asks, not for a while anyway. The
additional emotional shock of losing her husband might
impede her recovery, and we don't want to risk it. We'd
also prefer to have a close family member break the
news to her," he said, looking at me pointedly.

"I'm so grateful for the air bags that saved her life.
It's a shame they didn't save Marv's too."

"I was on duty when they brought them both in," the
doctor said. "The paramedics thought your dad might
have suffered a heart attack before impact, so that remains a possible cause of death, although there are other
things which must be ruled out as well. Air bags
wouldn't have made much difference in a case like that
though."

My dad? What a thought. Ugh! As I left the hospital,
I found myself picturing a grossly overweight Marvin
Pratt waddling through our lovely home, a blight on our
beautiful Blanchard House, stuffing himself with every
rich food he could get his hands on. Had his gluttony finally ended in a heart attack or stroke and consequently
caused his death? Had all that weight coupled with very
sedentary habits and a lifetime of performance pressure
as a concertmaster taken the ultimate toll? It seemed as
likely as anything else, I told myself firmly, refusing to
look at any other possibility.

And what did the doctor mean by Annabelle's "preexisting medical condition?" She was noticeably thinner than I'd ever seen her, but was it a medical problem or simply stress? Living with Marv Pratt could strain anyone's nerves, but living without him, I realized, might not prove to be so easy for her, either. Could it be that she'd actually loved the lout? Perhaps there was a tender side to him that only a wife could know, difficult as that might be to imagine.

My pragmatic self couldn't help but worry about how Annabelle was going to handle making funeral arrangements for her husband. How would she get around or feed and bathe herself? Maybe Annabelle wasn't technically my blood relation; however, I seemed to be the closest thing she had to family up here in Seattle, and I wasn't about to desert her at a time like this. Thank goodness we had those extra bedrooms. *It must be true that nature abhors a vacuum*, I thought, *because Blanchard House seems to be on the verge of filling up rapidly.*

Chapter 7

IT WAS NOON by the time I left the hospital. My first violin student of the day was due to arrive as soon as school ended at around three in the afternoon. That gave me *time* for a leisurely lunch, and I suddenly realized that I was ravenous, having completely missed breakfast. Conrad's car was still in our parking lot when I pulled in. It gave me a comforting feeling, knowing that my old friend and colleague was still hanging around Blanchard House, at least for a while. As I entered the house, the tender notes of a Debussy nocturne being exquisitely performed on Grace's grand piano floated down the stairs like a cascading wave of pure benevolence, filling Blanchard House with sublime and otherworldly music. Had Conrad heard about the accident already? Most assuredly, and this was his way, a true musician's way, of soothing us all. Even the animals seemed calmer than they'd been when I left.

There were more phone messages than usual on the answering machine. News of Marv's death had traveled quickly, and Oliver Siddon, my least favorite Seattle violin dealer, was among those calling for more details. I decided then and there to return his call and get it over with before I threw lunch together.

"Is it true that Marv Pratt's dead? You absolutely must tell me all about it!" demanded Oliver in his clipped and somewhat affected English accent, annoying and pushy as always. "Do the police know how it happened? Is Annabelle going to make it?" He seemed desperately overeager to hear all the grisly details.

"She doesn't look all that great right now, Oliver, but the doctor seems fairly confident that she'll pull through okay."

"Oh—" Oliver sounded slightly disappointed.

"By the way, who told you about Marv?" I asked him.

"It's all over the news. Haven't you been watching? 'Famous violinist dead in Kirkland in a spectacular traffic fatality. Wife critically injured as well.' Turn on your television if you don't believe me. King, Kong, Komo, Fox News, they're all carrying it."

"Ghouls ... all of them!" I said.

"Well, the public wants to know. I can't help wondering what's going to happen to Marv's violin collection. He always had the most exquisite taste in instruments! There's at least one Strad, a Guarnerius del Gesu, an Amati, several Roccas, a Storioni, and all sorts of fabulous treasures in mint condition. And the bows! My dear, he has untold numbers of the very finest, rarest bows in existence, Hills, gold-mounted Sartoris—Surely, Annabelle won't want to hold onto everything now that he's gone, will she?"

For a moment, I could hardly believe my ears. It took everything I had to be civil.

"Those decisions are probably pretty far down the road, Oliver. Right now, we have to concentrate on getting Annabelle well enough to survive on her own once she leaves the hospital."

"Well, how bad is she?" Oliver said.

"How bad is she?" I said, my voice rising. "Her arms and wrists are both broken. So are her ribs and her pelvis. I'd say that's pretty bad."

"Tsk, tsk. Such a shame," he said. "I can't imagine she'll ever want to play again, and in that case—"

"Personally, I plan to do everything I can to encourage her!" I said.

Oliver Siddon wasn't one to take a hint, no matter how archly delivered. "Marv's collection might be worth piles of money in the long run, but you know how difficult it is to sell instruments in this market. It'll probably take a year or more to sell any of them for their fully appraised value, and those auction people are just bloodsuckers, I swear. I'd really, really like to take a look at the entire collection as soon as possible just to help

Annabelle out, of course, so she knows what she can expect if she decides to liquidate them."

I had a vision of the harpies in *Zorba the Greek* cleaning out Bouboulina's bedroom as she lay dying. Oliver had always impressed me as being unpleasantly opportunistic, but it really shocked me to think that he was already making plans to pounce on Marv's violin collection. The man hadn't even been dead for twenty-four hours! And would Annabelle have any desire to sell instruments that she herself might enjoy playing in the future? It wouldn't exactly be like giving Marv's old clothes to Goodwill. The entire conversation felt weird and wrong. I couldn't get off the phone with this slime-ball fast enough, but he wasn't yet done with me.

"By the way, I understand you had an absolutely fabulous party over the weekend, you wicked girl! I adore parties, you know, so if you decide to throw another one any time soon, count me in."

Oh, right, I thought. *I didn't know weasels were considered party animals.*

"Just out of curiosity, Oliver, who told you about our party?" I said.

"Oh, let's just say a little birdie told me. I have friends all over, you know, and not just here in town. You of all people would be surprised to learn the identity of someone I consider to be among my nearest and dearest."

"Let me guess … Dracula?" I said.

"You're such a kidder, Althea. We have so many people in common, and I always hoped we could be better friends."

When pigs play Scarlatti, I thought.

"Naturally," he said, "I was more than a little distressed to hear that I hadn't been invited to your little soiree, I don't mind admitting, but then I realized it could only have been an unfortunate oversight. I mean, what string players in their right minds would give a party and not invite Seattle's premier violin dealer?"

I was speechless. Shocked, embarrassed, annoyed, but also speechless.

"Well, I must fly," he said. It wasn't a stretch to imagine him flapping away on long, tattered wings that matched his cheap salt-and-pepper toupee, flitting about his pretentious little shop, flailing against dusty glass cases full of rosin and metronomes as he attempted to become airborne. "I'm meeting an old friend for lunch," he added. "She's paying, and I find myself craving gin martinis and lobster. Think about what I said, Althea. Remember who your friends are. Ta-ta for now!" His phony British accent trilled almost a full octave too high as he clicked off.

While I'd been talking to Oliver Siddon, the piano music had stopped, leaving an echo of winter stillness in its place. Conrad shuffled into the kitchen and sat down heavily at the table, Winnie and Bert at his heels.

"Well, it's been quite a morning, Thea. Tell me. How's our Annabelle? I couldn't face the thought of eating breakfast once I heard about the accident. I'm pretty hungry now, though. Are you making lunch?"

I assured him that I was.

"Annabelle's going to have a hard time dealing with this, Thea. She and Marv were together a long time, and even though Marv was one controlling son of a bitch, I believe she loved him." Conrad sighed deeply.

"They haven't given her a prognosis yet, but I have to assume that she'll recover fully and be able to play violin again. At least that's what I'm hoping. I could never really understand Annabelle being married to Marv at all, let alone for so many years. What did she see in him? What could anyone have seen in him?"

Conrad picked up a teaspoon and polished it on his sleeve. "You know, he wasn't a bad-looking young guy," he finally said, "not the disgusting mound of flab he became later on."

"I can't begin to imagine him any other way," I said.

"Well, it's true. He compulsively ate himself into the kind of stature that a certain amount of sheer mass often provides. He wanted to be a 'big man,' a '*macher*' as they say in Yiddish, and he was, all six-foot-one and four hundred pounds of him. Marv truly came to embody that old phrase, 'throwing his weight around.'"

Marv had intimidated people with his size ever since I'd known him.

"No, he didn't become humongous until after he and Annabelle had been married for quite a while. Marv's problem was that he was ambitious, the kind of ambitious that walks all over anyone or anything that got in his way. Ruthless, I'd have to call it."

I'd certainly seen that side of him as well. It had made him one of the most detested men in Hollywood. When studio contractors eventually pushed younger players into the front of the orchestra to give the film composers "fresh young faces" to look at, thereby pushing the older players into the back of the section or reluctant retirement, no one was very sorry to see him go. Annabelle was another story. Although still a wonderful violinist in her own right, she was so identified with Marv that she suffered the same fate. The move to Seattle was a face-saving measure for them both.

"While he was still a young man," Conrad said, "he'd maneuvered himself into a concertmaster position at one of the major studios, and he held onto that rather successfully for the next forty years. I'm not saying he didn't deserve to sit in the chair. Just listen to some the solos he laid down on the biggest films of the fifties, sixties, and even the seventies and early eighties."

"Nobody ever said the guy couldn't play the fiddle," I said. He'd given recital after recital just to prove it to anybody who thought otherwise. Marv was well-known for accepting every concertmaster job that was ever of-fered to him no matter where he had to go or how far he had to drive to get there. To my knowledge, he never turned down a studio call, day or night. He never took a vacation unless the studios were on hiatus for the sum-mer, and he never called in sick. He taught at a couple of universities and played first chair with his own string quartet. Marv was seemingly unstoppable, but I always believed that he'd lost his humanity along the way.

"I remember how shocked everyone was when he was asked to step down as concertmaster of the string orchestra he'd practically put on the map," I said. "Imagine how battered his ego must have been when he was replaced a week later by some young violinist who didn't play half as well as he did. What a business!"

"Why do you think I left when I did?" Conrad said. "The cards were stacked against anyone with gray hair at that time, no matter how they played, and Whidbey Island seemed like a peaceful place to rest my aging car-cass. I've never looked back."

"So how did the lovely Annabelle Gardener wind up with Marv?" I asked. "She was a great, great violinist and a famous beauty. It always seemed kind of odd to me. I would have assumed that she could have had any-body or anything she wanted."

"Oh, she was a knockout all right, but for some strange reason, she seemed to be completely infatuated with Marv. Musicians rarely get to meet people who aren't musicians. You know that. We're a tight little clique with weird hours and strange habits, so maybe she never had a chance to look around and find a more appropriate version of Prince Charming. Still, the whole town was buzzing when she took up with Marvin Pratt in a serious way."

"I'll bet. Why would anyone do that to herself?"

"You've got me," Conrad said. "That's exactly what I asked my younger sister almost fifty years ago when she announced that she was going to marry him. Marv Pratt used to be my brother-in-law, you know."

"*What?*" I practically dropped the bread knife. "How come you never mentioned it?"

"Would *you*? Especially after the way it all turned out for my poor sister. Betsy died, you know. She was only thirty years old."

It was common knowledge that Marv had been married before and that his first wife had died, but I never suspected for a moment that she might be related to anyone I knew. It was a long time ago, years before I came to LA.

"Was this before you and I met back east?" I asked.

"Yes, way before. Betsy's marriage was the reason I took the faculty position in Boston. I wanted to get away from everyone in California, especially Marvin Pratt. She loved him right up until the end, if you can believe it, but I can't say the same for him. I always thought he behaved like a complete bastard."

I placed an enormous turkey, ham, and Swiss cheese sandwich with two dill pickle spears and some potato salad in front of Conrad and waited while he dug in. I poured an iced tea for him and waited some more. My curiosity finally won out over my patience. Conrad is a very thorough chewer.

"Well, what happened? How did they meet?"

Conrad looked up from his sandwich with a sad, far-away look in his eyes. "My sister and Marv? I wish you hadn't asked that. It was completely my fault," he growled. "I introduced them at a concert. I never imagined they'd be more than passing acquaintances, but you know how these things happen. Marv was over six feet tall, rather distinguished-looking in his tux, I suppose, and she was the beautiful Betsy Bailey, famous debutante, society's flavor of the month."

"Your sister was Betsy Bailey? *The* Betsy Bailey? I never would have guessed," I blurted out in my usual tactless way. "Not that there isn't a family resemblance, now that I think about it, but wasn't she an heiress or something?" Betsy Bailey, as I recalled, had become an icon among the beautiful people back in the fifties. Her wholesome good looks and elegance radiated old money and had graced magazine covers and society pages on coffee tables all over America. Then she'd disappeared from public view, or maybe I'd just stopped poring over my parents' collection of old *LIFE* magazines and moved on to more current newspapers and schoolbooks. "Wait. Doesn't that make you a pretty well-heeled guy?"

"You have no idea," he answered gruffly. "Listen, I never talk about money, and I don't want it to get around, do you understand? It didn't exactly bring our family happiness. In fact, I've always blamed the money for bringing us Marvin Pratt."

"And I always thought you were living from hand to mouth, as it were."

"That was no accident. I wanted it that way. I've seen firsthand what happens when greedy people decide you're going to be their ticket to the good life. Our great-grandfather was one of the railroad barons who made his fortune when money was money. Not a very nice guy, either. Just ask the Chinese coolies who worked for him in virtual slavery and died horrible deaths to build the railroads that made our family rich. Maybe Marv Pratt came to us as a certain kind of negative karma, the family curse."

He took a bite of his sandwich and washed it down with some iced tea. I sat back and appraised Conrad carefully, realizing that I'd never really known him at all. How many other people have I believed I've known very well, people who may have been carrying enormous secrets around inside themselves for years and years? Do we ever really know anybody?

Conrad took another big bite of his sandwich, and I just sat there, mesmerized by his narrative, waiting for him to finish chewing.

"Betsy showed up at a concert at the old Wilshire Ebell Theatre, where I was the soloist, and of course, she came backstage to see me afterward, all dewy- and wide-eyed, pretty as a picture," he said. "Marv was the concertmaster. *Beauty and the Beast.*"

Conrad sighed. I patted his hand.

"You didn't really stand a chance against someone as determined as Marv," I said.

"Maybe not, but I should have tried harder. The two of them eloped to Paris one day, and that was that," he said. "They didn't even send me a postcard. I'm sure I acted like a jerk at the time, but I thought I was doing it for her own good. Ha! We didn't have much to do with each other for years after that. That's when I took a position back east. It seemed like it was for the best."

I remembered Conrad from those years, a quiet and enigmatic bachelor. He didn't seem to be gay, but we never saw him with a woman, either. No one knew where he lived or what he did when he wasn't playing the piano or teaching. I'd been told that he'd been one of the most elegant and well-respected professors at the conservatory when he first arrived in Boston, but over time, he'd begun dressing down more and more, eventually impersonating a north woods lumberjack. His bespoke suits slowly gave way to old jeans and sandals, and his expensive haircut grew out into a scraggly beard and ponytail. I now began to understand that it was his way of physically expressing his detachment from the money and lifestyle that had brought about the fateful rift with his only sister.

"You can't blame yourself, you know," I said, placing my hand on his arm. "People, even very savvy people, fall in love with the wrong person all the time. It's a fact of life, Conrad. It's the universal cliché behind the romance of *Romeo and Juliet*, *Carmen*, *Tristan*, and *Isolde*, and all the great, immortal tragedies we make into our most beloved operas and ballets."

"Well, this one ended pretty badly, I can tell you," Conrad said, "and no one wrote any opera about it, either. Poor Betsy found a lump in her breast one day and was diagnosed with late-stage breast cancer. When Marv found out she only had a few months to live, he turned away from her and ran for the hills. That's when Betsy finally called me, and six months or so later, Marv began his affair, a very public affair by the way, with Annabelle Gardner."

"My God! That's pretty awful," I said.

"It was," Conrad said. "He didn't even come to her funeral. I was the executor of her will. She left a sizable amount to charity and the rest of her estate to Marv. She may have forgiven him, but I never did. How could I? Would you?"

"Probably not," I said.

"Betsy assured me over and over that she'd forced him to go. She said that if I'd only come to know Marv the way she did, I'd understand. They'd cried together and said their final good-byes, and then she sent him away. And he went, the bastard. So now you know."

We sat there for a few minutes, listening to the wall clock and the comforting stillness of Blanchard House.

"I'm so sorry about your sister, Conrad. I have to say, though, I'm surprised to learn something like that about Annabelle. She doesn't seem the type to have been involved with a married man. No wonder she looked so uncomfortable when she saw you last night."

"Thea, I never held any of it against Annabelle, not for a minute, although she refuses to believe that. She was very young, full of life, and completely infatuated with Marv just as Betsy had been. I don't know if she even realized Marv was still married when their affair began."

"Did you know her very well at the time?" I asked.

"Not really," Conrad said. "She'd only recently come to Hollywood from New York. Marv moved out of the Pasadena estate and into an apartment in Hollywood the minute Betsy told him she was sick. He may have insinuated to Annabelle that he was separated, getting a divorce—who knows? After Betsy's funeral, Annabelle left town for quite a while until some of the talk died down at least, and when she came back, the two of them seemed to take up right where they'd left off. A month or so later, they were married."

"It's hard to believe that Marv had that kind of effect on any woman, let alone Annabelle," I said.

"I'm embarrassed to admit that it hurt like hell to see them so happy together," he said.

"That's when you went back to Boston and started teaching?" I asked.

"I was so angry with Marvin Pratt that I knew I'd better get three thousand miles away from him or I'd be tempted do something I'd regret. How could he have gotten over his wife, that beautiful, darling girl, my own sweet little sister, so quickly? Nevertheless, Annabelle became the one true love of Marv's pathetic little life. She was quite a girl, our Annabelle. If things had turned out differently, she might have married me. I'd always had my eye or her, ever since I saw her for the first time."

"You had your eye on whom?" Grace asked, peeking around the corner of the kitchen. "What are we talking about, you two? Have I missed something?"

"Oh, no, just my entire life story," Conrad said. "You might as well tell her the whole messy thing, but could you wait until I've had my lunch? I don't think I could survive another telling of this grim tale. And listen, let's just keep it between the three of us, okay?"

"You've got it," I assured him. "And thanks again for sticking around while we sort this out. If you could manage another day or two here, I'd really appreciate it."

"Keep feeding me, ladies, and I'll think about it," he said and smiled at us, eyes crinkling at the corners. "I don't fancy leaving just now anyway. Not while Annabelle's in such a fix. Nothing I can do for her really, but I'd like to be close just in case."

After he polished off the last bites of his sandwich and pickle, Conrad went back upstairs to play some Beethoven sonatas, and I filled Grace in on what I'd just learned. She was as surprised and saddened as I was, but it didn't seem to affect our appetites. Not much does. And besides, I needed my strength for a long afternoon and evening of teaching. I made us two of the biggest sandwiches you ever saw, roast beef and Swiss cheese with cold slaw on them, and then slapped a scoop of potato salad and some pickles alongside each one for good measure.

Chapter 8

I WAS IN the middle of teaching the same tricky passage in a Mazas violin etude for the second week in a row to a gifted but sadly unprepared young man that afternoon when I heard the phone jangling in another part of the house. I purposely ignored it, and after four rings, the answering machine picked up. As the day wore on and one student after another came and went, I completely forgot about it. After my last student packed up her viola and was collected by her mother sometime after nine, I checked messages. It had been Detective Harry Demetrious, Kirkland PD, the man with the mellifluous voice, asking me to return his call.

It seemed pretty late to catch him at headquarters, wherever that was, but I placed the call anyway, hoping to leave a message. He must have given me his cell phone number because Detective Demetrious picked up on the second ring. He asked to see me first thing tomorrow morning.

"What does that really mean, detective? 'First thing tomorrow morning?' I'm a musician, so my 'first thing' might be a bit later than your 'first thing.' For example, I just finished teaching and haven't even had dinner yet," I said.

"Me either," he said. "Not the teaching thing. The dinner thing."

"I have an idea. How about you come over here in about fifteen minutes, and I cook something for both of us, and we can eat and talk? I don't mind whipping up a late dinner, especially if it means not having to get up early in the morning."

There was a long pause, and I wondered how far outside the bounds of propriety I'd just stepped when I heard the good detective burst out laughing. "Well, ma'am, I'm not sure I should be eating anything you cook without a taster present."

"Wha ... what?" I spluttered.

"It's just that, well, it seems that Marvin Pratt didn't technically have a heart attack after all. Not a natural one anyway. The cause of death has just been listed by the coroner as poison."

I was speechless, a highly unusual occurrence for me, but so far it had happened twice in one day. I was clearly on a roll.

"If I remember correctly, Ms. Stewart," the detective went on, "the deceased had just come from spending the

evening partying at your house. Did Mr. Pratt eat anything that evening? Anything that you can recall?"

Now it was my turn to utter an unseemly laugh.

"Are you kidding? That man ate everything! I was
surprised there was a tablecloth left when he was done.
There used to be a design on those plates, if you get my
drift. The man practically threw himself on the buffet
table with all fours and Hoovered everything in his
path."

"So I take it that the victim was an enthusiastic
eater," he said.

"You could say that," I said.

"I just did." The Marx Brothers would have loved
this guy. "Unfortunately, and much as I'm sure your
cooking might be *to die for*, I make it a habit never to
have dinner prepared by anyone I'm interrogating in a
murder case. Police policy. We're rather firm on that.
What if I drop by at, say, eight tomorrow morning, and
you can tell me what you remember about Sunday
night?"

It didn't sound like a request actually.

"Eight? Does anyone in the civilized world really get
up at that hour?" I asked, hoping for a reprieve. None
was forthcoming.

"Hasn't anyone ever told you about the early bird
catching the worm and all that?" Demetrious asked.

"Am I the worm to whom you're referring, detective? I guess that means you think I'm a suspect, doesn't

it? Too bad. And here I thought we were getting along so nicely—"

***

Sometime shortly after eight the next morning, Detective Demetrious and his partner pulled up in a dark gray Ford Taurus, my least favorite make, model, and color for a car. My face screwed itself up involuntarily as I watched it lumber up the gravel and grind to a stop. I'd made a fresh pot of coffee and thrown myself in the shower, but I'm not exactly a morning person in case you hadn't guessed, certainly not like Grace. She'd been up for hours already, making tea, practicing the cello, and puttering around the kitchen, singing Italian art songs. This aspect of Grace's personality was almost enough to strain the bonds of friendship, but I tried to overlook her propensity for early morning cheerfulness by keeping my eyes half-shut until the first chug of strong coffee slid down my grateful throat. It was all I could do to grope for the newspaper on the front stoop and feed the cat. Winnie and Bert had been out to Doggie Heaven, the wooded ravine on our property, to do what dogs do first thing in the morning. They'd already enjoyed their breakfast biscuit, and were now lying together on a small Oriental carpet in front of the entryway of Blanchard House, ready for company.

I don't know what I'd been expecting to see when I opened the door, but Harry Demetrious wasn't it. Mischievous dark blue eyes, black curly hair, dimples, and a body that worked out a whole lot more than I did flashed a badge and stepped confidently over the threshold. He was probably forty, more or less, but he looked disgustingly trim. Suddenly, I wished I were ten pounds thinner. I reminded myself that I was still a size six and relatively fit. At least I was wearing my good black jeans and my best black turtleneck sweater, and my shoulder-length hair was freshly washed. Had I remembered mascara? Of course. At least living in LA had taught me that much. With him was a tall but pudgy young man, straight sandy hair and bad skin, stuffed into a defiantly rumpled sport coat, a man who Demetrious introduced as Sergeant Matt Ziegler.

"Well, c'mon in and make yourself at home," I said, trying to sound more chipper than I felt. "This is Bert, the big baby."

Bert wagged his huge, shaggy tail while his lips curled up in a tooth-baring grimace that I'm sure he intended to present as a fetching doggie smile. The sergeant wasn't so sure.

"And this is Winnie, my little Aussie shepherd girl," I said, patting her head and giving her a scratch behind the ear. She had nothing to wag, her tail having been docked in a cruel and unnecessary breeding practice practically at birth, but she wiggled her rump attractively anyway.

"Hi there, guys." Detective Demetrious reached down and let the dogs sniff his outstretched left hand. There was no wedding ring there, I noticed. He smiled at me and flashed perfect teeth and enormous dimples. Are police detectives allowed to have dimples? I offered coffee and Christmas cookies. Both men declined when I passed the silver tray under their noses, but they didn't look happy about it.

"First of all, Ms. Stewart, may I ask … what is your connection to Marvin Pratt?"

"None, thank heavens! I mean, I've known the Pratts for years and years as colleagues, and I consider Annabelle a dear friend. We were all musicians in Los Angeles. You see, my friend Grace and I decided to celebrate our purchase of Blanchard House by hosting a small Christmas gathering for friends and colleagues who'd, for one reason or another, left LA and moved to Seattle. It seemed like a good idea at the time—"

"And it wasn't?" Demetrious asked.

"No, not so much. You see, in an incredible lapse of judgment, Grace and I thought it might be a nice gesture to invite the Pratts. I probably shouldn't say this, because he's dead now, but no one liked Marvin Pratt very much, except maybe Annabelle. He has … had," I corrected, "a way of getting on people's nerves. By the end of the evening, all we wanted was for him to go away and never come back."

"He was very obliging then, wasn't he?" Demetrious said dryly.

I shot him a look that said … oh, I don't know what it said, but it was a look.

"Did Marvin Pratt have any *known enemies*? See, that's how they say it on *CSI*. Pretty good, huh?" he said, giving me the full-wattage Demetrious smile. It was dazzling. I'd never met a dimpled police detective before, and I found the experience highly unnerving. His navy blazer matched his eyes. His blue shirt was perfectly pressed, and his tie had colorful little figures on it like a UNICEF greeting card. I couldn't think of even one man I'd met in the last three years, or maybe my entire life, who could wear a tie like that at eight in the morning and manage to look so incredibly sexy.

"Nice tie, detective," I said.

"Thanks," he said. "My mother gave it to me." *Touché*.

"Let's put it this way, detective," I said. "Marvin Pratt had no real friends that I know of at this particular party, although he had a wide circle of acquaintances, and I believe there were people in Seattle who the Pratts saw regularly for dinners and concerts. Marv got himself around in the top tiers of the music industry. We come from kind of a 'kiss up, kick down' business."

"What does that mean exactly?" Demetrious asked.

"If you're a concertmaster," I said, "which Marv Pratt was for many years, other musicians often feel they have to tolerate or even pretend to admire you. He pretty much made up the string section lists for every motion picture or television show or record date on which he sat principal for over forty years. That's real power. He decided who made a living and who didn't."

"Hard to make friends that way," he said.

"Yeah, but he never gave the impression that he cared about friendship much one way or the other," I said. "He treated most of his colleagues like dirt, if you must know. For his part, though, Marv was completely obsequious to conductors and contractors or to wealthy arts patrons."

"Sounds like a delightful man. And what about his wife?"

"Annabelle? Poor Annabelle's a completely different story, although I know she's often been painted with the same brush as Marv. Annabelle Gardener Pratt was already a pretty famous violinist before she married her husband. Everyone loves her. She's done her best to make Marv behave like a human being whenever possible, but it must have been an uphill struggle. She married beneath herself, I always thought."

"She certainly feels close to you, Ms. Stewart. You're the only person she asked us to contact when she went to the hospital. In fact, she listed you as 'next of kin.' Am I correct in assuming that you're actually no such thing?"

"Well, yes, you are, but please don't mention that little fact to anyone at the hospital, or they'll never let me in to see her. I couldn't bear it if she were stuck in there all alone day after day!"

"Now why would I do that?" He smiled at me with those dark blue eyes and his deep, deep dimples. My stomach lurched. "Can you tell me about the other people who were present that night? How many of them knew the deceased?"

"Most of them. In fact, the only two who didn't have some dealings with Marv are music teachers who've always lived up here in Kirkland, and even they'd heard of him. What's that saying? 'Bad news travels fast?'"

"We're going to have to talk to your, um, partner, too," he said.

"You mean Grace? She's my housemate and *business* partner. We're best friends."

Suddenly, it seemed rather important that Detective Demetrious have no questions about my sexual orientation. In another second, I probably would have blurted out, "Men! I like men!" Subtlety has never been my strong suit. I fluttered my eyelashes at him, though, just in case he had any remaining doubts. I can be shameless.

"Ah, I see," Demetrious said, getting out his pen. Did he really, or did he think I'd merely gotten a bit of dust in my eye? He was strolling through the library now, looking with interest at the rows and rows of psychology books lining the walls.

"Are you ladies holding a psychiatrist hostage somewhere in Blanchard House, Ms. Stewart? No? Are these all yours then?"

I nodded in the affirmative. "It's my hobby."

"You must be one smart cookie, Ms. Stewart. I'd better watch my step, or have you analyzed me already?" He lifted an eyebrow in my direction and turned back toward the living room, all business once again. "We'd like to talk to the other guests as well. Do you happen to have a guest list handy?"

"Not a formal one, but I can certainly write one out for you later today. I assume you'll need phone numbers and e-mail addresses too." I found myself unwilling to mention the fact that one of those guests, a certain Conrad Bailey, was currently reading *The Seattle Times* while settled comfortably in a high-backed wing chair just off the sunroom, well out of sight.

"A list with contact numbers would be very helpful," Sergeant Zeigler said. "Was this a dinner party?"

"Sort of. It was an early evening holiday tea. A buffet. We had lots of little sandwiches, you know, things like egg salad, shrimp salad, chicken curry with apple and walnut salad, ham and cheese, and cream cheese on nut bread. The usual. Then we had fabulous Victorian scones, which are Grace's specialty, with clotted cream and jam. Oh, and Christmas cookies, of course."

Zeigler looked over at the empty buffet table and sighed mightily. I wondered if he'd had breakfast.

"Were those the ones you just offered us? They looked delicious," Demetrious said. "By the way, what happened to the leftover food from the party?"

"Gone," I said. "We ate every bit of it, what little Marv Pratt left for the rest of us, that is. Except for the cookies. Allow me to point out that both Grace and I are still here, healthy as two horses."

"Too bad," Demetrious said. "Not too bad that you're still alive and kicking, but too bad that all the food is gone. I was hoping to take away a few of those little sandwiches and cakes for the toxicology lab."

I stopped breathing for a moment. "Oh, my gosh!" I said. "That's exactly what Marv did the night of the party. I just remembered. He made a few piles of those sandwiches and tea cakes on paper napkins and took them with him, probably for the ride home. You don't think that's what killed him, do you?" Suddenly, I felt sick.

"Well, it could be." Harry Demetrious stood up, and he and his partner headed for the door. "That, and a rather large dose of strychnine," he added over his shoulder.

Chapter 9

ANNABELLE LOOKED ONLY slightly better the next day. Her black eye now sported some dark purple and yellow discolorations. The breathing tube had been removed from her throat. The last specks of blood had been washed away, and she was sitting up in her hospital bed like a real person. Her swollen eyes opened slightly when she heard me nearing her bed.

"Thank heavens you're here," she whispered hoarsely. "I couldn't call you. My arms ... I couldn't remember your number. It's Leopold! You've got to save Leopold!"

"Leopold?"

"My baby. My beautiful Persian cat, Leopold. He's just a kitten, not even a year old. He's all alone in the house with no one to feed him. Marv will never remember. He's got dry food and a bowl of water, but he needs his wet food twice a day, and his litter box will need cleaning by now, too."

Her swollen eyes filled with tears, and she looked up at me imploringly.

"Oh, honey, please don't cry," I said, reaching for a tissue to wipe away her tears. "You know I'll do anything I can to help. Just point me in the right direction."

"There's a key to the house in my purse. They took away all my things, but the nurse told me they put everything in that closet over there. You have to go and save him, Althea. He's probably wondering where I am. What day is it?" Annabelle was becoming more and more agitated.

"It's Wednesday, Annabelle. Honey, you and Marv were in a traffic accident Sunday night. Do you remember that?"

"Not really," she croaked. "I remember being with you and Grace at your new house, and then nothing. My God! That means that Leopold hasn't been fed his wet food for three days already! My poor baby." Tears slid down her cheeks. I wondered if she knew that Marv was dead and wouldn't be feeding cats anytime soon, but I had no idea how to approach the subject again. Clearly, my first attempt had failed miserably. While I searched through her locker for her purse, I caught sight of the day nurse and slipped out into the hall.

"Excuse me, but has anyone informed my mother about her husband's death? I don't know how much she knows or what to say."

"The staff had a meeting this morning and discussed how the situation should be handled," she said, looking down at her crepe-soled shoes. "Your mother seems to be in complete denial and cuts us off any time we try to approach the subject. We were wondering if perhaps you might be better able to get through to her."

Not really, I thought. In fact, I was probably the very worst person there could possibly be, especially if you took into account my final, rather explosive encounter with Marv only an hour before he died. Hey, maybe I'd be asked to deliver his eulogy, too. Things were just getting better and better.

Annabelle was waiting for me to come back to her bedside, eager to give me instructions as to the care and feeding of Leopold. I'd never even been to the Pratts' house in Queen Anne, something I'd managed to avoid for three years, but I assured her that I could Google the address for directions and be there within the hour. I straightened her pillows and smoothed her sheets as best I could without jostling her.

"Listen, Annabelle, you shouldn't talk anymore," I said. "Your voice is giving out, and you need to rest. There's something I have to tell you, though. I've encouraged the hospital staff to believe that I'm your daughter. I hope you don't mind. Since you listed me as next of kin, I thought it would be all right with you. The hospital rules only allow immediate family members in the intensive care unit, so I fibbed ever so slightly—"

Annabelle tried to smile at me, but it looked more like a grimace of pain than anything else. "Of course, Althea, my sweet girl," she whispered. "I always knew I could count on you to do the intelligent thing."

Her house keys jingled safely in my pocket, and I decided to say good-bye quickly and run for the parking structure before she could ask about Marv. Normally, I'm ready and eager to face any situation head-on, but this was way beyond awkward and something I was unprepared to deal with at the moment. Neither, it seemed, was she. Was Annabelle still in shock? Perhaps, but she was pretty darned lucid about her cat. She knew she'd been in an accident, and she knew today's date, so what was going on here? Had the violence of the accident brought about some sort of selective memory, or was she simply afraid to ask the dreaded question? In any case, I wasn't about to pry open that door until I had to.

Chapter 10

"WOW, YOU'RE COMPLETELY out of breath. Did you run all the way back from the hospital?" Grace asked as she looked up from her laptop. "How's Annabelle? I probably should have gone with you, shouldn't I?"

"You couldn't have gotten in to see her anyway. I'm the only person she listed as family, and they're quite strict about visitation in the ICU."

"You're listed as a member of her family? That's pretty weird, isn't it? What's that all about? And you haven't answered my question. How is she? How is she taking Marv's death?"

"That's just the thing, Grace. She hasn't mentioned him at all, and I didn't bring him up, either."

"Whew! This could get tricky. What are you going to tell her when she asks?"

"The truth," I said. "I'm going to tell her the truth." *At some point, anyway,* I thought. Perhaps I should have been firmer today at the hospital and told her in the gentlest way possible that Marv was dead, but something held me back. She looked so pitiful, and so worried about her cat. Or was I just making excuses?

Grace looked up at me from her laptop with an expression I can only describe as pity. "I'm just glad that I'm not listed as a member of anybody's family."

"Rub it in, why don't you. Well, you're not getting off that easily. You're a member of my family, Grace, closer to me than a sister, and don't you forget it. I'm counting on you to write my heart-wrenching obituary and cast my ashes from the top of the cliff overlooking Kalaupapa on Molokai. I just hope you're still up to it when we're in our nineties."

"What is it with you and the leper colony?"

"It's my favorite place on earth, Grace, and so peaceful! So don't go thinking you can just toss my mortal remains under a bush across the street in Juanita Beach Park or into Lake Washington from the deck of an Argosy tour boat. I will know, and I'll come back to haunt you, I swear."

Grace rolled her eyes and shook her head. She'd feel differently, I knew, if she'd ever been to Molokai. This was one way of getting her there to see for herself how astonishingly beautiful the topography is. Too bad I wouldn't actually be with her. Well, at least part of me would.

"So what have you been doing while I've been busy impersonating a relative?" I asked.

"Me? I'm working on an ad to put in the Kirkland paper. How's this? *Haven't you always wanted to play the cello?* It's aimed at all those adults who fantasize about playing an extremely romantic instrument. People are always asking me what I do for a living, and when I tell them I play the cello, it seems like half of them say, 'I've always wanted to play the cello.' Well, here's their big chance."

"I think we could design a fantastic ad campaign around that idea," I said. "Something like *'Fulfill your secret desire to master the G string. Learn to play the cello.'* We could take a sexy glamour shot of you and your cello on a Victorian fainting couch with the wind blowing through your hair, satin dressing gown falling seductively around your shoulders revealing the slightest bit of cleavage. I can see it now." And I could. A picture like that could sell almost anything, not just cello lessons.

"Stop right there, missy," Grace said. "You'd have me dress up like Barbara Eden in those old *I Dream of Genie* TV episodes, wouldn't you? You missed your calling. You'd have been great in advertising."

"Just tryin' to help, ma'am," I drawled, "Unfortunately, you'd probably have a whole different type of clientele lining up for 'lessons.' Seriously, Grace, are you hoping primarily for adults, or are you willing to teach kids too? We should get your name on the public

school music department lists as soon as possible if you
want to teach kids."

"Honey, I'll teach anything with opposable thumbs.
We have to pay the utilities and eat, don't we?"

"Good point," I said. "Listen, I have to run over to
Queen Anne to pick up Annabelle's cat."

I filled her in on the Leopold wrinkle, and she insisted on coming along. Grace has always had this thing
for pug dogs and Persian cats because of those pushed-in
faces, which is definitely not my favorite look. I always
thought it made the poor animals look as if they'd run
into a plate glass window face-first, but if she was eager
to meet Leopold, that was fine by me. I was hoping for a
love match. One less litter box for me to clean. Poor
Lydia wasn't going to like this one bit, I suspected. It's
always awkward to have two members of the feline no-
bility ruling one kingdom, no matter how large.

The Queen Anne neighborhood encompasses an
enormous hill in Seattle, overlooking Puget Sound on
one side and Lake Union on the other. Marv and
Annabelle Pratt's three-story Georgian mansion was sit-
uated at the very end of one of the most desirable streets
on Queen Anne Hill, offering a jaw-dropping view of
Elliott Bay from the gardens and from every window on
three sides of the house. This remarkable edifice bore no
relation to the aging pile Grace and I called home. We
couldn't help but notice that every shrub was expertly
trimmed and the lawn was manicured. The brass plates

and beveled glass of the imposing front doors gleamed
beneath two enormous Christmas wreaths. I put the key
into the lock and heard a satisfying click as I pressed
down on the brass latch. The door swung open easily on
well-oiled hinges.

As architecturally pleasing as the freshly painted exterior of the house appeared, the interior far surpassed it
in sheer grandeur. Rich Italian brocade draperies, highly
polished teak floors, and elegant "Louis Something"
pieces were juxtaposed with oversized linen couches and
heavy glass and wrought-iron end tables, defining the
spacious ground floor rooms by providing cozy seating
arrangements. A floor-to-ceiling, carved limestone fireplace dominated one end of the house. Marv's art collection filled the walls, and I had to admit the man had exquisite taste. There was a Joan Miro abstract on the far
side of the dining room and a large David Hockney oil
dominating the vestibule.

The reality of Marv's death hit me then and there.
No longer would he be coming home at the end of the
day to this magnificent refuge and his elegant wife.
Whatever pride he'd enjoyed from collecting his various
treasures was at an end. There would be no joyous
Christmas morning at the Pratt household this year. It
suddenly became impossible to imagine Annabelle re-
suming her life all alone in this big, perfectly conceived
paean to the Pratts' worldly success. The man, even considering his lack of personal charm, had always been a

huge presence, and his death would leave a gaping void. *Can Annabelle find a way to go on without him?* I wondered.

A tiny, plaintive mewing coming from the general direction of an oversized sofa had Grace down on all fours before I could even say, "Here, kitty, kitty." Good thing I didn't waste my breath. No amount of coaxing could lure Leopold out from under the heavy furniture. In the dance hall disguised as a designer kitchen I found a can of what was obviously Leopold's favorite food, because there were several dozen identical cans of the pricey stuff stacked neatly on one end of the wide marble counter. The distinctive snap of the cat-food lid worked its magic and out shimmied a gray and white fluff ball ready to dine. Leopold was up on the polished countertop before I could even plop the food into a dish. We could have been jewel thieves or terrorists for all Leopold cared. This was one kitten that had his priorities well in order, and wet food was right up there at the top of the list as far as he was concerned. A rabid pit bull standing between him and a dish containing his favorite meal might not have given him more than a moment's pause.

"Isn't he gorgeous?" Grace said. "Look at those big, golden eyes, and that superb tail. No wonder Annabelle named him Leopold. He looks as if he could be the re-incarnation of Mozart's father, you know, fluffy gray hair, powdered wig, regal bearing. All he needs is a silk waistcoat!" She could hardly keep from petting the eager little glutton as he gulped down his chow.

"Was Mozart's father a world-class slobberer?" I said, watching him devour every morsel in his dish. "Leopold sure is."

"Don't be harsh, Thea. Remember, the poor little thing hasn't eaten in a few days."

"Maybe not this canned gourmet stuff, but there's enough dry kibble in his feeder to get him through the siege of Troy." And there was. Despite the immaculate condition of the rest of the house, and apart from the obvious fortune someone had invested in hand-painted English cabinetry, I was amazed to see that one entire slab of countertop was devoted to Annabelle's beloved cat. His dry food feeder, several bowls of water, dishes, and grooming aids were spread out on the white marble. It made me a little queasy to see him up there, dribbling chicken and some sort of disgusting fish in gravy by the smell of it, all over the place, but who was I to say? If Annabelle could put up with Marv, who ate pretty much the same way, I could understand how she might easily learn to love a good-looking cat with atrocious table manners. In fact, it was pretty obvious that Grace was quickly falling under Leopold's spell as well.

Getting Leopold into his carrier was another matter altogether. He was perfectly content to snuggle in Grace's arms after a hearty meal, but at the sight of the hated travel crate he stiffened, stretching all four legs in opposite directions, claws extended dangerously. He was willing to literally fight tooth and nail to keep us from putting him into that thing. The little monster clung fiercely to the edge of the hinged doorway of the despised crate, hissed, scratched at us, and began to foam at the mouth. Finally, we just plain gave up. We wrapped Leopold in an oversized bath towel that I'd borrowed from the linen closet next to the powder room, and Grace held him securely on her lap all the way home. We stuffed the entire backseat of my car with the carrier, the wet food, the dry food, the litter box, the toys, and his brushes. Grace was purring louder than Leopold, scratching him behind the ears and under the chin. I remained relatively uncharmed by the little ingrate, cursing under my breath at the snarl of traffic we hit as we headed toward the floating 520 Bridge and home.

Chapter 11

ANDREW LITZKY, FRESH from his afternoon Seattle Symphony rehearsal, was sitting all bundled up in his Toyota Camry. He'd obviously been waiting for us in the parking lot of Blanchard House as we drove up. I wondered just how long he'd been there, because his windows were completely fogged up and it took me a minute to realize that there was someone inside the car. He'd been huddled in there, listening to a remastered CD of Itzakh Perlman, an early recording of the Tchaikovsky Concerto I realized as soon as he opened the door and the music poured out, along with a few McDonald's Big Mac wrappers, an empty red container of fries, and some greasy paper napkins. Andrew looked cold and miserable.

As soon as I turned off the engine, Grace clasped the towel-wrapped Leopold tightly to her chest and ran for the front door. I followed at a more leisurely pace, dragging the carrier, the food, the toys, and a bad attitude.

Already, I could make out the sounds of barking and hissing emanating from inside the house. Yeah, this was gonna be lots of fun. Good luck, Leopold.

"I hope you haven't been sitting out here long," I said over my shoulder to Andrew as he shrugged himself out of his car, tossed the errant food wrappers back in, and followed me to the front door of Blanchard House. "We had to pick up Annabelle's cat all the way over in Queen Anne. The traffic was hideous. Conrad would have let you in if you'd rung the doorbell. What brings you over this way?"

"Man, I'm glad you finally got home," he said. "I was thinking about making a second trip to McDonald's for some hot coffee when you drove up. I didn't think anyone was here, and your car was gone. We just had a visit late this morning from a Kirkland Police detective and his chunky pal. Have you met them yet? Rosencrantz and Gildenstern."

"Ah, you mean Demetrious and Zeigler," I said.

"Yeah, that's them. Marilyn's pretty shaken up, and frankly, so am I."

Andrew was indeed looking harried as he removed his parka and plopped himself down at the kitchen table. Before we bought this place, I'd envisioned myself graciously entertaining guests in front of the fireplace in our elegant living room, but so far, everyone seemed determined to head for the same old spot at the kitchen table. It was ever thus. Oh, well.

"This guy asked a whole lot of questions about my relationship with Marv Pratt," Andrew said. "I didn't tell him a whole lot, but he seemed very interested in the fact that I'd been Marv's violin student in college. Thea, there's something I didn't bring up during the interview, but if the police dig a little deeper, they might just stumble across something that could lead them to believe that I was implicated in some way with Marv's death."

Andrew put his elbows on the table and rested his head in his hands. I put on some water for tea and waited for him to continue.

"You have to promise me not to say anything about what I'm going to tell you," he finally said. "When I'm finished, if you think I should say something about it to the police, then I will. I just need to talk it over with someone first. Marilyn is too freaked out to be much help right now, but I've always felt you'd be a good person to confide in. You're always studying psychology and stuff like that, aren't you? I trust your judgment about these things."

Ha! I thought. *You can fool some of the people some of the time.*

"I'm making some coffee," I said. "You look like you could use a cup. Go ahead. Talk. I'm listening."

"Okay, here goes," Andrew said, taking a deep, re-storative breath. "When I was in my sophomore year of college, my stepdad was diagnosed with lung cancer. He'd always smoked. So did my mom. Anyway, my mother asked me to come home and help her deal with everything. She was pretty overwhelmed. I have three younger half-brothers, much younger than I am actually, and they were a handful. Mom went to the hospital every day to be with my stepdad, and the boys were going wild on their own."

"It sounds like it was pretty tough on your family," I said.

"It was. I was on a full scholarship at that point and working part-time at a department store to pay for living expenses, so I had no extra money for a flight back to Rhode Island or anything else for that matter. I was afraid I'd lose my scholarship if I took a leave of absence from school and went home, but how could I refuse to help my mother and my stepfather? He was a really good guy, you know? He didn't really 'get' me, but he was always there for my mom and the kids."

"How does Marv figure in all this?" I asked.

"I remember being pretty upset when I went to my lesson with Marv that afternoon. When I told him about my stepdad's cancer, he tried to talk me out of going home. He got really angry with me and told me that, if I went, I'd be jeopardizing my scholarship and any possible career I might eventually have. I persisted, though, and he finally came up with an idea."

Andrew took another deep breath while I took the whistling kettle off the stove and brewed a large carafe of filtered coffee.

"Here's where it gets ugly. My very first violin teacher, Bernice Schulman, had given me private lessons since I was six years old back in Providence," Andrew said. "She'd never had children, and she treated me like a son. When she died of a heart attack sometime during my freshman year in college, I learned that she'd left me her fabulous Testore violin in her will. I never imagined that I'd own an instrument like the one she left me. It was pristine, the most remarkably preserved Testore you ever saw, and the sound was sweet and complex but extremely powerful too. More than that, it had belonged to my teacher."

"I'm sure you'd made her very proud," I said.

"When Marv saw that fiddle, he practically salivated," Andrew said. "He asked to play the Testore at every lesson, asked me about its provenance, and told me all about the maker. He had quite a number of illustrated volumes relating to violins and violin makers in his studio, and he'd pull out color photos of other Testores and compare them with mine."

"It was Marv's big thing, learning as much as possible about violins," I said.

"There was more to it than that, though. I didn't suspect at the time how much Marv craved my violin for himself. When he offered to lend me three thousand dollars so I could make the trip back to Rhode Island and be with my family, I was too relieved to second-guess his generosity. In my naiveté, I thought that perhaps all

music teachers must have some special feeling of kinship
with their students, a bond between them, the kind Mrs.
Schulman had felt for me. What an idiot I was!"

"You certainly were not!" I said. "It was a loan, for
heaven's sake. Anyone would have been touched and
grateful for an offer like that from his teacher."

"Wait. It gets better. Marv suggested that I leave my
violin with him as collateral, since I still had my old violin to practice on at home, and told me that he had no
doubt that I'd be back soon, and then I would repay him
as soon as I could. My mom sounded desperate, and I
was so worried about my stepdad and my brothers that I
jumped at the offer."

I could see already where this story was heading,
and it wasn't good. I poured coffee for us both and put
out a plate of cookies while Andrew continued his
narrative.

"My stepdad suffered a lot. Lung cancer's a hell of a
way to go, Althea. He lingered another six months or so,
and I took a leave of absence from school for a semester.
After the funeral, I came back to California only to learn
that Marv was refusing to return my violin."

"How could he justify something like that?" I asked.

"You know Marv. He could justify anything. He insisted that he'd bought it from me for three thousand
dollars, and a deal was a deal. In fact, he refused to teach
me anymore or take the money I tried to send him on in-
stallments or even take my phone calls."

"I wish you'd dragged him into small-claims court," I said.

"Me too, but I was completely broke, and only twenty years old at the time. Eventually, I managed to buy a passable modern fiddle, but nothing remotely comparable to my Testore. You know, I've tried hundreds of violins since then, but nothing has ever moved me like the sound of that particular instrument." Andrew drank some more black coffee and fidgeted with his napkin.

"Where was I?" he said. "Oh, yeah. I remember. As soon as I graduated from college, I took the audition for the Seattle Symphony and made it into the first-violin section. Marilyn and I got married a few weeks later, and we moved up here, relieved to be out of Los Angeles and away from Marv Pratt. I knew he'd see to it that no one ever hired me for studio work."

Andrew was right, of course. I'd seen Marv destroy my own husband's career on a whim. Andrew would probably have fared far worse.

"In a strange way, of course, if it hadn't been for Marv, I might not have taken a chance right out of college to audition for the Seattle Symphony and gotten lucky. Still, Althea, I have hated Marvin Pratt every day of my life since then. I've often dreamed of squashing him like a bug or pushing him over a cliff. Never poisoning him, though. That would have been too easy."

"Have the police suggested that you killed him?" I asked.

"Not yet, I don't think, but if they knew about all this, they might. He still has my violin, as far as I know, and I'm sure it's appreciated enormously in value over the years. It wasn't enough for him to own a Strad, a gorgeous Amati, and rooms full of fabulous instruments. No, he had to have the only instrument I've ever played that I felt was my authentic musical voice, the only thing of value I've ever had."

"That's not true, Andrew. You still have your integrity, which is more than anyone could say about Marvin Pratt, and you have your talent, not to mention your wife, who loves you very much, and your beautiful little Amelia. Still, I see your point, and I'm so sorry."

"It really sucks, doesn't it?" he said.

"It's a terrible story, Andrew," I said, "and just one more reason to despise Marvin Pratt. Still, I don't have any brilliant advice in this case. You didn't kill him, so I don't see why you should have to tell the police every gory detail of your past. I'm certainly not going to tell anyone."

"Tell anyone what? Hi, Andrew. Did I miss something?" Grace headed for the plate of Christmas cookies, selected a gingerbread man, and gleefully bit his head off. "For your information," she said, "Lydia and Leopold are sitting on opposite sides of my bedroom right now, eyeing each other. Leopold isn't too happy with the dogs, but he hasn't hissed at Lydia once. She looks ready to eat him, but I think they'll settle down in a few days. So what's going on?"

Andrew shook his head dejectedly. "Just tell her, okay?" he said to me. "But no one else. It's a mess, isn't it?"

He stood up and pulled on his parka. "I honestly hope Annabelle's going to come through this okay," he said. "She had no part in the doings between Marv and me as far as I can tell. I think he kept a lot of his underhanded dealings to himself. She'd have been appalled if she ever found out. Not her style, and Marv would have been too afraid of losing her good opinion, I think, to let her see what a bastard he truly was."

Andrew thanked me for the coffee, made his goodbyes, and left in time to hit the end of rush-hour traffic. I didn't know if unburdening himself to me was worth the trip, but this seemed to be my week for manning the confessional.

"Where's Conrad?" I asked Grace as she seated herself at the kitchen table. "His car is still here, but I haven't seen him"

"Oh, he's up in my room, mediating between the cats. First, he strokes Lydia and tells her how beautiful she is. Then he shuffles over and picks up Leopold and pets him for a while. I told you it'd be all right, and that was before we knew we had a cat whisperer among us." Grace accepted a cup of coffee, loaded it up with low-fat milk and sugar, and settled in to hear all about Andrew's violin and Marv's treachery.

"Well, now we know two people with plenty of motive, but I doubt either of them are murderers," she said. "In fact, I'd bet my life on it."

"Would you really? Me too," I said. "I mean, I wouldn't bet *your* life, just *my* life. But someone poisoned the man, and it wasn't me. And I'm pretty sure it wasn't you, either, Grace, so where does that leave us?"

"Us? It doesn't leave us anyplace. We're not the police, Thea. Let them handle it. Bad enough you're hearing more confessions than a parish priest the day after Mardi Gras, but I don't think you should try to solve a murder too."

"Still, I can't help but wonder who poisoned Marv Pratt. Don't you? Everyone may have wanted to, but someone actually went right ahead and did it. The question is ... *who?* Who hated him that much, and who had the guts and the smarts to pull it off? I don't know if you've thought about this, but are we absolutely sure that Marv was really the intended victim, or could it have been someone else entirely? Maybe one of us even. Would anyone we know want to kill us? I don't really think so, but there's another question that's been nagging at me. Did we invite a murderer to our tea party, Grace?"

"I told you they'd be talking about our parties for a long time to come, didn't I?" she said. "Here's the question that's been nagging at *me*, Thea. Will parents feel reluctant to drop off their little darlings at the scene of a murder? Would you feel entirely confident if it were your child?"

"Do you think we're going to lose students over this?" I said.

"We may," Grace said. "Once word of this gets out, and even if it isn't directly our fault, everyone may start looking at us with suspicion and wonder if we're somehow responsible for poisoning one of our guests."

No doubt about it. Murder isn't good for business. We were both plenty worried, and with good reason.

Chapter 12

"NICE, VERY NICE," Detective Demetrious growled at me early the next afternoon as he grabbed my elbow and steered me past the doorway of Annabelle's new room on the ninth floor. "You didn't tell her, did you?"

"You mean about Marv?"

"No, about the NFL playoffs. Of course I mean about Marv! You let me barge in there like an idiot and start questioning the poor woman about her husband's death before anyone had the decency to tell her he's gone!"

I bit my lip and squirmed a bit as he continued.

"She looked at me blankly as I went on and on about 'the deceased,' and it suddenly hit me that she didn't have a clue. This was the first she'd heard that her husband was dead, wasn't it? I came off like an insensitive jerk in there!"

"Well, at least she knows now," I sort of mumbled into my collar. "Wait a minute!" I looked up into the handsome face hovering menacingly near mine. "That means *you* told her. Detective, I'm counting this as an early Christmas present." I smiled up at him brightly. "You can cancel whatever else you may have been planning to give me, the diamond earrings, the Lexus. So how did she take it?"

"Do you really want to know?" he said, glowering right back at me, apparently less than charmed by my unrepentant cheerfulness. "She was strange, positively strange. She stared at me like I was some alien creature from a distant galaxy. Then she said, and I quote, 'Don't be silly. Marv's fine. He's always fine.'" Demetrious mimicked Annabelle's hoarse whisper in a wickedly accurate version. "'He just hates hospitals, or he'd have been in to see me already.' It was spooky. Tell me ... has she always been like this?" The detective fixed me with a piercing gaze, as if I had all the answers.

"Has she always been like *what*? Like a woman who's been through a terrifying ordeal and lost her husband of forty years? No, I don't think so, detective. Generally, Annabelle is the most responsible, pragmatic person I know. Now she's got casts on both arms. She's probably in a lot of pain, pumped full of drugs, and scared out of her wits. She's extremely traumatized. I'd hate to be judged under those circumstances. Wouldn't you? As for telling her about Marv's horrific death, well, there just didn't seem to be a good time, you know what I mean?"

I leveled a glare at him that would have given Medusa a run for her money. To tell you the truth, I was surprised to see him still upright and breathing.

"When I first saw her in the intensive care unit," I said, "she was crazed with worry about her cat, and now at least that's taken care of."

"What a relief," Demetrious said, wiping his brow dramatically with the back of his hand.

"Don't be such a wise guy," I said. "I thought that perhaps today if she asked about Marv, I'd break the news as gently as I could. Who knew Torquemada was on his way over to hoist her broken carcass onto the rack?" I could feel myself getting worked up, but I was determined to give as good as I got.

Harry Demetrious took a deep, calming breath. You could see him wrestling with his annoyance, trying hard not to bite my head off, but it was clearly a struggle.

"Look, Ms. Stewart, I have a job to do here. You're not making it any easier. Believe me, I have no intention of acting like the Grand Inquisitor of Spain, at least not with the unfortunate Mrs. Pratt." He shot me a menacing scowl, making his dimples all but disappear. "I'll come back tomorrow and speak with her in my most dulcet tones, all right?" he said. "Meanwhile, if you could just convince her that her husband is really quite dead, it would really help me out here."

"I live to serve, detective." I couldn't help smirking, but he deserved it. To think that just the day before, I'd found this obnoxious creature mildly attractive! It boggled the mind. "I'll see what I can do, but you know as well as I do that denial is an important survival tool, the human psyche's way of protecting itself from something truly unbearable, and she may not be willing or able to take the whole situation in for weeks or months. She'll probably need a good therapist to get her through all this. I'll bet you would, too," I added.

"You really did read that wall of psych books, didn't you? Yeah, well, she's waiting for you in there, Dr. Freud, and you'd better figure out a way to tell her pretty darn quick." He smiled ever-so-slightly, seemingly changing his tactics. "I'm counting on you, Ms. Stewart. You seem to be the one person she's able to connect with right now. Don't get me wrong. I think it's great that you're here for her. I really do."

Was there truly a human heart beating inside that impressive chest, or was this a merely the standard police line for gaining the confidence of a suspect? In any case, I wasn't in the mood.

"Thanks, detective. You're a peach," I said coolly. I turned on my heel and left him standing there in the hallway between two rolling carts full of dirty lunch trays. Seconds later, there followed the satisfying sound of a smart-alecky detective bumping into several awkwardly placed carts of plates and flatware. *Serves him right*, I thought as I proceeded into Annabelle's hospital room.

Annabelle's new roommate, a tiny, gray-haired, African-American woman surrounded by an impressive display of Christmas and "get well" cards, was dozing. As I tiptoed past a bedside table, I found my friend propped up in her hospital bed, looking out the window. There was a glass bowl of white narcissus and a potted red amaryllis in full bloom sitting on her windowsill. I wondered who might have sent them.

"Althea! How kind you are to come every day, and thank you for the beautiful amaryllis plant. You and Grace are always so thoughtful."

Annabelle's voice was still barely a hoarse whisper, but I welcomed hearing it. *Thank heavens for Grace*, I thought to myself. Why hadn't I thought to send Annabelle flowers or something? What kind of fake daughter was I, anyway?

"Who sent these delicious narcissus blooms?" I asked, sniffing the delicate white petals. "They perfume the entire hallway."

"I can't imagine. At first, I thought they were from Marv, but there's no card. He always includes a hand-written note, so I know they couldn't be from him. They just arrived a short while ago, but the young woman who carried them up had no idea who sent them, either."

I pulled the visitor chair closer to the bed so Annabelle could talk without straining her voice.

"Speaking of the mysterious," she said, "I've just had the strangest visit from a very insistent police detective, a rather good-looking fellow in an athletic body-builder sort of way, but annoying as hell. Overdeveloped muscles generally equate with very little brain, I believe. I think he's cuckoo, as a matter of fact."

"You must mean Detective Demetrious," I said.

"That's the one. He thinks Marv is dead. What a joke! I assured him that Marv is just fine. Between you and me, Marv's probably out having a lovely lunch with his new paramour."

I looked at Annabelle carefully to see if her eyes were dilated from heavy drugs or if she'd gone completely mad. What on earth was she talking about? I took her fingertips gently into my own and looked into her eyes.

"Huh?" I said.

"Marv hates illness and hospitals," she said. "He always told me that if I ever became truly ill, he'd have to leave me, and now it appears that he's done just that!"

I took a deep breath and plunged into the job I dreaded most. "Darling, I have something to tell you," I said, stroking her fingertips. "Something difficult and terrible. I don't know if you're ready to hear it, but I think I have to be the one from whom you hear it first. Annabelle, Marv never survived the accident. The police and the paramedics all concur. He died instantly. He never felt a thing. I'm so sorry."

Annabelle looked at me and blinked. Then she did the very last thing I expected. She let out a raucous bark of laughter.

"What ridiculous nonsense!" she said. "Marv's not dead. This is all a ruse."

"But the police report—"

"Let me tell you something, Althea. When I first met Marvin Pratt forty-five years ago, he flat-out lied to me. Yes, that's right. He lied. He told me that he was newly single, that he was a widower. Six months later, I learned that his wife hadn't been dead at all!"

I flashed back to my conversation with Conrad. I wondered what he'd think about what Annabelle had just told me.

"Imagine," she said, "what it was for me to stumble on her obituary in the newspaper, Betsy Bailey Pratt, the rich and famous Betsy Bailey, knowing that I'd been carrying on a passionate love affair, the first of my life, with the husband of a dying woman! Are you shocked? I certainly was. And the worst part is that everyone knew but me. It was beyond humiliating."

"Oh, honey," was all I could manage.

"It took me a long, long time to forgive myself and to forgive him," she said. "I've certainly never been able to forget it. No, Althea, as dreadful as it is to admit this to myself and everyone else, I know that Marv planned this. He's moved on. He's dead to *me*—that's all."

I realized that I'd been biting the inside of my mouth when I tasted blood. This wasn't the way our little talk was supposed to go. Things were veering farther off course every minute, and I had no idea how to stop them.

"Oh, I knew this would happen eventually," Annabelle said. "It's Marv's way. Did you know that I never even let on when I had the flu or a bad cold because I thought he might just up and go?" Her lips began to quiver. "Oh, Althea, I happen to know that he's already started seeing someone else, and I even know who she is." Tears were now streaming down her bruised face and spilling onto the hospital gown.

I whipped out a few tissues from the box by her bed and blotted her tears. I held a plastic cup full of water and a straw to her parched lips and urged her to sip.

"Oh, my poor Annabelle," I said, gently smoothing her hospital gown and straightening her pillows. "How can you even think such a thing? He's always been completely devoted to you. He's never left your side for a minute in all these years."

It was true, I thought. Marv had hovered around Annabelle like a well-fed honeybee in a clover patch, jealous of any attention she showed others. I was actually surprised that he tolerated sharing her affection with a cat, let alone with friends. He'd managed to insinuate himself into every conversation I ever tried to have alone with her, even showing up at, and completely sabotaging, several frivolous lunch plans we'd made so that we could enjoy a little "girl talk." Surely, Marv hadn't strayed, and not at his age.

"You don't believe me, do you?" she said. "That's because you don't know what I found in his datebook.

He had a luncheon tryst with a pretty young thing as recently as last week, and he thought I wouldn't find out."

I didn't know what to say. It all seemed so unlikely, but what did I know?

"Marv told me he was going to talk to someone about his violin collection," she said, "but after he left the house his '*meeting*' called to say she'd be late, only I was the one who answered the phone." Annabelle was now crying so hard that she could barely speak. "The young woman sounded flustered, to say the least, when she heard my voice, but she didn't say, 'Hello,' even though she knows me. Did she think I wouldn't recognize her voice? I'm a musician. I never forget a voice!"

At least that much was true, I knew from experience. I never forget a voice either.

"As soon as she hung up, I looked in his datebook," she said, "and there she was, penciled in for lunch at Marv's favorite restaurant. I knew right away something was up. Violin collection, my foot! His slutty little girlfriend plays the oboe!" Annabelle finished on a huge sob.

"Who was he meeting, Annabelle?" I couldn't imagine anyone wanting to sit across a lunch table opposite Marvin Pratt for any reason, watching him stuff his face as he rattled on about himself, let alone contemplate for one minute a pretty young woman wishing to engage in a hot and heavy romance with the most boring, annoying man on the planet. Of course, one can never explain affairs of the heart, can one?

"You know her," Annabelle insisted. "You know her very well. She was at your house the night of the party. It's Marilyn Litzky, the hussy!"

An absolute torrent of tears gushed down Annabelle's already wet cheeks from her swollen eyes. Her shoulders heaved. It must have hurt like hell to cry that hard while she was wearing all those casts and wrappings. At least she was finally showing some emotion concerning Marv, even though I was convinced that it was for all the wrong reasons. How could a smart guy like Detective Demetrious miss the signs of a proud woman suffering from a broken heart? Men!

I grabbed the box of hospital tissues on her bedside table once more and dried her eyes and nose and whatever else was dripping, careful not to injure her black eye, bump her casts, or disconnect the intravenous tubing that was hanging in the way.

"There's got to be some simple explanation, Annabelle," I said. "I know Marilyn's in love with her husband."

Actually, I realized with a start, I knew nothing of the sort. Sure, the Litzkys seemed happy together in public, but who knows what really goes on inside any marriage? Had Andrew bumped Marv off in a fit of jealous rage? Had Marv gone after his wife as well as his violin? It just didn't seem possible, but stranger things have happened.

"Andrew and Marilyn have a beautiful little girl, Amelia, who's only a toddler," I said. "As far as I can tell, Marilyn's a completely devoted mother. I can't imagine her doing anything to jeopardize her family life."

"There are many things a person like you can't imagine, Althea. You've always been such a straight arrow. You stood by Dennis longer than anyone expected you would, and even then he was the one who did the leaving, the fool! Not every woman's so levelheaded, so steady. You'd be surprised at what a woman is capable of when she's truly mad about a man. She'll sacrifice her home, her child, her dignity. Love makes people do truly insane things. Do you really believe Marilyn's incapable of making a mess of her life if the right man came along?"

"I really don't know," I answered truthfully. I thought back to a time before I'd met and married Dennis Littleton. I'd been engaged to a well-known Hollywood composer. It was my first real love affair, and it had ended badly. The beginning and middle weren't so hot either. I'd felt suicidal and helpless, and I had behaved like a ninny. The shame of it still lingered. *Dear, dear Annabelle*, I thought, *I could write volumes about the loss of dignity and the insanity of love.*

"More to the point, Annabelle, everyone in the world knows that you've always been the love of Marv's life. He would never abandon you, no matter what."

"Ha! Marvin is well-off, a fine figure of a man, and he's still someone of influence in the music industry. He's just as susceptible to flattery as the next person, perhaps more. Maybe Marilyn Litzky thinks he can help her with her career. You'd be surprised how many women have thrown themselves at Marv over the years just to get into a studio orchestra."

Boy, would I. I remembered Conrad's recollections of Marv as a good-looking younger man but still couldn't imagine it. Somehow, it seemed more likely that Marv had done the throwing of self, but perhaps Annabelle had actually been in love with her revolting husband and was not immune to jealously where other women were concerned. I began to see why Annabelle seemed incapable of accepting the reality of Marv's death. If he were merely having an affair, the marriage might not be over. He might eventually grow tired of the other woman or find to his surprise that he missed the comfort and companionship of his loyal spouse and, chastened and remorseful, feel compelled to return home. Annabelle might yet win him back. Death, on the other hand, was devastatingly final.

"You know, Althea, everyone else may believe that Marv is a cold and judgmental man, and perhaps to the outside world he has been, but not with me. He's always been so thoughtful, so generous about anything I might have wanted. Not a holiday or birthday or anniversary has gone by without Marv giving me a fabulous piece of custom jewelry that he designed himself. This may turn out to be the first Christmas in all these years that he won't be surprising me with something exquisite from Tiffany or Cartier that he's been planning for months."

If that were true, I thought, *there is probably a small but extremely valuable box hidden away among Marv's things.* If I could find it and bring it to Annabelle, would she at last accept her husband's passing? It was worth a try. I still had her house key in my bag, and perhaps to-night after my last afternoon of teaching before the Christmas and New Year's vacation, I could drive back to Queen Anne and take a look.

"Annabelle, by any chance, did you mention your suspicions about Marv and Marilyn Litzky to Detective Demetrious?"

"Absolutely not! Why would I? It's no one else's business, is it? Especially not that nosy detective's. I just told him that Marv hated hospitals." She looked past me and out into the gray morning that shrouded all of Seattle and beyond. "I didn't mention that I was dying, either," she whispered softly.

"What do you mean ... dying?" I asked her. Suddenly, there was a solid lump in my throat as I looked at this frail, still-beautiful woman in front of me. At that moment, I could clearly see it, the wasting away of flesh, the skin so white and papery that every blue vein was apparent. What surprised me was that I hadn't allowed myself to acknowledge it before now. Perhaps I just hadn't wanted to look beyond what was readily apparent, the shrinking frame of a formerly robust, vital woman. The sheer depth of my affection for her took me by surprise, and once again, I was reminded how powerful denial could be as a shield for the fearful individual psyche.

"Annabelle, please tell me what's going on. I'll keep it to myself, I swear, but you must have someone on your side, an advocate, someone you can talk to."

"Don't tell Marv. I beg of you," she said, hiccupping slightly. *Not bloody likely*, I thought to myself. "He suspects, I'm sure of it, but he doesn't know for certain," she went on. "Earlier this year, I had a few fainting spells, just a couple of times at first but with more frequency as time went on. I've always had energy, lots of it, but I have no stamina at all anymore. The simplest things tire me out."

"Oh, Annabelle, I wish you'd called me," I said. At that moment all I could do was berate myself for not having called her as well. I felt deep remorse for having allowed our friendship to suffer, Marv or no Marv.

Annabelle looked off in the distance and went on. "Thank heavens for Leopold! I told Marv I was taking Leopold to the vet for his shots. My poor husband hates doctors and needles. Even the thought of sitting in a veterinarian's waiting room makes him nervous. This was the one time I knew he'd be glad to let me go alone, although he hates having me drive by myself, so I took

Leo as a decoy, so to speak, and was able to see my internist and get blood work done. Althea, I have leukemia. Acute promyelocytic leukemia to be exact."

The stillness in the room was unbearable. I could hear the clock ticking and the vague hum of traffic nine stories below but nothing else. Annabelle looked up at me with those soft amber eyes and held my gaze with her own.

"Now you know, my dear Althea, and you have to keep it to yourself. Only one other person in the world knows besides my doctor, and that's my very oldest friend in the world, Babe. She's also sworn to secrecy, of course."

"Does she know you've been in an accident?" I said.

"That's just the problem. I thought it would be okay to confide in her because she lives so far away, but now she's flown all this way because she heard I'd been injured. She's already been here at the hospital today."

I wondered why she'd never mentioned Babe to me before, but I suppose we all have friends from our past that others know nothing about, former school pals, playmates, next-door neighbors, and the like. The woman's name itself held a certain caché, reminding me of that famous society darling "Babe" Paley. I imagined a wealthy *grande dame*, perhaps a former debutante.

"I must say it was strange seeing her in person after more than forty years," Annabelle said. "We were roommates at Juilliard. She became my accompanist. For a while, we even shared a huge apartment on Riverside Drive."

"Wow!" was all I could say.

"I still can't imagine who told her about the accident," Annabelle said. "I'm sure Marv didn't because he never had anything to say to her other than a quick 'hello' when he answered the phone, but you know the music business. Rumors spread like wildfire. It was probably that miserable little worm of a violin dealer Oliver Siddon. He's such a gossip, and he's known Babe forever because they come from the same town in the Midwest."

Somewhere in my jumbled little brain, two wires sparked, and a distant memory tingled, but not strongly enough to make a connection. Oh, well.

"Actually, Annabelle, you made the news all over Seattle and who knows where else, so I'm pretty sure she could have seen it on TV," I said.

"Oh, no! Now I have to hope that Babe and Marv don't run into each other," Annabelle went on, biting her lip in anguish. *No worries on that score*, I thought. "If Marv thinks I'm dying, he'll never come back to me, and I couldn't bear that. I always hoped I'd be the first one to go, and go quickly. I don't want to die alone."

I leaned over and kissed her on the brow.

"You won't," I promised her. "You mustn't think like that. We'll get you better, and no matter what happens, I'll be here."

All of the emotion of the last half hour must have exhausted Annabelle. Within minutes, she closed her eyes and fell asleep. I slipped quietly into the hallway, armed with a key to the Pratts' house and a keen interest in getting to know Marilyn Litzky a little better.

Chapter 13

AFTER I NEGOTIATED a hallway full of patients hobbling around with walkers, and nurses' aides wheeling dangling IV bags alongside them, I hightailed it to my car and raced to the Bellevue Shopping Galleria. Christmas was less than a week away, and I hadn't bought anything for Grace or Conrad or anyone else for that matter. Seeing the beautiful amaryllis in Annabelle's room jolted me into the realization that Grace, the sender of countless and timely handwritten "thank you" notes, had certainly already purchased a Christmas gift or two for me. What could I get for her at this late date? I'm no shopper. Enclosed places like malls and department stores make me queasy. Still, I had less than a week to find something, and I was on a mission.

And then there was Conrad. He'd shown little or no interest in moving back to Whidbey Island any time soon. It wasn't just loyalty to Grace and me, I realized, but his concern for Annabelle that kept him here. He hadn't complained once about being in a strange house, sleeping in a strange bed, and being without his own things around him. I wanted to put something special under the tree to thank Conrad for hanging in there with us during this most trying time.

Annabelle could certainly use some cheering up too. Unfortunately, all she really wanted was Marv. Much as I disliked the man, I would have dug him up with my own two hands and tried CPR if I could have restored him, living and breathing, to Annabelle.

Perhaps, I thought, *it would be fun, albeit inherently wrong, to find an amusing little gift for Detective Demetrious as well.* He looked like a man who could use a present under his tree. Unfortunately, my thoughts in that department kept drifting to a pair of shiny new handcuffs and something in black leather. Down, girl.

I needn't have worried about getting claustrophobia at the mall. I couldn't even get inside. The parking lot was completely full. Of course, this was Bellevue, an even politer version of greater Seattle, so no one pushed or screamed or threatened violence over parking spaces the way they do in LA. They just waited patiently in line, car after car. It hardly seemed like Christmas.

I pulled an illegal U-turn and headed away. I thought about fighting the crowds at Redmond Town Center but decided on Parkplace Books instead. It's important to support local independent merchants, and this particular bookstore is a Kirkland treasure. I found a space on the far side of the parking lot near Starbuck's and walked toward the bookstore. By now, a gentle rain had turned my hair into a mess of long, wet frizz. My parka was pretty well drenched as well, but we consider it bad form up here to run from the rain or, heaven forbid, use an umbrella. Good sport that I am, I have tried repeatedly to fit into the local scene by strolling at a nice, even pace from my car to my destination despite my natural inclination to make a run for it. Today was no exception. By the time I stepped inside Parkplace Books, unfortunately, I smelled like wet dog and looked about as appetizing.

"Althea! Over here!" Delilah Cantwell trilled in her rich mezzo-soprano. She was still wearing the same rumpled outfit she'd worn to our party, but now it was damp and, I noticed as I drew closer, musty-smelling. As she motioned with one arm from the cookbook section, she tried to balance a perilously tall stack of books with the other.

"Have you been visited by the police yet?" she asked. "James and I got the third degree from them, and we didn't even know Marvin Pratt. By the time that detective got through with us, we were both looking at *each other* with suspicion. He intimated that Marvin Pratt had been poisoned. But we didn't even suffer from the slightest bit of indigestion that night, and we ate everything but the shrimp. It wasn't the shrimp, was it?"

"No, I don't think it was the shrimp, Delilah." I said. "In fact, I don't believe it was anything we served at all.

Between Grace, Conrad Bailey, and me, we ate huge amounts of everything left over from the party, and we're just fine."

Delilah began to color slightly and looked off to the distance.

"The detective asked us if anything unusual happened at the tea, and we didn't know what to say. James was his normal, discreet self, but I was a little more nervous than usual. Before I knew it, I'd blurted out the whole story about you and Marvin Pratt, including the awful things he'd said about your ex-husband. Althea, I'm sorry. I didn't mean to make trouble for you, and James and I know you had nothing to do with the poor man's murder. It just sort of came out," she said, looking away in embarrassment.

"Don't worry about it, Delilah," I said. "It was bound to come out sooner or later. Detective Demetrious has that effect on people. I find myself babbling like an idiot whenever he's around."

Oh, and mentally undressing him, I thought, but I didn't mention that part.

"Anyway," I said, "I'm looking for some meaningful, last-minute Christmas presents, and they're going to be books from this store or nothing at all, so please excuse me while I shop my brains out. Promise me you won't feel bad about mentioning that little 'incident.' I consider you a dear friend, Delilah, and if it makes you feel any better, I told the police *you* killed Marvin Pratt."

Delilah Cantwell looked up in horror. I waited a few seconds and then gave her my best hundred-watt smile. She guffawed and promptly dropped her enormous pile of books on both of our feet.

"Cleanup on aisle four!" Delilah said, giggling as we bent to retrieve them.

I looked at the titles of her prospective purchases with interest. There were several volumes on kayaking in the Northwest, probably for James, a vegetarian cook-book, and more than a few books pertaining to adoption. Delilah, of course, noticed me reading the book titles as I piled her selections one by one into her arms.

"Yes, James and I are finally considering adoption. We've been on the fence for years. But I'm not getting any younger, and we've been trying to conceive forever. We tried a fertility clinic, but nothing worked. Frankly, we're both a little scared about how to even start the pro-cess, so I thought we could read up on it over the holidays."

"Wow! That's wonderful and very brave of you both. It could be great! I envy you and James. I really do. Somewhere between my career and my now-famous marital disaster, I completely missed the baby boat. I've almost reconciled myself to the realization that having my own child isn't going to happen for me. After all, I'm forty-three years old, and there's no man on the horizon. It's too bad. I always thought I'd make a good mom."

"I had no idea, Althea. I'm so sorry." Delilah patted my arm, almost dropping her books again. "We've felt the same way for years, but now we've finally decided that it's time for us to do something about it."

"Some little child will be incredibly blessed to have you and James for parents, Delilah. Anything I can do, a letter of recommendation, hand-holding through the process, you just let me know."

We hugged somewhat awkwardly, almost toppling those books once more. I wished Delilah Cantwell a Merry Christmas and the best of luck in their baby quest and resumed my shopping.

Now if I could just recall which authors Grace enjoys most I'd be all set. Then I spotted a shelf of Alexander McCall Smith books and remembered his series based on daily life in Edinburgh. I knew they'd be just right for Grace. I also threw several Mary Daheim books on the pile for good measure. With any luck, Grace would have plenty of time to enjoy lounging in front of a crackling fire this winter, enjoying a good read and a cup of tea rather than dwelling on the interminable drizzle outside while cursing the insane friend who dragged her up here.

What did Conrad find amusing these days? How about a book or two about Whidbey Island? I noticed a darling rubber duckie in the children's section and, remembering Conrad's love of the bath, it wound up on the counter too. I bought Annabelle several narrated best sellers and music CDs, because she couldn't turn pages to read books or magazines with her arms in plaster casts. Of course, she couldn't work a CD player either, but I figured that with the help of the hospital staff we'd manage something.

It occurred to me that Harry Demetrious might enjoy reading something about the surviving Templars and crime-solving in the Middle Ages. On a whim, I selected a Michael Jecks paperback mystery for him, threw it onto the ever-growing pile, and whipped out my trusty debit card. At least now I could face Christmas with some measure of equanimity. Of course, Winnie and Bert, perfect dogs that they are, had earned something juicy and chewy for their stockings, and Lydia and Leopold surely deserved a few catnip mice apiece. Next stop, the pet store! I was on a roll.

My little Honda actually seemed lower to the ground than usual from all the gifts piled up in the back as I pulled into Blanchard House's parking area. Conrad must have heard the car crunching on the gravel, because he came hobbling out to help me wrestle with the shopping bags.

"Have you seen Annabelle? How is she?" he asked anxiously.

"Better, I think. She doesn't look like her old self, though. She's so thin and very weak. She has a big black eye that's swollen almost shut and casts on both arms. The most frightening part is that she's in complete denial about Marv's death. She says he's just avoiding coming into the hospital because medical things make him uncomfortable."

Conrad shook his head as he shuffled to the door with the bags. "She really adored him, didn't she? I guess I always knew it, but there was a time when I hoped otherwise."

"Someone sent Annabelle a beautiful bunch of white narcissus, but there was no card attached. Those flowers wouldn't have come from you, would they, Mr. Bailey?" I asked him gently.

"Maybe," was all he answered as he slowly climbed the stairs to the guest room for his afternoon nap.

Chapter 14

THE LAST STUDENT of the night, my very last student before the Christmas vacation, was packing up his viola. In one corner of my studio stood a seven-foot-tall artificial Christmas tree covered with tiny white lights. Every young violinist or violist that had come for lessons, and even quite a few parents and siblings, had written wishes for the New Year on shiny pieces of colored foil origami paper. Then we'd tied each one to the tree with silver curling ribbon. Our studio's "wish tree" looked magical, especially as the afternoons darkened to evening. There was also a small pile of gifts beneath the tree from students and their families. Some packages, I knew from Christmases past, contained homemade candies and cookies. Others were music-related ornaments, gift cards, and handmade items. I'd baked brownies and many different kinds of Christmas cookies for everyone to enjoy during the last two weeks before vacation, and those were just about all gone.

I stood back and marveled at the handsome young man shrugging on his leather jacket before picking up his viola case and music bag. Just three years ago he'd come to me as a short, chubby, eleven-year-old beginner. Now he was a slim six-footer, his smooth skin and perfect Chinese features set off by an appealingly shy smile. He was currently the principal violist of a local youth symphony and well on his way to becoming a fine musician. So was his thirteen-year-old sister. Yes, it was good to have these lovely young people in my life, even if only until they left for college. I felt happy and extremely blessed as I unplugged the tree, closed the studio door for the night, and headed upstairs to the kitchen.

"Althea, you have to try this soup I've made!" Grace was happily ladling her steaming creation into large china bowls. "You know, I don't mean to be immodest or anything like that, but I think I really may have a talent for making something delicious out of nothing. I'm not kidding. We're out of almost everything, but I just kept throwing in bits of this and bits of that and *voila!* Fantastic soup!" She'd already set the table and had cut the bread and put together a salad. As a result of her most recent domestic efforts, the kitchen looked like a bomb had exploded behind her. Ah, well, I was happy to clean up if she was kind enough to cook and then wait until after nine at night to eat dinner with me. Grace is, unlike me, a morning person, and just keeping her eyes open this long was a major sacrifice for her.

"Where's Conrad?" I asked Grace as I sat down and opened my napkin. His place was empty. I found this unsettling, as he'd shown himself to be quite prompt about mealtimes.

"He left for Whidbey Island about an hour ago," she said. "He told me not to worry, that he'd be back tomorrow with some clothes and some trio music for us to play. I guess he's tired of rinsing out and wearing the same thing four or five days in a row. Not that it matters. All his plaid shirts look exactly alike. So how do you like my soup? I'm thinking of calling it Blanchard House Chowder." Grace was right to be proud of it. It was terrific.

"It's great," I said. "What's in it?"

"That's the problem, Thea. I can't remember. There's corn and fresh clams and then a whole lot of fresh vegetables, diced potatoes, cream, and some sherry. It's really the herbs that make it, though, and for the life of me I can't recall what and how much of everything I used. I just let myself sink into a trance and threw stuff in. I was channeling Julia Child at the time."

"How would you like to channel Captain Kidd and go on a late-night treasure hunt inside the Pratts' house?" I said. "I'm headed there right after dinner, and if you'd like to join me, I'd be grateful for the company."

I explained to Grace the nature of the search, omitting any reference to Annabelle's suspicions about Marv and Marylin Litzky. I was also careful not to tell her about Annabelle's diagnosis, either. I was beginning to understand how therapists feel carrying their patients' secrets. Confidentiality can be a terrible and lonely burden.

Winnie and Bert hadn't seen much of me all day, except for their walk in the rain, dragging poor Grace and me behind them through all the biggest, muddiest puddles. They absolutely love car rides, though, and wagged their rumps and ran for the door when they heard my keys jingling. If only I had that effect on everyone.

"Who wants car treats? Then get right into the back, and no shilly-shallying," I said. The dogs were very obedient and hopped up and onto their bed in the car. Grace and I got right in too. The wind and rain lashing at us through our clothes to our skin moved us along rather briskly. We popped a CD of Medieval Christmas carols into the car stereo to set the mood and drove carefully through the wet streets of Kirkland and along Lake Washington on our way to the 520 Bridge. Our town was a vision. Twinkling Christmas lights and fanciful holiday displays had turned Kirkland into a fairyland after dark. Traffic was unusually light this late in the evening, so we were able to take our time and enjoy the scenery.

"If I haven't said it yet, then I've been seriously remiss," Grace said. "Thank you, thank you for urging me to come up here, Thea. I love this place!"

Grace had been drinking in the beauty of Christmas in the Northwest with every fiber of her being for the last two weeks. She'd spent an afternoon ice-skating in the temporary ice rink in Bellevue Park. She'd spent an afternoon photographing local toddlers pulling on Santa's beard and squirming off his lap when he came to the Waterfront Marina a few weeks ago. Blanchard House was garlanded, illuminated with twinkling white lights, and festooned with red velvet bows and swags, thanks to her cheerful ministrations. Despite the shadow of a murder hovering over us, Grace was working hard to make Blanchard House a welcoming place we could call home.

***

The Pratts' house and yard were pitch dark when we arrived. The nearest streetlamp was a full block away and no help at all.

"Guard the car," I told the dogs, locking them in. They seemed to understand. I'd forgotten to bring a flashlight, so we struggled in the inky blackness to get the key into the lock. Finally, we were inside, feeling around for a light switch. Grace stumbled into an occasional table, knocking a lamp practically into my hands, or we might be there still, feeling around for a wall switch.

The view of the city lights against the inky water of Puget Sound beyond was, if possible, even more breathtaking at night than during the previous afternoon. Grace and I wandered from room to room, turning on lights and admiring the furniture. The bedrooms all seemed to be on the second floor, so we headed up the curved staircase to the master bedroom to search for a hidden jewelry box.

We were taken aback by the dimensions of the room itself. The upholstered, king-sized bed hardly seemed imposing at all in such a grand space. On the taller dresser, obviously Marv's, was a beautiful photograph of Annabelle holding her violin, taken when she was probably in her twenties. Her lustrous ash-blond hair hung down onto her bare shoulders, and her face was luminous, even in a black-and-white photograph. No wonder Marv had fallen for her, and fallen hard. On Annabelle's dresser, however, was a picture that completely took our breath away. There was Marv, but not the Marv that Grace and I knew. This photograph captured the image of a young god, possibly in his early thirties, looking into the distance, posed with his violin. He was nothing short of stunning. Who would believe that under all that extra flesh, there lurked a potential movie star? This youthful Marv reminded me of someone, but I couldn't put my finger on it. Gary Cooper, if he'd ever played the violin. Rumors of Marv's early successes with women became instantly plausible. Marv Pratt had been an extremely handsome man. I stood and stared for quite a while as Grace continued her search.

"Thea, look at this!" Grace called from across the room. She was thumbing through a stack of leather-bound albums on a shelf near the bed. "Here's a collection of programs from every concert the Pratts ever attended. Annabelle must have made them into scrapbooks. The dates go all the way back to when they first met. Here's a Jascha Heifetz trio recital, with Gregor Piatagorsky on cello and Virginia Majewski on viola. These must be worth a fortune! Oh, my gosh! Here's a whole separate scrapbook of programs from your duo concerts with Dennis. Annabelle must have attended every recital you two ever played!"

"I believe she did," I said. I was now feeling horribly guilty about not making sure to see more of Annabelle once I'd moved up to Washington state. I'd shied away from anything that reminded me of Dennis, or our duo, and, I realized, that entire portion of my life excepting my friendship with Grace. Annabelle, it seems, had become a painful reminder to me of what I'd lost.

Grace had moved on to the various drawers of Marv's bureau, careful not to disturb the folded contents. "No little boxes in here," she announced. The closet yielded nothing, either.

"Let's see if Marv had an office or a practice studio," I said. Across the upstairs landing were two full bathrooms and three more bedrooms. One was clearly a guest room, judging from the basket of soaps and guest toiletries on the wicker dresser. The other room was pink and feminine, with a wooden music stand, an oversized, pink-and-white-striped reading chair and ottoman, a pink-and-white chintz daybed, and a small but elegant French writing desk facing the windows. Annabelle clearly had her own space in which to practice, read, and nap if she felt like it. The middle door led to a small guest room impersonally furnished with two twin beds and an empty dresser.

Not so for the room at the end of the hallway. This last door opened into a large, magnificently wood-paneled study worthy of an English country squire. Not only was the carved mahogany desk huge and imposing, but the built-in, sliding shelves contained case after case of violins. There were wooden file cabinets full of music and several two-sided, wooden music stands. There was an entire wall of CDs. This was the central location for the stereo system that served the entire house, judging by the labels on the panel doors. The room was also climate controlled, obviously to protect the violin collection, remaining several degrees cooler, I noticed, than the rest of the house. If home were truly a man's castle, then this was the command post.

"Don't you feel weird about going through Marv's things? I do," Grace said as she gingerly examined the contents of the desk drawers, gently lifting papers and folders in search of a likely jewelry box beneath them. Interestingly, nothing was locked. One might think that a violin collection valued in the millions of dollars would be protected by an alarm system or enclosed in a vault. *Musicians are truly eccentric to a fault*, I thought.

Perhaps Marv had wanted access to his violins and bows whenever he wanted to play them or show them to someone. Couldn't he be bothered with unlocking a vault? Did he believe that the force of his personality would keep out burglars?

On the desk, beside a framed silver picture of a smiling Marv and Annabelle in what appeared to be the Italian countryside, was a hefty pile of mail as well as some previously opened letters. One, I noticed, was from Oliver Siddon's violin shop. Another's return address was from the manager of the Los Angeles Philharmonic, and a third came from the office of the music director of the Seattle Symphony. Yes, Marv may have been retired, but he was still someone of influence in the music world. I didn't even know where to start in a room this complicated. A small jewelry box might be stashed anywhere—in a music cabinet, in a violin case, or behind the books and CDs that lined the walls.

A relatively small but captivating oil painting in a gilded antique frame caught my eye. It was hanging by itself on a far wall between the casement windows that overlooked the garden. As I moved closer to it, I recognized the serene face of Betsy Bailey gazing out at me. The face was youthful and sweet, set off by sandy-colored hair worn in a soft pageboy curling just beneath her chin. This wasn't the glamorous, lush beauty of the young Annabelle Gardner but a refined and gentle loveliness that spoke of summers in the Hamptons and winters in Swiss boarding schools. It was easy to see a family resemblance between the young Betsy Bailey and her brother, the once-elegant Conrad Bailey I'd first met at the conservatory so many years ago. It surprised me to see that Marv still kept a place in his heart and on his wall for his first wife, and that Annabelle was so obviously tolerant of that affection. *People are always more multilayered, more intriguing than one first imagines*, I thought, *even Marvin Pratt*.

"Nothing," Grace said. "Not a thing. It would take several days to go through all these files and cases. Maybe we should come back another day when we're not so tired and it's not so dark." Grace was feeling discouraged, as was I.

"I can't help wondering if Andrew's Testore violin is somewhere in this room in one of these violin cases," I said. "There's a part of me that would love to find it and simply return it to him. Of course, that would be so wrong and completely unethical, but it's certainly tempting."

"This entire collection now belongs to Annabelle, doesn't it?" Grace said. "If she knew the truth, I have no doubt she'd restore it to Andrew, or at least allow him to buy it back from her."

"Telling her the whole story might sully her memory of her husband, though, wouldn't it," I said, "so how could I do that to her? And how do we know that Andrew's version of the story is the absolute truth?"

There were all sorts of ethical questions inherent in the situation, questions which could not easily be ignored. I was torn, though. I could still picture Andrew sitting at our kitchen table, his head in his hands, telling me about the loss of his precious violin so many years ago. Could he have been mistaken in his original understanding of Marv's intentions? He'd undoubtedly been under a lot of pressure at the time, and people do tend to hear what they want to hear. So much of what I thought I knew about Marv and Annabelle had changed, even during the last hour. Could there really be something going on between Marilyn Litzky and Marvin Pratt? Stranger things have happened, I realized, but being in this house and in these rooms assured me that Marv had always been deeply in love with his wives, both of them.

Grace and I left on a few lights, strategically illuminating various rooms to be seen from the street just in case someone had been watching the house for signs of occupation, and then we carefully locked up. Marv may not have been nervous about leaving all of those instruments unprotected, but I was.

"Do you think Marv really bought something for Annabelle and then hid it in the house?" Grace said, stopping in her tracks as a new thought occurred to her. "What if he left it at the jeweler's until just before Christmas? It would be safer that way, and Annabelle wouldn't find it by accident. That's what I would have done, if I were Marv."

"If you were Marv, we definitely wouldn't be having this conversation, but you've got a good point there, Sherlock," I said. "Perhaps there's a jewelry receipt among Marv's personal effects, the things he had on him at the time of the accident. The police must still be holding them. We should ask them to check his wallet for a jewelry receipt, don't you think?"

The thought of calling Detective Demetrious produced alternating waves of pleasure and anxiety. Did he still regard me as a murderer suspect or merely an annoyance?

By the time we got back to Blanchard House, it was after midnight. The rain had finally let up. Winnie and Bert climbed stiffly out of the rear of the car and wandered through the wet shrubbery, doing what all good dogs do before retiring for the night. We waited for them on the front porch, wrapping our coats around ourselves and shivering a bit. The heavy marine layer hanging over Kirkland blocked out any possible glimmer of starlight, and Grace and I found ourselves staring up at a black, moonless sky. The interior lights from our upstairs windows and the twinkling white Christmas lights wrapped around the porch pillars were comforting against the inky darkness that surrounded us. The dogs didn't seem to mind, however, and were taking seemingly forever rustling around in doggie heaven, so I whistled to get them back to the house. They charged out of the bushes and into the house with their usual gusto, barely missing our legs as they headed for the hall. After we got them safely inside, Grace and I eventually dragged ourselves upstairs to our respective bedrooms.

It had been a long day—the rain-soaked dog walk, the confrontation with Demetrious in the hospital corridor, Annabelle's emotional revelations, hours of teaching, and the final disappointing treasure hunt through the Pratts' household. Lydia jumped up on the bed, purring softly, demanding her usual bedtime ritual of petting and stroking before settling down snugly against my legs. The house was quiet, and I was exhausted; however, sleep eluded me. There were too many unanswered questions.

Was it possible that Marv Pratt had indeed been romantically involved with Marilyn Litzky? Could Andrew Litzky have found a way to get his wife and his violin back with one well-planned murder? Had Marv known or at least guessed about Annabelle's illness, and was he planning to leave her? Was there a piece of jewelry that held the answer to Marv's last intentions concerning his wife, and if so, where was it? Who had poisoned Marvin Pratt, and why? Finally, there was what seemed to me to be the most pressing issue, the one that kept my eyes from closing until dawn. If the doctors' diagnosis was correct and Annabelle indeed had acute leukemia, what would become of my dear friend?

Chapter 15

"HO! HO! HO! Santa's a wee bit early, but good, good dogs that you are, he left these for you!" Conrad pulled two enormous, basted beef bones from behind his back and handed them to Winnie and Bert, who'd been sniffing his pant legs and making happy snuffling noises ever since he'd come through the front door. Both of them immediately ran off in opposite directions with their disgusting Christmas loot firmly gripped in their appreciative little jaws. "And Santa has something for you two ladies as well," Conrad said. Hopefully, he wasn't handing us more chew bones. He'd taken the midmorning ferry back from Whidbey Island, and he was standing in our front hallway, beaming. "I hope you're not busy this evening, my lovelies, because we have third-row orchestra seats at Benaroya Hall. The Seattle Symphony is playing Tchaikovsky's 'Nutcracker Suite Overture' and Beethoven's Ninth in one glorious program! How can you beat that?"

"Are you serious, Conrad?" Grace said. "I haven't heard the Seattle Symphony play one live note yet, and I've been dying to go to a concert ever since I got here! How did you ever manage to get tickets for the week before Christmas?" She was thrilled, and so was I.

"Santa has his ways. And lots of ill-gotten family money, remember?" Conrad winked. "Santa even owns a tux, so you two had better get dolled up if you want to be seen with him." He shuffled back out to the car for his suit bag and another carryall, but not before we gave him a few hugs and some hearty pecks on his grizzled cheeks. Meanwhile, I could hear Winnie and Bert contentedly gnawing in the distance, grinding their massive beef bones into slobbery pulps. We all express appreciation in our own way, I suppose.

Grace was up the stairs in a flash. I could hear the hangers rattling around in her closet as she searched for the perfect thing to wear. Of course, if you look like Grace, almost anything becomes the perfect thing. I followed her up to her bedroom a few minutes later and stood in the doorway. Leopold was sleeping, stretched out on the canopied bed among Grace's pillows, looking like a fluffy gray pasha. Lydia was fast asleep on an overstuffed chair near the window. There was definitely a "live and let live" attitude prevalent among the furry residents of Blanchard House.

"I have to go out for a while, Grace," I said as she emerged from her closet with an armload of shoes and evening purses. "Can you make lunch for Conrad? I probably won't be back until sometime after four this afternoon. There are steaks for dinner tonight, and I'll be happy to broil them and throw together a salad before the concert, or we can grab a bite on the way to Benaroya Hall."

"Where are you headed? Are you taking the dogs?" Grace dumped an armload of accessories in a pile on the bed and began holding up all sorts of flashy outfits in front of the full-length mirror. Leopold opened one eye, surveyed the small mountain of evening bags and shoes that had momentarily disturbed his nap, and went promptly back to sleep.

"I have some shopping to do," I said. Well, I sort of did. The best excuse I could come up with for visiting Marilyn Litzky was to drop by the Litzky household with a Christmas gift for little Amelia. "The dogs seem pretty happy just chewing away on their new bones and drooling on the oriental carpets, so I'll leave them here. They've had their big walk already, so they'll be okay until I get back." I probably should have been selecting my own evening shoes and jewelry, but I knew from experience that it would only take me a few minutes. Some women can spend days planning their attire for a big event. I have a ten-minute attention span where wardrobe is concerned. Like Flora Poste in *Cold Comfort Farm*, I'm content with looking "elegant and interesting" rather than drop-dead gorgeous. I'll admit that my self-esteem took a major plunge as Dennis's disinterest in my womanly charms became increasingly evident over the course of our marriage. It's made me a little afraid to put myself out there. I sometimes remind myself that I'm still selling a worthwhile product, competence and character. Talk about cold comfort.

Where do people buy toys for children these days? My parents used to take us to actual toy shops just before Christmas when I was a little girl, those magical wonderlands filled with everything a child could possibly dream of receiving from Santa. How else could a child who'd been relatively good all year compile a suitable list of things she couldn't possibly live without? The aisles, I recalled with some nostalgia, had been crammed with exquisite dolls from all over the world, doll carriages and strollers, and elaborate dollhouses. Of course, tomboy that I was, I wanted, and to my astonishment got, a Daisy air rifle for Christmas, but that's another story. It occurred to me that I hadn't seen an old-fashioned toy shop in years, but I supposed that now most people hit the big chain stores. The thought of going to yet another mammoth, overcrowded, overheated shopping center only a few days before Christmas made my skin crawl, so I drove myself back to Parkplace Books.

Today, it was crammed with last-minute shoppers, but I managed to make my way to the children's book room without stepping on too many feet or knocking over the holiday displays. There were small groups of unattended children sitting on the carpeted floor with picture books in their laps, creating an adorable, squirmy obstacle course. In a corner beyond the fantasy section, a beloved old friend named Raggedy Ann caught my eye. She appeared to be exactly like the Raggedy Ann doll that I'd loved almost to death as a child. *Surely, a colorful little rag doll would be appealing to a toddler*, I reasoned. Who could resist that big, heartwarming grin and floppy yarn hair?

I grabbed a boxed version of my old childhood pal and several classic Raggedy Ann and Andy picture books and then joined the line of customers at the register. As the clerk at the customer service desk wrapped my purchases in Santa-themed Christmas paper, I stepped outside under the store's awning and called Marilyn Litzky on my cell phone. She answered on the third ring and assured me that I was more than welcome to come over for lunch, not just to deliver Amelia's presents, but to meet her own mother, who was still visiting from San Francisco. Oh, goody! How do you coax a woman to come clean about her extramarital love affair while her mother's chowing down across the lunch table? *Too bad*, I thought. I was already committed to making the visit, so I stuffed the presents into my Honda and drove through the steady rain over the 520 Bridge and onto the 5 Freeway North toward the Green Lake section of Seattle.

The Litzkys' historic, foursquare bungalow sits only a short block away from the actual lake in the middle of Green Lake Park, which places it in a very desirable section of the city. None of the houses in the neighborhood have much front yardage, but most of the old craftsman homes still retain the original front steps and covered porches and have been lovingly maintained. The Litzkys' house was no exception. It was painted chocolate brown with pale cream trim. The conifer plantings around the small front garden were remarkably lovely, even on a wet winter's day. Someone had placed a life-sized, inflatable Santa on the porch, and the door was wreathed in garlands of fir and red velvet ribbon. Everything seemed pretty jolly, so I was unprepared for the dour face that Marilyn Litzky wore as she opened the front door.

"Come in. Come in!" she welcomed me in hushed tones, carefully closing the massive oak door as I stepped inside. The house was warm and smelled of fresh pine and cinnamon. "I'm so glad you're here, Althea," Marilyn whispered. "I know it's Christmas and all, but I'm not in a very good mood at the moment. I could use some cheering up. Amelia's down for her nap, but my mom and I are getting lunch ready in the kitchen."

"That's a shame," I said. "I really missed seeing Amelia at the party. My timing isn't the best, I'm afraid."

"She's been fussy all morning, so I was glad when she finally conked out," Marilyn said. "Here, let me take your jacket. You're sopping wet! You haven't met my mom yet, have you?"

Marilyn looked pale and tired. Her eyes were red-rimmed. Had she indeed lost a lover when Marv had died? I couldn't help but wonder. She led me from the front hallway past a cozy craftsman-era living room, decorated with a fresh noble fir Christmas tree in the far corner, and into her large and newly renovated kitchen.

"Hello. I'm Paula Sachs, Marilyn's mother." A pretty, slim woman in her midfifties stopped putting out plates and cutlery long enough to offer me her hand. Her professionally cut chestnut hair and smart gray pantsuit only served to highlight her daughter's lack of makeup, uncombed mop of hair, and generally disheveled appearance. I'd never seen Marilyn look anything but well put-together and bouncy. I found myself wondering if this sudden change in grooming might be the result of depression. She'd seemed her usual perky self less than a week ago at the tea, but her appearance had changed radically since then.

"Do sit down and make yourself comfortable," Paula said. "We're having tuna sandwiches. I hope that's all right." Paula Sachs was a "take charge" kind of woman, no doubt about it. "Here, let me put those pretty packages underneath the tree. It was so kind of you to bring them. Our little Amelia's very anxiously awaiting Christmas this year, thanks to all those television commercials and holiday specials on the Disney Channel."

"We've read *The Night before Christmas* to her so many times that we all know it by heart," Marilyn said.

"She'll be very, very excited to finally see something underneath the tree," Paula said. "Marilyn and Andrew have hidden all of poor little Amelia's gifts until Christmas morning, so she's been a bit worried, you see. This will be reassuring for her." There was a slight but unmistakable undercurrent of disapproval in her tone as she moved briskly toward the living room with the boxes.

"Amelia is Mom's only grandchild," Marilyn whispered to me, "so it's been a case of overkill in the toy department. My family's actually Jewish, but not religious. I was raised with the old Chanukah tradition of small presents and those gold foil chocolate coins on eight subsequent nights after the lighting of the menorah. Not Andrew. His mother was Catholic, and his dad was Jewish, so they celebrated everything, but they hid the presents until Christmas morning."

"So did my family," I whispered back.

I aimed my best smile at Marilyn, but she was looking down at her hands and twisting her wedding ring.

"It's going to be a very strained holiday this year," she said. "All my plans have been ruined. Whoever expected Marv to die like that? It's changed everything." Her eyes grew misty, and her mother, having returned to the table, reached out to touch her daughter's hand.

"I know, honey. It's so disappointing. It really is." *Paula must be the most understanding mother in the world*, I thought. What plans had been ruined? Had Marilyn been planning to leave Andrew for Marvin Pratt? Was her mother also her confidante in an illicit affair? It seemed that Annabelle might have been justified in her suspicions after all. Poor Annabelle. Poor Andrew. The thought of trying to choke down a tuna sandwich with these two women was horrifying, even though I'd been famished until a moment ago.

I was thinking up a likely reason to excuse myself from lunch and run for the door when Marilyn pulled herself together enough to continue.

"My Christmas gift for Andrew has completely fallen through now that Marv's dead. I tried my best to make this a perfect holiday for him. I really did. Andrew's been so down lately. He's been tense and distracted for the last few months." Marilyn looked forlornly out of the kitchen window. "I was going to give my husband back the one thing he's ever really loved, Althea, his Testore violin. It was all worked out. I'm sure that Andrew told you the whole sordid story of the wonderful violin his first teacher gave him and Marv's acquisition of it, but he doesn't know that we've been trying to buy it back."

"And we almost did," her mother said.

"You see, my father died last year," Marilyn said. "I was his only child, and he left me quite a sizable inheritance. My mother flew up here a few weeks ago to help me make an offer to buy it from Marvin Pratt."

Marilyn looked over at her mother and gave her a fond smile.

"Mom's a real estate attorney and a pretty shrewd negotiator, so I asked her to help me. We met with Marv, who agreed to sell the damned violin back to me. We set a price, and I was going to pick the instrument up a few days before Christmas at the Pratts' house and hand over a cashier's check. It was all settled."

"And suddenly Marv died in the accident," I said.

"It's unbelievable!" Paula said.

"Annabelle's in bad shape now, too," Marilyn said, "and as far as I can tell, she knows nothing about the deal we made. Everything Marv owned is now solely hers, I believe, and she may not be willing to sell the Testore to me. Why should she? Besides, she's all banged up, and she's just lost her husband. I couldn't possibly ask her about it for months and months, if at all."

No wonder Marilyn was depressed.

"To make matters worse," she said, "I barely said 'hello' to either of the Pratts at your party, because I didn't want Andrew to suspect anything. We've never been very friendly with them anyway, not after what happened with the violin, but in retrospect, it must have come off as being downright rude."

Well, that explained the expensive lunch date in Marv's daily planner. Marilyn and her mother really were having a business lunch with Marv Pratt about his violin collection. So much for a red-hot love affair. The tuna sandwich on toasted rye began to look slightly more appetizing, but only slightly. The gloom in that kitchen was ankle deep.

"You know, I could put in a word for you with Annabelle about the violin," I said. "I'd be happy to. It's not like she doesn't own at least forty other violins at this point. I'm just not sure how to explain the whole deal without making Marv look like a jerk, though. It isn't considered polite to speak ill of the dead, is it?" This had certainly become a delicate situation, I realized, and I'd just put myself firmly in the middle of it. Oh, well, I could just add it to the ever-growing list of uncomfortable situations in which I seemed to be finding myself.

"I couldn't expect you to do that, Althea," Marilyn said. "It would be ghoulish. And then there's the possibility that Marv had already included the Testore in the collection he was planning to bequeath to the Seattle Symphony. If it's already listed in the will as part of his posthumous gift, that's the end of it, isn't it?" She stood up suddenly, grabbing for a tissue from the box on a nearby shelf, spilling her coffee and mine.

"Oh, God, Althea. I'm so sorry. Here, let me get that," she apologized, blowing her nose while she attempted to wipe up the spill with her napkin before the river of hot liquid wound up in my lap.

I probably should have jumped up as well to escape the steaming coffee that was rapidly surging my way, but I was too stunned by this latest development to move.

"Did he tell you that, Marilyn?" I said. "Did Marv actually say that he'd planned to will his entire collection to the Seattle Symphony?"

"No, he didn't. Not at first, anyway. Oliver Siddon found out that Marv Pratt had asked Horst Beckman to come out from Chicago and appraise his entire collection prior to bequeathing it to the orchestra."

Everyone knows Beckman's fine reputation as a recognized violin expert and appraiser, so I wasn't surprised that Marv had sent for him. *Oliver must have been miffed*, I thought, *to be left out of the deal*. Appraisals are one of the most lucrative parts of the instrument business.

"Oliver Siddon has always claimed to be *the* local string instrument expert, as you know," Marilyn said. "He couldn't stop ranting about it the day Andrew went to his shop to buy a set of strings. You can imagine how devastated my poor husband was by the news."

Marilyn was right about Marv's bequest, I realized. Once Andrew's Testore violin went into the settlement as part of the collection, it would be virtually untouchable.

"He came home from Oliver's shop, feeling sick to his stomach," Marilyn said, "refusing to talk or eat for several days. He wouldn't tell me why until a week later, and only because I coaxed it out of him. That's when I got the idea of trying to buy that stupid, stupid violin from Marv, no matter what the cost."

Marilyn wasn't touching her lunch, and neither was I. This was the first I'd heard that Marv had planned to bequeath his instrument collection to anyone, and I wondered how Annabelle felt about it. Did she even know? Had she been consulted, or was this yet another one of Marv's high-handed schemes?

"I'd never spoken with Marvin Pratt before we all three met for lunch," Paula said in a soft but precise voice as she poured fresh coffee into our cups and handed them around the table. "He seemed pleasant enough at first, if a tad pompous. He'd made reservations at a very upscale restaurant and insisted on picking up the check, but he wasn't exactly what I would call warm and gracious."

"No one has ever called him that," I said.

"Mr. Pratt didn't seem receptive to the idea of selling us anything at all," Paula said, "but we had a good deal of money at our disposal, and Marilyn was very determined. Ultimately, he came around to agreeing to let it go for what Marilyn believes was a fair price."

"It wasn't about the money, it seemed to me," Marilyn said, "but more about the prestige of handing over all those extraordinary instruments to the Seattle Symphony in a very splashy way and being acknowledged for it by his peers."

"I take it that LA wasn't kind to the Pratts," Paula said. "I sensed that he wanted to be remembered as a great man by his fellow musicians while making the 'powers that be' in Los Angeles regret having driven him out. This may turn out to be quite a legacy for the Seattle Symphony, don't you think?"

I was speechless, contemplating the enormous ramifications this endowment might have and how it would contribute to the prestige of the orchestra. Management would be thrilled by the publicity alone that such a gift would generate. If someone in the upper echelons of the organization knew about this in advance, would he or she be tempted to make it happen sooner rather than later by poisoning Marvin Pratt?

"You're right, Mom," Marilyn said, "so what was one measly little Testore violin compared to Marvin Pratt's Stradivarius, his Guarnerius, his Amati, the Gaglianos, the Villaumes, the Storionis, and all the other gems he was about to hand over? That's what I asked him, Althea. Then I looked him square in the eye and inquired if Annabelle knew the whole story of this particular violin."

"I wish I'd been there," I said.

"I asked him if she knew how Marv had gotten his hands on it," Marilyn said. "That was my trump card, and I played it. She must have had no idea whatsoever. Judging by the horrified expression on his face, Marv wanted it to stay that way, too. If that's blackmail, then so be it. I'd do it again in a heartbeat!"

Marilyn looked at me so fiercely that I felt momentary frightened. *Like mother, like daughter*, I thought.

Marilyn wouldn't have made a bad attorney herself. No, there was no love lost between Marilyn Litzky and Marvin Pratt. That much was certain. She'd simply met with Marv because she'd wanted to save her husband from his ongoing obsession over a lost violin, and now it looked as if she'd never be able to do it.

I recalled the countless ways I'd practically turned myself inside out trying to make things better for my husband during the last years of our marriage. To what lengths would I not have gone to save Dennis from his demons? How many books had I plowed through about alcoholism and depression, hoping to find a way to save my husband? I had nothing but admiration and sympathy for Marilyn Litzky.

"I think the hardest part for my daughter has been trying to conceal this from Andrew," Paula said. "When that police detective and his partner came over to question the two of them about their relationship with the deceased, Marilyn claimed that she barely knew Marvin Pratt. It was an understandable behavior at the time, considering the circumstances. She still believed we might be able to recover Andrew's violin, and the hopelessness of the situation hadn't fully sunk in yet."

"It must have been a terrible shock to her, finding out about Marvin Pratt's death that way," I said.

"Of course," Paul said. "but Marilyn's initial denial makes the situation very precarious. As soon as the police begin looking into Marvin Pratt's personal items more closely, they're sure to find her name in his calendar and learn all about that lunch meeting. I've advised her to call the detective in charge of the investigation and tell him the whole truth of the matter as soon as possible. She hasn't been willing to make the call because she's afraid that it might implicate herself and Andrew in the murder."

"I would think that just the opposite is true," I said. "Marv's death only serves to end a deal that was beneficial to both of you, Marilyn. Couldn't you just tell the police that you were trying to buy a wonderful violin for your husband as a Christmas surprise without mentioning its history? That would explain sufficiently why you didn't speak up about it in front of Andrew, wouldn't it?"

"Oh, Althea, of course you're right, and I will," Marilyn said. "I have to, don't I? If Andrew knew that I'd come so close to getting his Testore back and that we'd lost it once again, this time maybe for good, I'm afraid he'd just make himself sicker over it. I don't want to do that to him. He's been through enough with that damned instrument. I can't help but resent the thing. Honestly, I wish his teacher had never given it to him in the first place!" Marilyn said, slamming the tabletop with her open hand.

A sharp, piercing wail cut though all discussion. "Now I've awakened Amelia. Mom, could you please get her? I'm so tired, and I don't want to take it out on her. I feel like a terrible wife and a complete failure as a mother." Marilyn did look awful and obviously felt worse.

"Please listen to your mother's excellent advice, Marilyn," I said as Paula left the room to attend to her granddaughter. "Go call Detective Demetrious and tell him everything. Maybe you can ask him not to share this information with Andrew, at least not right now. Andrew probably senses something's very wrong, too. He's a big boy, Marilyn. He'll deal with it. In fact, I think he'll be proud of you for having the gumption to try getting the violin back. Personally, I think you're a terrific wife and mother!"

I hugged my rather limp friend and pushed her dark hair out of her eyes as if she were a little girl. At that moment, I had only tender feelings for this unhappy young woman who had tried so hard to make everything turn out right for the man she loves, but to no avail. This was a situation with which I could identify completely.

"I promise I will speak to Annabelle when the time is right," I said. "Now go enjoy your holidays and your beautiful family. Thank you for lunch, Marilyn. Please make my good-byes to your mom for me. I hope Amelia likes her present, no matter when she opens it."

With that, I headed back to Kirkland and the hospital. I hadn't taken a bite of lunch, and there was a dark coffee stain on my new beige slacks, but I felt better for having made the trip to the Litzky household.

What could I say to Annabelle that would bring her some peace of mind? I could certainly relieve her worst fears by assuring her that there was no affair going on between her husband and Marilyn Litzky, but that might interfere with a very necessary coping mechanism that her subconscious mind had created for her psyche's protection. *How emotionally fragile was she? Would she ever be able to face the fact of Marv's death?* I wondered.

Chapter 16

I SPENT A few restful minutes slumped in my car in the parking lot of Evergreen Hospital, watching rain-drenched visitors come and go. It was damp but peaceful in the Honda, and I took this rare opportunity to simply sit still and think. There were so many questions that only Annabelle could answer, but I wasn't sure how to approach any of them. Was Annabelle in on Marv's plan to bequeath millions of dollars' worth of instruments to the Seattle Symphony? Was there a will already drawn up that would immediately go into effect in the event of Marv's death, or was the gift to be given posthumously by both of them? No wonder Oliver Siddon was so eager to get his talons into Annabelle and those instruments. If Horst Beckman hadn't already submitted the appraisals, and if the gift to the symphony hadn't already been for-mally entered into Marv's will, Oliver might yet be able to persuade Annabelle to allow him to sell off the entire collection privately, piece by piece.

I found myself considering whether or not the vast amount of money and prestige involved in such a sale might be considered a credible motive for murder. Still, Oliver hadn't been present at Blanchard House on the night of the crash. Was it possible that the poisoner had somehow placed something in the Pratt's car while the guests were inside? Marv and Annabelle had lived in Los Angeles too long to ever leave their car unlocked, I knew with reasonable certainty. I was sure that whatever car they owned would always have been alarmed, or at least locked. Even my little Honda Fit, "Bluesette", was locked and alarmed every time I left it for even a moment. LA trains you to behave self-protectively, so I was confident that I wasn't alone in my car-locking routine. In fact, Annabelle had made such a habit of locking herself out of her own car while she was shopping that Marv was always driving to various shopping malls or sending the Auto Club to rescue her from her latest predicament. He finally had numeric keypad locks installed on both of their cars. I'm sure the Auto Club was grateful.

After ten minutes of heavenly solitude, I forced myself to leave the warm but moist cocoon of my beloved car and dashed for the hospital entrance, head down against the wind and rain. Of course, I ran right into the rock-solid chest of Detective Demetrious as he prepared to step out into the storm.

"You again," he said. I looked up into a pair of blue-gray eyes brimming with humor.

"Yes, me again. No, I wasn't looking where I was going. Sorry," I said, but I didn't mean it. "Have you finished torturing Annabelle?" I said, staring straight up at him. "Did you leave any marks?"

Why did I always have to joust with this man? Couldn't I have just sincerely apologized for almost knocking him over? My mouth seemed to have a life of its own where Detective Demetrious was concerned.

"Really, Ms. Stewart, you have a poor opinion of police work, or is it just me that you enjoy disparaging?" he said. "By the way, I make it a point never to leave marks."

I felt myself coloring under his gaze. There was a slight twitch in the corner of his mouth, but no dimples showing whatsoever. My knees went a little wobbly, but I held my head high nevertheless.

"Well, that's a relief," I said.

We were facing each other in the doorway of the hospital, and neither of us was moving; however, my mind was racing. Why hadn't he interrogated me more thoroughly? He'd certainly grilled everyone else who'd been at the party that night. Did he believe I was innocent, at least of murder? Was I currently dripping rainwater on his shoes?

"Your *mother* had a lot of visitors today for a woman who's supposedly alone in the world," Demetrious said. "I had to wait my turn to see her. First, there was an older woman from out of town, and then a skittery little man with an English accent. Do you happen to know an Oliver Siddon by any chance?"

My grimace probably told him everything.

"Yeah, unfortunately, I do" I said. "He's a Seattle violin dealer. He has his own shop downtown."

"I take it you don't approve of him. Has he been a friend of the Pratts? Listen, we're clogging up the works here," he said as a number of visitors pushed past us on their way in and out of the hospital doorway. Demetrious took me by the elbow and maneuvered me gently away from the crowd. "You look like a woman who could use a coffee. They have a coffee shop here on the ground floor, if we can believe the signs. I'll treat."

"Normally, I'd say, 'No thanks,'" I said, "but lunch was a bust, and as you can see, I'm wearing the coffee portion of the meal on my slacks. I'd kill for a latte. Oh," I said, wincing, "forget I said that, okay?"

"Really, Ms. Stewart, you'd make a very likable killer. Anything with that latte? How about a biscotti or a muffin?" the detective offered as he steered me into the little coffee nook.

"You'd do that for me?" I said. "Then I'll tell you everything I know about everything. In fact, I'll make up stuff."

As I shrugged out of my wet coat, Detective Demetrious stood at the counter and ordered lattes and blueberry muffins. His stock was going up by the minute. You know, they say that the way to a man's heart is his stomach, but the way to a woman's is the midafternoon coffee or tea break with a nice bit of pastry thrown in.

"Now where were we?" he asked, deftly carrying the goods back to our little bistro table in two trips. "Ah, yes. Oliver Siddon, the violin dealer. What do you know about his relationship with the Pratts?"

"Why? What did he say?" I asked.

"He called the station asking about the accident, and he assured the duty desk that he was as close as a brother to Mrs. Pratt. I didn't see him on your guest list, so I'm assuming that he wasn't part of the merry throng at your little tea party on the night of the murder."

"You'll never see him at my house, ever," I said. "He's a bit slimy for my taste. I hate to say this, but he's worked some pretty shady instrument deals since I've been up here, and those are just the ones I know about personally. Once I got wise as to how he cheated people who didn't know any better, I began sending my students and their parents to other violin shops. Oliver has never forgiven me."

"Does this sort of thing happen a lot in the music business?" he asked.

"All the time," I said. "Buying and selling the really fine, higher end instruments leaves even more leeway for unscrupulous dealers. Oliver isn't the only guilty party, either, not by a long shot."

"It sounds a lot like the art world and gallery owners," he said.

"Exactly. Even if there are papers of provenance and certificates from reputable dealers, there are those who will tell the owner that the instrument isn't what he's always believed it to be, appraisal letters be damned. Sometimes they're right, but often it's just a ploy to cheat someone out of his or her instrument. The so-called expert can then buy it himself and resell it later at a higher price. Believe me, it's a dirty business, and there's hardly anyone you can trust these days," I said.

"It sounds as if you're speaking from personal experience," he said.

"Oh, I am. I am," I said.

"So tell me some more about this Oliver Siddon character," Demetrious said.

"If you must know, I hadn't heard from Oliver for over a year, but that didn't stop him from calling me the day after the accident, ostensibly to ask after Annabelle and to make sure Marv was really and truly dead. He made my skin crawl. It was pretty obvious that he only wanted to get his hands on their instruments before the competition could get a good look at them and sell them for a big fat profit. Marv's collection is worth a fortune."

I took a sip of my latte and daintily broke off a small piece of muffin. I noticed that Detective Demetrious had elegant table manners for a policeman, or for the king of England for that matter. Seeing him cutting up his dessert into bite-sized pieces with a plastic knife was the only thing that stopped me from taking a nice, healthy

mouthful of blueberry muffin. Spoilsport. Oh, well, perhaps he'd had lunch already, so he could afford to be polite. I, on the other hand, would have happily polished off
my own muffin in several unladylike mouthfuls, and his
too, if no one were looking.

"Have you had any indication that Mrs. Pratt might
wish to sell her instruments to Oliver Siddon or anyone
else?" Demetrious said. "Has she discussed this with
you? I'm not sure why I'm asking, but everything may
be tied to the murder in some way. At least, we think it
was murder."

"You only *think* it was murder?" I said.

"Well, it might have been suicide, but would Marvin
Pratt have tried to kill himself with his wife in the car?
Unless they'd made a suicide pact, or he truly hated her,
it seems highly unlikely. From everything I've learned so
far it seems they were a devoted couple. Do you know
anything to the contrary, Ms. Stewart?" he asked, looking directly into my eyes. He caught me mid-bite, and I
had to chew a bit and swallow and wash down a dry
piece of muffin with my latte before I could continue. He
seemed content to sit and wait.

"Far from it," I finally said. "In fact, they were probably more in love than I realized, even after all these
years. Marv used to give Annabelle a special piece of
jewelry every Christmas, she told me yesterday, something he'd have custom made for her. I'm assuming that

this year he was planning on doing the same thing, and perhaps he'd already done it."

"Quite the romantic, wasn't he?" Demetrious said.

"I suppose," I said, but it was hard for me to picture Marv that way. "Anyway, Grace and I went over to the house to look for it last night. I thought that it might help Annabelle to accept Marv's death if we could produce it, his last gift to her, you know what I mean?"

The detective was staring at me with rapt attention. "Did you, in fact, find it?" he asked.

"No such luck," I said. "Grace had an interesting idea, though. What if Marv had something made, and then left it with the jeweler until just before Christmas? The more we thought about it, the more likely it seemed. That's what most people would do, right?"

"I have no idea," Demetrious said. "How many people do you know who can afford to spend that kind of money on custom jewelry?"

"Not nearly enough," I said, "but I'd be happy to meet a few."

"Wouldn't we all," he said.

"Tell me, detective, did the police find anything in Marv's wallet, a receipt of any kind when he died?"

"Actually, there were a few things of interest," he said. "There's a receipt from somewhere. Could be a jeweler. We haven't followed up on it yet, but I could certainly do that this afternoon."

"Wouldn't that be amazing?" I said. "I mean, if it turned out to be a receipt for Annabelle's Christmas present, a final declaration of love from beyond the grave."

"It sounds like something Edgar Allan Poe would write," he said.

"You might try Tiffany and Cartier." I said, ignoring his last comment. "Annabelle mentioned that he's ordered things from both of those stores before. It must be incredible to know that someone loves you enough to do something like that for you year after year." I felt myself blushing the moment the words left my mouth. I can be such an idiot sometimes.

I didn't mean to sigh. Really, I didn't. Suddenly, Detective Demetrious reached across the small bistro table and covered my hand with his own. It was warm and dry.

"So I've heard," he said, looking at me intently. "You've been very kind to your friend, Ms. Stewart. She's lucky to have you in her corner."

"Thank you," I said. "And you've been more than kind to me, detective. My stomach thanks you. Now I'd better get up there before Annabelle thinks I've abandoned her." I reluctantly removed my hand from beneath his and got up to go.

"Oh, by the way, do you have the security code for the Pratts' house?" he said nonchalantly. "I forgot to ask Mrs. Pratt for it, but I'd very much like to go through

Marvin's things later today if she doesn't mind. Otherwise, I'll have to get a court order to search the premises and deal with the alarm company directly."

"I'm sure she wouldn't mind," I said. "Why should she? She has nothing to hide. Wait. What security code? Grace and I just used the key to open the front door. Twice. Are you sure there's an alarm system? I didn't notice one when we went over there last night, and I'm absolutely certain we didn't set anything off."

"Oh, I'm sure," he said. "There appears to be a rather expensive system in place along with a security surveillance patrol. There's a panel on the wall next to the front door and a sign on the lawn. I'm surprised you didn't see it. We hoped to gain access yesterday, but there was no talking to Mrs. Pratt about anything, let alone asking for her permission to examine her husband's personal effects."

"It was pitch dark last night. Grace and I couldn't see a thing, but no alarm went off. I was kind of worried about their security measures or lack of them, what with all of those priceless instruments in there. The first time we drove over, it was during the afternoon, and we were busy searching for Leopold, Annabelle's cat. Again, the key gave us entry. No alarm went off then, either. Tell you what. I'll ask Annabelle about it when I go up to her room. Would you like me to have her call you with the code, if there really is one?"

"That would be great, worth the price of a latte at least. I wonder what lunch would buy?" he said with a smile. There were those dimples at last.

"For a substantial lunch, I'd be willing to solve the whole case for you," I said. "Of course, then you'd be out of a job. No need to risk your career, detective. Better to stop with a latte. Thanks again." I stood up, offering him my hand for a businesslike shake, and headed for the elevators. I could feel him watching my backside as I traipsed through the lobby. I prayed silently that the coffee stains on my slacks were only visible from the front.

Chapter 17

THE HOSPITAL'S NINTH floor was fairly quiet today. It was even more plastered with holiday cutouts and
tinseled decorations than the day before. Silver garlands
now festooned the nurses' station and the entire hallway.
A familiar nurse waved at me as I passed the desk on my
way to Annabelle's room. I smiled and said a cheery
"hello" to Annabelle's roommate, who was sitting up and
watching *Oprah* as I stepped across the room on my way
to my friend's bed. The birdlike lady, who, according to
the name on the door plaque, was Marvella Sykes, pretended not to see me. Annabelle, I realized, was watching *Oprah* too, but on a different elevated television.
Unlike her roommate, however, Annabelle seemed glad
when I poked my head in.

    "I heard you've had a busy day," I said. "Detective
Demetrious just met me on the way in, and he told me
that Oliver Siddon was here to see you, and that someone
else came by before that. Anyone I know?"

I hung my coat over the back of the visitor's chair and kissed my friend's pale cheek. Annabelle wasn't looking any better than she had the day before.

"Actually, it was my friend Babe," Annabelle said. "She looks quite hale and hearty, and I was so glad to see her after such a long time. We were very close all through Juilliard, you know."

"No, I didn't know," I said. "I've never even heard you mention her before yesterday, come to think of it."

"I'm sure you're right," she said. "We don't really know many of the same people these days, Babe and I. She lives in the Midwest with her husband. We've stayed close, though, through letters and phone calls."

"Tell me about her," I said.

"Hmm. Let's see. We first met at school. She became my accompanist, and then we concertized in New York and up and down the East Coast after we graduated, wherever they'd have us. We even had a lovely apartment together on Riverside Drive."

"It's sounds divine," I said.

"Yes, it was … rather. It seems like only yesterday when I think back on those times. It's been over forty years, though, since we've seen each other, but we still write fairly often and talk on the phone every week."

"You must share quite a history," I said.

"I owe her a great deal, Althea. You know how it is when you perform music with someone on a regular basis. You get to depend on each other in all sorts of ways, not just musical. She did something extraordinary for me once upon a time, and I'll never be able to repay her for it. She reminds me of you more than a little. Steady. Reliable."

Annabelle smiled at me with her eyes. I've always liked that about her.

"I still can't believe she's come all this way to see me, though," she said. "I'm embarrassed to have her make such a fuss over me. As for Oliver Siddon, that little snake, you can't imagine the nerve of that man! He swore up and down that he didn't tell anyone about the accident, that Babe must have seen it on the news, but I didn't believe him for a minute. I'm sure he was on the phone to her the second he found out."

Again, that little connection in my brain tingled, but nothing was coming through that made any sense.

"You know, that ridiculous British accent of his is completely phony," she said. "He was born in the Midwest, I happen to know, and went to Switzerland for a few years to study violin making. Then he spent a few years in London, working at a very prestigious violin shop, and when he returned, *voila!* he had that cloying accent."

"It's always grated on my nerves," I said, "but I assumed he'd been raised over there."

"Ha!" she said. "Can you believe that he came here to convince me that Marv is dead so that he can get his greedy little hands on Marv's violin collection? What kind of lowlife would do a thing like that? I called for the nurse to throw him and his greasy toupee out of here. I threatened to get a restraining order against him if he comes back."

"Good for you! Yes, I know exactly how much nerve he has. He called *me* the day after the accident for heaven's sake! I can't believe he came to the hospital to bother you at a time like this. But really, Annabelle, as awful as it is to hear things like this, I need you to understand that Marv really is quite dead," I said, feeling pretty cruel myself. "It's terrible, I know. I can hardly believe it myself, but it's true."

Annabelle didn't respond.

"By the way," I said, "I went to see Marilyn Litzky today."

Her eyes widened, and her mouth opened; however, no sound came out.

"Before you upset yourself all over again, I have something to tell you, and I need you to believe me. There was no affair, Annabelle," I said. "Marilyn and her mother had lunch with Marv because they were trying to purchase a specific violin for Andrew from Marv's collection. Marv agreed to a price and everything. It was going to be Marilyn's Christmas gift to her husband."

I heard Annabelle's sharp intake of breath.

"Do you believe her, Althea?" Annabelle was intensely focused on my face. I couldn't tell if she wanted me to believe Marilyn or not.

"Yes, I do," I said, looking her square in the eye. "Her mother was there today and corroborated everything. It also explains why Marilyn didn't spend any time talking with you and Marv at the tea. She didn't want Andrew to suspect that she was buying him a violin from your husband. It was supposed to be a surprise."

"Ha! I knew something was up, didn't I tell you? I always know. Why didn't Marv mention it to me, though? What's the big deal about selling a violin? Which violin by the way?"

"A Testore, I believe," I said.

"I didn't even remember that he had one of those," she said. "They're usually very lovely, Testores, but not as valuable as some of the other instruments in the collection. I guess that's why he agreed to sell it," she said.

"Well, Andrew has always wanted one," I improvised, "and Marilyn inherited some money and wanted to give her husband a really fine violin for Christmas. She and her mother approached Marv about buying one of his violins after learning that he had a beautiful Testore, and they came to an understanding."

"An understanding. Hmm," Annabelle said. "Well, that does seem to explain the lunch, but the story still seems fishy to me. On the other hand, she wouldn't bring her mother along to a romantic rendezvous, now would she? I suppose Marilyn Litzky's on the up-and-up after all, but that doesn't mean I have to like her. Every time I see her she's so revoltingly perky."

"You wouldn't have thought that if you'd seen her this afternoon," I said. "She looked haggard and awful."

"Good," she said. "That's the best news I've had all day."

"Annabelle! That's so unlike you," I said.

"Tough," she answered grumpily.

Clearly, this wasn't the best time to approach Annabelle about Andrew Litzky's violin, so I shut up.

"So now where can Marv be, if he isn't with Marilyn?" Annabelle asked, looking worried. What was I supposed to tell her? That he was in cold storage? She didn't want to hear the real answer any more than I wanted to reiterate it.

"I'll have to get back to you on that, Annabelle," I said. "By the way, is there an alarm system at the house? Detective Demetrious would like to get inside to look through Marv's things."

"Of course there is. But why would he want to do that, and why should I let him? I don't want any strangers, especially that nosy detective and his minions, snooping around our home. Our alarm system exists just to keep people like them out! Did you really think we would be careless enough to leave all of our instruments and valuables unprotected, Althea?"

"I was hoping you hadn't," I said, "but then, how did Grace and I manage to get inside without setting off the alarm when we rescued Leopold?"

"I asked the day nurse to call our security company for me, of course. She held the phone up to my ear, and I gave them our access code. I forgot to reenter it until this morning. Marv will be furious with me when he finds out."

Wow, I thought. *Grace and I could have gone to jail last night. The security patrol and the police might not have gone for the phony daughter routine as willingly as the hospital staff had.*

"Why didn't you just give me the code when you sent me over there?" I said. "I could have punched it in and then reset it. I'm not as dumb as I look, you know."

"Althea, darling, I was so out of it that I forgot until after you'd left. And honestly, I didn't want to bother you with unnecessary complications, remembering all those numbers. It's enough that you had to drive over and that you've saved my darling baby kitty. How is my sweet little Leopold adjusting to a strange place?"

"Actually, little Leopold has made it an even stranger place," I said. "I expected flying fur and lots of kitty attitude the minute he arrived at Blanchard House. Instead, we have our own version of *Peaceable Kingdom*. Leopold and Lydia have been hanging out in Grace's room since yesterday, more like an old married couple than two territorial cats. I suspect it's all Conrad's doing. He's a bit of a magician with animals."

"Conrad? Conrad Bailey? Why is he still at your house? I thought he lived on Whidbey Island," she said.

How could Annabelle be so sharp about everything going on around her and still cling so fervently to her fantasy about Marv having survived the accident? Denial's one powerful coping mechanism, I have to say. Freud may have been wrong about a lot of things, but he knew his stuff when it came to that.

"He does ... normally," I said, "but I asked him to stay with us for a while, at least until we sort everything out with you and Marv."

"Does Conrad know where Marv is?" Annabelle asked, brightening. "He might be just the one to ask. They weren't close friends, of course, but they've known each other forever. He might have some idea where Marv is lying low."

She certainly had no idea what she'd just said, I reminded myself, almost choking. I remembered just in time that Conrad had sworn Grace and me to silence about his past relationship with Marvin Pratt, so I said nothing. It was getting harder and harder to say nothing.

"Well, I'd better go, but I'll ask him," I said. "Conrad is taking Grace and me to hear the Seattle Symphony tonight, and I promised to be home in time to make dinner before we leave. Can I bring you anything tomorrow?"

"Bring Marv," she said. "I know he hates hospitals. I know they terrify him, but I need him here, Althea. I need to see him. Maybe he's gone back to the house by now. He can let that snoopy detective in himself if he wants to. He always said he couldn't stand to be alone in the house without me, that he'd never stay there by himself, but maybe he's decided to try anyway. My poor Marv. If you only knew—"

Knew what? Perhaps I should have asked; however, it was getting late, and I needed some time to cook dinner and dress for the concert.

"Please, Althea, ask Conrad about Marv," Annabelle said.

"I will," I said, "and please think about giving that security code to the police. They really do need to look through Marv's things."

"Ha!" she said.

At least I'd been able to reassure Annabelle that her husband wasn't cheating on her with a perky little oboist. I'd felt reassured myself, learning that there was indeed an alarm on the Pratt's house. *Annabelle could have trusted me with the access code. She really could have*, I thought. She probably would have trusted her old pal Babe with it, so why not me? Did she think I was too dim-witted to punch in a few numbers? Maybe she really did just plain forget to give it to me, though, and only remembered after I was on my way over. That had to be it. Still, I had an uneasy feeling in the pit of my stomach every time I thought about that alarm code. Something in Annabelle's glib explanation felt slightly "off." Oh, well,

I was headed for a lovely evening. The best thing I could do was to put it out of my mind for the time being. At least, that was what I believed then.

Chapter 18

WINNIE AND BERT greeted me happily at the front door of Blanchard House. I've observed over the years that dogs quickly learn the sound of every car that pulls up, sometimes even before it turns into the driveway. My furry pals were more than ready for their afternoon walk, so I quickly slipped their leashes on their collars and headed back out into the filthy weather. Rain doesn't deter these two. They were prancing through puddles for the next half hour. Bert always waits until he's well inside the front hallway again before he shakes himself off all over the polished wooden floor and the oriental carpets. Winnie likes to throw her wet self against my legs and then shake. Ugh! All I could think about after our walk was a hot bath and a big, sizzling steak.

"Hi!" Grace greeted me as I shrugged myself out of my wet coat. "Have you picked out an outfit for tonight yet? I can't wait to show you what I'm wearing, Thea. It's something I bought on a whim in London several years ago. I never thought I'd get to wear it, but I found it this morning behind a bunch of concert gowns. Wait until you see it!"

Grace was buzzing around the first floor of Blanchard House in her sweats, plugging in more twinkling lights than you're likely to see at Disneyland. She stepped on several foot-operated switches, and our living room became a shimmering diorama of colored lights, bathing us both in a surreal glow. The twinkling white lights on the porch were on a timer, and these blinked on within minutes as well. Thank heavens I'd remembered to buy Christmas gifts, no matter how last-minute. I may have been a slouch about decorating, but at least I wasn't going to be seen as the Grinch this year.

"I can't wait to get into a hot bath, Grace. It's been quite a day."

"Good luck, honey," she said. "Conrad's been in there soaking himself in the claw-foot tub for an hour already. He must look like a bearded prune. I hope he's still breathing. That's all we need next, a drowning in our bathtub!" Grace rolled her eyes back in her head. It was funny, but not funny, if you know what I mean.

"Heck. I'll take a shower then," I said. I don't really enjoy taking baths in those shallow 1960s shower-tub combos we have in the rest of the bathrooms. My idea of heaven is the deep, old-fashioned kind, but I wasn't going to fight Conrad for it. *Anyone who's taking us to the symphony should be able to laze around in our best tub for as long as he wants*, I told myself. I was trying my best to be gracious.

"Did you say you were making dinner before the concert, Althea?" Grace asked. "I'm not really hungry, and I made Conrad and myself a huge lunch, so maybe we should hold off until after the concert and go for a bite then."

Oh, great, I thought. *No leisurely soak in the tub and no dinner.* So far today, I'd had a blueberry muffin and a latte.

"Sure. I'll rummage around in the fridge and grab a snack," I said. "Maybe there's a stale cracker and a glass of tepid water I can have to hold me over."

If I was grumpy now, just imagine how pleasant I'd be in about three or four hours. Fortunately, I found a nice wedge of camembert cheese, so I slathered a piece of rosemary bread with some of it and ate an apple. It wasn't exactly the juicy steak that I'd been dreaming about all afternoon, but it was probably enough to keep me from taking a bite out of a fellow audience member's leg during the concert. I was heavily into one of my carnivorous modes at the moment, which generally lasts a full month before I reawaken to the hideousness of chomping on my fellow creatures and return, somewhat chastened, to the tofu. Still, during those meat-craving episodes, you don't want to get between me and a rare burger, or find yourself stranded in Donner Pass with me during a blizzard. It could be deadly.

At least the water in my shower was hot and plentiful. I'm a two-minute-shower girl, though. Al Gore would be proud. I get wet, lather up, rinse, and go, unless I'm washing my hair, which takes a bit longer. Did I mention that I always finish my shower with an ice-cold rinse? It stimulates the lymph glands, makes your skin glow, and even makes your hair shiny. It's also guaranteed to scare the living daylights out of houseguests the first few times they hear the inevitable screaming and gasping. I like to think it earns their respect, too. Only a fool would mess with a woman who takes ice-cold showers year round.

By the time I'd washed and blow-dried my hair, applied body lotion, moisturizer, and makeup, thrown on a dark red velvet dress, dug around at the bottom of my closet for a pair of strappy gold heels and a gold evening bag, and sifted through my earring collection until I found a pair of long gold dazzlers, I wasn't hungry anymore, just excited. I had to admit that I looked pretty good all dressed up. I put my hair up. I took it down. I put it up again. This is what we women do. We don't bore easily as long as there's a mirror. Finally, I decided to leave it up in a classic French twist to better show off the earrings. I floated downstairs while humming, "There she is, Miss America," ostensibly to wait for everyone else to assemble. I'm always early, but then, as I soon learned, so are Conrad and Grace. Musicians, you know.

Grace was already in the kitchen, scooping cat food into several ceramic bowls on the sideboard, too high for the dogs to get into, or so we fooled ourselves into believing. We have since been proven wrong over and over by Bert, who stands on his hind legs and pushes the dishes onto the floor so he and Winnie can share in the spoils.

"Don't get any of that on your dress, Grace! Your sleeves are almost in the cat food. Here, let me do that," I said, pulling Grace's ivory lace sleeve away from the stinky, emulsified fish that cats seem to adore. Lydia was already gulping down her share of the grub, while Leopold watched anxiously from the sidelines.

"Where can we feed Leopold? You'd like to eat on the counter, Leopold, like you do at home, wouldn't you?" Grace asked the pacing fur ball. "Not a chance, buddy. Sorry, but only we humans get kitchen counter privileges in this house."

"Thank you for your excellent judgment, Grace. I couldn't live with smelly cat food where we prepare our own meals. Can't we put his dish in the little bathroom or something? What about up here next to Lydia's?" I said.

"Well, we can try it, but Lydia may not go for it," Grace said as she handed me the can. I no sooner put Leopold's dish up on the sideboard than Lydia hissed and spit at me. I guess eating areas are sacred to cats, too.

This was her personal food place, and she wasn't about to share it with some newcomer.

Grace looked around the kitchen before she headed into the butler's pantry. "How about up here?" She was pointing to the marble counter of the cabinet where we kept the glassware. We put Leopold and his smelly little bowl on the cool surface and watched him gobble down his dinner. "Maybe the marble reminds him of home," Grace said.

"As long as I don't have to have him on our kitchen counters, Grace, I don't care where he eats. Lydia has never been allowed up there, and Leopold is going to have to live by the rules of the house."

"Good luck with that," she said.

Now that the cat crisis had been successfully averted and I could get a better look at Grace in all her finery I was very impressed. She was elegantly turned out in an ivory top and a floor-length ivory silk skirt that came down in a gentle A-line. The blouse had full bell sleeves and a scooped neckline. She'd put her hair up, except for one long curl that cascaded down one side, and the whole effect was set off becomingly with a string of creamy white pearls at the throat and pearl and crystal drop earrings, very Julie Christie indeed.

"You look like a Christmas bride! It's gorgeous, Grace!"

"Oh, no! Do you think this color makes it look too much like a wedding gown? I can change," she said, coloring slightly.

"Don't you dare!" I said. "It's really stunning."

"You look beautiful yourself, Thea," Grace said. "I love your auburn hair against that deep burgundy."

"Thanks," I said. "Too bad no one will actually get to see what we're wearing in that crush."

"I don't care," Grace said. "This is the first time I've gotten to wear this getup since I bought it." She twirled around slowly, the skirt moving gracefully with her every step.

"What about me?" Conrad asked as he hobbled into the hallway in his tux. He wore a huge grin. "This is the first time I've put on the monkey suit since I retired. You ladies should feel honored."

"We do! We do! You look handsome, Conrad," we said, and he did. It's always surprising how good most men look in tuxedos. Of course, some men are hopeless, no matter what they're wearing, but Conrad wasn't one of them. Looking down at his feet, I noticed that he was even wearing patent leather shoes rather than his usual socks and sandals. No wonder he was having trouble walking. Those feet hadn't seen a real pair of shoes in years. He'd actually trimmed his beard as well. Would wonders never cease?

The sound of tires on gravel coupled with Winnie's sharp howling and Bert's low "woof" announced that a car had just driven right up to the front door of Blanchard House.

"They're here, and right on time," Conrad said as he checked his gold Piaget watch. Who suspected before tonight that he even owned such a thing? He threw open the front door to reveal a gleaming black town car complete with a uniformed driver. "Ladies, your chariot awaits!" he said happily.

Grace and I patted Winnie and Bert on their doggie heads and reminded them to watch the house. Then we grabbed our black velvet coats and evening bags and hurried out into the waiting town car. The rain had finally let up. Conrad sat between us in the heated backseat. The limousine had a minibar, so he poured each of us a cream sherry. "Merry Christmas, me beauties!" he growled in his best pirate impersonation.

"When did you dream this up?" I asked him. "I've been expecting to drive downtown through holiday traffic and worrying all day about the parking. Honestly, I've been dreading having to walk very far in these high heels, too. I'm good for about a block or one garage floor before my feet start to scream at me."

Conrad just looked at me and winked.

"This is absolutely first-class, Conrad," Grace said, "and I love having our very own driver! Can we keep him? He can sleep in a cardboard box on the floor of my room. I promise to feed him and take him out for walks."

"No, I'm afraid the limo turns into a pumpkin after midnight, and the footman, as I recall, turns back into a big fat rat," Conrad said.

"Just like all my dates," Grace said. "Why am I not surprised?"

"Honey, if you can't rope in a better class of date in that getup, you don't deserve to date at all," I said. And I meant it.

Chapter 19

SEATTLE'S BENAROYA HALL is really worth a
visit. The wide staircases on each side of the lobby are
graced by enormous white blown-glass Chihuly sculp-
tures that hang down between the floors like milky sea
flowers. Grace couldn't get enough of looking at them
from various angles. Of course, the entire building was
twinkling and garlanded to the hilt for Christmas, which
made it even more spectacular.

A smiling young woman handed us programs, and
an older male usher guided us to our seats in the orchestra section, three rows from the front, dead center.

"I know people," Conrad muttered in explanation as
we gasped in amazement at our fabulous seat locations.

"Who? The Pope?" I said.

Conrad helped us out of our coats and carried them
back to the coat-check room, something I never would
have thought to do for myself. Conrad really had come
from a very cosmopolitan family, I realized, and his

manners were still impeccable when the occasion called for them. Grace and I smoothed our dresses and settled in to read the program while we waited for him to return. At least, I did. Grace's head was swiveling around like a bobble doll, taking in the hall, the patrons, and the orchestra members that were drifting onto the stage to warm up.

"Don't the Pratts have a season subscription?" Grace said. "I wonder where their seats are and if anyone's using them." She craned her neck to get a good look at the balcony section.

"Of course they do," I said. "I don't think they've ever missed a program. I'm sure they purchased the best seats money can buy, and, yes, the seats are probably empty."

"What a waste," Grace said.

"I can't imagine that Annabelle has thought for one moment about her symphony subscription," I said. "She's been acting as if Marv's just disappeared offstage momentarily while the scenery's being changed. The way she talks about him, I almost expect him to reappear myself!"

Conrad, meanwhile, could be heard muttering, "Excuse me. Excuse me. So sorry," as he made his way past the concert patrons already settled in our row. There was a lot of commotion as people half-stood to let him through. Sitting dead center is always a mixed blessing, as far as I'm concerned.

"Thea, look around," Grace whispered from behind her program. "We're probably the most formally dressed people here, except for the orchestra members. I mean, in LA for a Saturday night concert at Disney Hall, everyone gets pretty spiffed up. Not here. Just look at that woman in the ripped jeans and black T-shirt."

"I know," I said. "And what about the guy two rows up in the ratty-looking plaid shirt?"

"I don't know how upscale clothing stores stay in business in Seattle. I really don't," she said.

"Face it, Grace. We're LA girls at heart. We stand out, but I'd like to think it's in a good way. Our mothers would be proud!"

"Not my mother," she said.

"Okay, not mine, either," I said. Neither of us were our mothers' favorites. It was a shared bond. "Nevertheless, it's disrespectful to show up for a concert looking as if you'd just finished running a few laps around a muddy soccer field. I think we look just right."

"Well, well, if it isn't Seattle's newest party girls, Althea and Grace," a familiar voice with an equally familiar, phony British accent trilled shrilly from the aisle. "What brings you two wild things here?" Oliver Siddon made sure that he'd be noticed, leaning into our row and waving a program in our direction. Of course, his ill-fitting brown and gray toupee, even now sitting slightly askew on that overly large head and spindly body, would have guaranteed a certain amount of comedic attention anyway. Concert goers sitting close enough to hear his ridiculous description of Grace and me craned their necks to look at us, undoubtedly surprised to learn that two aging call girls with their elderly John in tow were nevertheless classical music devotees.

"Excuse me," I said, turning to Grace. "Do you know this man?"

"Oh, and if it isn't Conrad Bailey. Lucky thing, you," Oliver said, snickering and rolling his eyes lewdly.

"What's he doing here? Trolling for unsuspecting widows?" Conrad growled somewhat loudly, refusing to look in Oliver Siddon's direction.

"Oh, you silly man!" Oliver said. "I never miss Saturday nights at the symphony. Everyone knows that."

"Everyone knows that he wanders off at intermission to get blotto across the street at the local bar," Conrad said to Grace and me without bothering to lower his voice. "The man is completely tone deaf."

"Oh, I do believe I see an old friend," Oliver said, standing on tiptoes and scanning the nearly full auditorium. "I must go and pay my respects before the lights dim."

"Well, you'd best hurry along then," Conrad said, holding up his program so that it covered his face and blocked his view of any and all annoyances. Oliver, however, was already grinning wolfishly, preparing to descend on his next social victim, looking right past us and into the cavernous auditorium as he disappeared into the crowd.

"What a blight on humanity Oliver Siddon is," Grace said, shaking her head in disbelief. "The man doesn't even realize that he's just been treated to a first-class snubbing."

I had to disagree with her. Oliver knew. He just refused to care. I'd often heard it said that Oliver Siddon was "uninsultable," but I was sure that he'd made a conscious decision many years ago to allow nothing to pierce his professional armor.

My own skin, unfortunately, wasn't nearly as thick as Oliver's. It took every bit of my often sadly lacking self-control to refrain from pointing out to everyone within a few rows that Grace and I were really classical musicians, not ladies of the evening. I hunched down into my seat and reread my program in an attempt to avoid further notice. Not Grace. If anything, she sat up a little straighter, tilting her head and smiling demurely at a middle-aged man sitting directly in front of her who'd turned completely around in his seat to look us up and down. I knew instinctively that my best friend had just made the internal shift from being Grace Sullivan, classical cellist, to becoming the brave, tragic heroine of Verdi's *La Traviata*. I could almost hear the pianissimo string tremolo underscoring the heartrending moment as she batted her lashes at both the rude and the curious seated around us. All her young years spent studying method acting in New York tend to kick into high gear at moments like this. We each have our own ways of navigating the choppy waters of life, I suppose. I go home and try to make sense of things by reading Rollo May and Carl Jung. She revels in the drama of the moment by becoming Camille, right down to the delicate little cough. *All she needed*, I thought to myself, *was a blood-spattered lace handkerchief.*

Soon, the huge hall was filled, and the symphony musicians seated themselves in their respective sections of the orchestra, instruments in hand. The house lights dimmed. The stage grew brighter, and the conductor, Gerard Schwarz, made his way to the podium to lead the orchestra in Tchaikovsky's "Nutcracker Suite". As the ensemble stood for his entrance, I scanned the group on-stage for familiar faces and counted quite a few people we knew. There was Andrew Litzky, of course, seated on the fourth stand outside of the first violins. I wondered if Marilyn Litzky came to see her husband play his symphony concerts these days or whether she'd succumbed to the apathy that seems to hit so many orchestra spouses sooner or later. One of the orchestra wives I'd known well in LA told me she waited all week for Friday and Saturday nights so she could do her nails, read a book, and go to bed early.

Suddenly, Grace looked over at the bass section and slapped her hand on her chest directly over her heart. It looked as though she were having a spasm. Her mouth fell open, and her eyes went wide.

"Who's *that?*" she finally hissed at me, continuing to stare in the direction of the basses. Just then the orchestra began to play the first notes of the overture to the "Nutcracker."

I might have enjoyed Tchaikovsky more had Grace not been clutching at my arm for the next forty-five minutes. It was still a lovely performance, punctuated as it was by my friend's unconscious pinching and squeezing. She could barely contain herself until the music ended and the house lights went up and before she demanded to know who was playing on the first desk of double basses.

"Do you mean the short, chubby, bald guy with the gold tooth?" Conrad said blandly. "That's Larry Grable. You'd like him. He plays a mean game of chess."

Grace was in no mood to be toyed with. "What are you talking about? Are you blind? I mean the dark-haired Adonis playing next to him. That has to be the most gorgeous man I've ever seen in my entire life!" Her lips were almost bitten through, and her whole body was trembling. Grace enjoyed the occasional histrionic moment, but for once, she wasn't playacting.

"Do you think she could be talking about Emile, Thea?" Conrad asked me, leaning across Grace and giving me a covert wink. "You remember Emile Girard, don't you? He was at the conservatory when you were there. You probably haven't seen him in years, but he still looks the same, doesn't he?"

Or course I recognized Emile Girard. No red-blooded woman in her right mind would have forgotten who he was.

"He married a crazy woman, a Hungarian, if I remember correctly," I said.

"They're getting a divorce, though," Conrad said. He may be retired, but as I said before, he never misses a thing.

"I knew him very slightly," I said. "He was always very good-looking but completely dedicated to the bass. So many young women had a crush on him back then that he could have had a date every night, but he spent all his time practicing. I haven't had any contact with him in over twenty years, but he's still rather good-looking, if you're into the craggy, intense type."

If anything, Emile Girard had become even handsomer. He still had a full head of shiny black hair with a few streaks of gray, and he'd maintained his youthful physique; however, I couldn't help but hope that he'd grown less serious with age. Somehow, I doubted it.

"Can we go backstage?" Grace begged. *"Please*? I have to meet him! Conrad, you know him. Can you introduce us?" She sounded way beyond eager, not at all like the self-possessed woman I knew, the one who could walk past a gang of whistling construction workers and wave back, smiling.

"Whoa, there, Grace," Conrad said. "I'm happy to take you backstage, but you have to promise to behave yourself. No drooling." Conrad chucked her under the chin. Grace wasn't amused. "Come this way then," he said.

As we turned to face the rest of the hall, I allowed my gaze to take in a full sweep of the mezzanine and the balconies. This was one gigantic place, all right, larger than I'd remembered from my last visit, and it was packed to the rafters. Nevertheless, a face leapt out at me from the boxes on my right. For one startled moment, I was sure that I'd recognized a white-haired woman in an apple-green suit and that she'd recognized me as well. Then she buried her face in the program, and I wasn't so sure anymore. *No*, I thought to myself, m*y imagination is working overtime*. How many occasions have there been when one thinks that someone across the room or down the street is an acquaintance, only to realize upon closer scrutiny that the person is a complete stranger? I thought briefly about heading up to the mezzanine just to reassure myself and get a closer look, but Grace was already tugging at my arm. Instead, being the loyal friend that I am, I permitted myself to be dragged backstage. Later, I wished that I'd followed my initial impulse.

Conrad, indeed, "knew people," and this included the ushers guarding the backstage entrance to the artists' lounge. Apparently, Conrad attended the symphony often, and he was a backstage regular. We entered the high-ceilinged room behind the stage where the members of the orchestra store their cases and other belongings and headed toward the green room. Emile Girard wasn't among the many musicians vying for coffee cups and tea bags. Lots of friendly colleagues exchanged greetings with us, though, including Andrew Litzky. I waved to the formerly kitty-phobic trombonist who'd quickly become Lydia's personal chin-scratcher at our Christmas party. After he thoroughly appraised the assembly, Conrad firmly ushered us out into the larger backstage area. In a far corner, we spotted Emile sitting alone at a long table full of open violin cases, intently reading a book.

"Well, if it isn't Emile Girard! How are you?" Conrad bellowed at the startled man as we bore down on him. Only Conrad could get away with feigning surprise at seeing him there. It was Saturday night, and Emile Girard was a member of the Seattle Symphony. Where else would he be?

I felt Grace's hot, sweaty hand grab for my arm as Conrad shoved us forward.

"You remember Althea Stewart, don't you?" Conrad said. "Weren't you in the same class or thereabouts at the conservatory? She's been up here three years already, teaching in Kirkland. And this is her friend Grace Sullivan, a cellist from LA."

Conrad stepped aside to reveal the lovely Grace, who for the first time in memory, found herself unable to speak. Apparently, so did Emile. He just stood up and looked at Grace, appraising her from head to toe in one swift glance, nodded slightly in her direction, and then turned quickly to me with the beginning of a smile.

"I remember your name, and you do look vaguely familiar," he said. "Weren't we in the conservatory orchestra at the same time?"

"Absolutely!" I said. "Don't you remember recording 'Ein Heldeneben' and 'Francesa di Rimini?' How about when the orchestra played at Carnegie Hall?" I asked him.

"Sure, I do, but I don't really remember you very well at all," he said.

"That's the story of my life," I said. "I've been everywhere and played with everyone, but I seem to be invisible. Maybe it's a good thing, considering all the evil deeds I've perpetrated during my lifetime."

"Oh, like what?" Emile asked, suddenly showing more interest.

"Remember the cartoon of our esteemed conductor, Viktor Schnitzer, the one that found its way into the *Boston Globe* the day after we performed Bruckner's Fourth Symphony?" I said. "The one showing a small child with his pants down around his cowboy boots, a ten-gallon hat over his eyes, a handlebar mustache, and waving his lasso over his head for all he was worth? Unfortunately, that was my handiwork."

"Schnitzer was fired right after that cartoon was published, you know," Emile said.

"I always felt terrible about that, but I couldn't help myself," I said. "The man was a menace on the podium."

"True, but remind me never to cross you in the future," Emile said with a lopsided grin and a raised eyebrow. "That cartoon was the funniest thing I ever saw in my life. I sure never suspected it was the handiwork of some little girl who played the violin. Usually, brass players do things like that, but not violinists!"

"You see why it pays to be less than memorable?" I said. "Not you, though. You were the boy wonder of the bass."

"Oh, I don't know about that," he said, looking down at his hands, "but here I am, still living the dream, only now I'm pretty tired of it, and I'd rather be fishing. And how are you, Conrad? I haven't seen you in a tux in years. I almost didn't recognize you."

"As you can see, I have a hot date with, not one, but *two* gorgeous women this evening," Conrad said, "so I dragged this old relic out of mothballs for the occasion. Don't expect to see it again, though. I'd forgotten how much it itches."

Conrad waited for a further comment from Emile that never came. The silence seemed interminable. "Well," Conrad finally said, "we'd better get back to our seats. We wouldn't want to miss Beethoven's Ninth, now would we?" Conrad and Emile shook hands.

"Good to see you after all these years, Althea," Emile called after us as we headed toward the stage door.

I waved and smiled brightly in reply. What else could I do?

Grace, meanwhile, looked as if she'd been smacked in the face with a halibut. She'd abandoned her usual, regal walk, and he was holding up her skirt and practically running through the outer hallway and into the auditorium itself as we made our way back to our seats.

"He's just shy, Grace," I called after her. I grabbed her hand when I caught up with her and gently eased her through the crowded hallway and back toward our third-row seats.

"Do we have to stay for the whole concert, Thea? I feel awful," she whispered to me as Conrad led the way down our row through the half-standing, knee-twisting, but nevertheless accommodating concert goers. I'd stopped worrying about whether or not they still believed us to be high-priced call girls, although several dowagers eyed us with unmistakable curiosity.

"Yes, we do, unfortunately," I said. "Conrad has gone to a lot of trouble to make this evening special for us. The least we can do is smile and try to enjoy it."

"Okay," she said, "but I feel like an idiot. That was so humiliating."

"Honey, you're taking this way too personally," I said. "What did you expect the man to do? Fall on one knee and propose?"

Her face was extremely pale but with a bright splotch of red on each cheek. "You're right, of course," she said. "I don't know what's going on with me. I just felt this jolt of recognition when I saw him. I can't explain it, but I instantly thought Emile Girard just might be *the one*."

"Oh, Lord, save us from the myth of soul mates," I said.

"I guess you're right," said Grace, "but he could have at least said 'hello'." She hunched down in her seat.

I rummaged around in my evening bag and dug out some hard candy. "Here, have a Lifesaver," I said. "Butterscotch, your favorite."

"No thanks," she said. Things were worse than I'd feared. Grace never turns down butterscotch.

I couldn't resist turning to see if the white-haired woman in the apple-green suit might still be up in the balcony. Her seat was empty, though, and it remained so for the rest of the concert. Perhaps she didn't have the stamina for Beethoven's long, long, long Ninth. I wasn't sure at this point that Grace or I did either; however, the house lights dimmed, and Maestro Schwarz resumed his place on the podium.

The Seattle Symphony, like so many other orchestras these days, seats its string sections in my least favorite arrangement, with the second violins on the opposite side of the stage from the first violins, the celli on the inside next to the firsts, and the violas on the inside next to the seconds. This assures that the violins are almost never quite together on the most difficult passages, being separated by both time and space, and that the second violins are rarely heard clearly because their instruments' F holes are facing the back wall. This is a conductor's prerogative, and I can only imagine that Maestro Schwarz's background as a trumpet player is partially responsible for this choice. True, the orchestras in the time of Mozart were often set up in this way to give the audience a stereophonic effect; however, these orchestras were tiny by comparison to today's, and the concert venues were intimate drawing rooms or ballrooms. There weren't forty or fifty violinists attempting to play intricate passages together in a concert hall the size of an airplane hangar.

Beethoven's Ninth Symphony presents another logistical problem altogether. The piece requires a large mixed chorus of singers, which is added to the orchestra for the final chorale. This makes for a splendid visual effect from the audience but cramps the instrumentalists onstage quite a bit. Thus, the bass section was pushed even farther forward on the proscenium and toward the audience than usual for the second half of the concert. I couldn't help but notice that Emile Girard never looked out into the audience during the performance, always keeping his eyes glued on the conductor or the music in front of him, the quintessential professional.

Grace, for her part, barely looked up from her lap during the entire symphony, including the rousing chorale at the end, something I knew she'd always loved.

She remained slouched in her seat, pouting and looking bored. The vitality of the music and the uplifting theme of the last movement rang out gloriously through Benaroya Hall, moving the audience to wild applause at the end, all except for Grace. She clapped, of course, but with no real enthusiasm. She didn't spring to her feet with the rest of us for the standing ovation until I took her gently by the arm and helped her up. I knew Grace well enough after all these years to be certain that she'd feel terrible by the next day if she thought she'd hurt Conrad's feelings tonight. She just couldn't seem to pull herself together.

"Smile, Grace," I said.

"Look, I'm smiling," she said, forcing her lips into a determined, if inauthentic smile.

"Now walk," I said. "That's it. One foot in front of the other. Pretend you're headed for the guillotine."

"With pleasure," she said. And with that, the Grace I knew and loved straightened her posture, lifted her chin, and moved nobly out to the lobby. *Years of method acting*, I thought.

I looked up into the balcony one last time for the woman in the apple-green suit, but she was long gone, if she'd really been there at all.

Chapter 20

I SILENTLY CURSED Emile Girard for his social awkwardness as we made our way to the waiting limousine, which now had all the holiday atmosphere of a tomb on wheels. To make matters worse, our driver inched out into traffic only to become stuck in the lane closest to the curb. For the next half hour, we sat in the same spot as drivers all around us idled their engines to keep warm. We could clearly make out police cruisers and several paramedic trucks filling the intersection at Third and Pine, their blue and red lights flashing dramatically through the night sky.

"What's going on?" Conrad asked our driver after he tapped on the glass separating us from our chauffeur. "Can you see anything from up there?" The man shrugged and shook his head. After a while, he got out, leaving the motor running, and spoke briefly with a Somali taxi driver who was several cars ahead of us on the one-way street. He then sauntered back to our car and cut the engine.

"We're going to be here a while, folks," he said, sliding open the glass partition. "Some poor old guy stepped out in front of a bus and got himself squished a little while ago."

"Oh, no! The poor thing," I said.

"Do you think it's too late for me to join him?" Grace said to no one in particular.

"He was probably a drunk or another suicidal tourist," our driver said. "Seattle natives don't usually jaywalk or cross against the light, especially downtown."

"You're so right," I said. The first time I stepped off a sidewalk against the light here in Seattle, it was practically the middle of the night. There were no cars coming in either direction, but I was the only pedestrian who budged off that curb until the "walk" sign came on. It was eerie.

"You might as well make yourselves comfortable back there, folks," our driver said. "It looks as though we're stuck here for at least another few minutes. The police are preparing to move the body, as far as I can tell, and then they'll let us through. It must have happened right there at the corner." He pointed down the block to where the police were clustered. Unfortunately, there was no way to detour traffic around Benaroya Hall from this point.

"At least we're not stuck in the garage like most of the people behind us," Conrad said.

"There's a full bar on the seatback directly in front of you," our driver said. "Just pull down that brass handle and pour whatever you want ... on the house."

"I'll take a whiskey, straight up," Grace said.

"Are you sure about that, Grace?" Conrad asked.

"I'm sure," she said.

This should be good, I thought, handing her a glass containing a small portion of Canadian Club that Conrad had poured for her. We watched her wince as she threw it down her throat in one fiery gulp. It looked painful, but she held her glass out for a second pour.

Conrad and I exchanged worried looks, but Grace was insistent. He splashed a bit more in her tumbler, and we watched her lift the glass quickly to her lips and chug it down. The woman is no drinker. Her second swig put her out for the rest of the evening. Eventually, I knew, we'd have to drag her well-dressed carcass upstairs to her bedroom, but at least we'd be spared her rotten mood on the ride home. I wanted a drink desperately myself at this point, and there was a bottle of Harvey's Bristol Cream staring at me from the portable bar. I finally asked Conrad to pour me a sherry, which took the edge off our long wait. Conrad was soon chatting up the driver about the man's former life in Iraq as a doctor. Grace was softly snoring in the corner of the backseat.

After a while, my curiosity, which was mixed with a hearty helping of boredom, got the better of me. I decided I needed to stretch my aching lower back and leg muscles and got out of the limo, uncomfortable gold sandals and the evening chill notwithstanding. I forced myself to limp painfully through the sea of unmoving traffic to the end of the block. If this had been Los Angeles there would have been a whole symphony of cursing and honking, but here in Seattle, the drivers merely turned off their engines and waited politely for the police to do whatever was required.

As I hobbled toward the intersection and got a better view, it became clear that the paramedics were in the process of loading a sinister-looking leather body bag into the back of an ambulance. A tall young policewoman who looked very no-nonsense with her dark blonde hair pulled back severely into a low ponytail and a brimmed police hat that rode low over her eyes sternly ordered me away from the scene and back to my car, but not before I noticed what appeared to be a flattened squirrel lying on the dark street next to the body. *Poor squirrel*, I thought. *Wrong place, wrong time.* It didn't occur to me until sometime the next day what that mangled pile of fur in the middle of Third Avenue actually was.

Chapter 21

GRACE WAS UP early next morning as usual. She hadn't combed her hair, though, and she was all wrapped up in a tattered pink terry-cloth bathrobe, something that should have been reserved for shoveling out coal cellars. I recognized it as the rag Grace had used to cushion her Chinese porcelain table lamp during the move from Southern California. It was clearly meant to be the ulti-mate statement of self-loathing. A cold cup of tea sat untouched in front of her, and Leopold was rubbing him-self and purring against the leg of her chair to no avail. Grace paid no attention either to him or me. The Sunday *Seattle Times* was spread out on the table in front of her, and she was halfheartedly doing the crossword.

"Good morning, Grace," I said.

"Ha! What's another word for 'over the hill?'" she asked.

"How many letters?" I said.

"Who the hell cares? I mean *me!* I made such a fool of myself," she said, slapping herself on the forehead. "All I can think of is how stupid I must have looked in that ridiculous getup, like some desperate, middle-aged bride who'd been left at the altar!"

"Don't you think you're being just a wee bit hard on yourself?" I said. "Is that what you really think? Do you care to know what *I* think, Grace? I think you looked fantastic, and if Emile Girard didn't notice it's certainly not your fault. And you didn't make an idiot of yourself, honey, at least not until afterward. No one but Conrad and I had any idea that you'd suffered a momentary lapse of sanity over some moronic bass player. Now you have to get over it."

Grace made as if to throw a spoon at me but then thought better of it. "You used to be so sympathetic, Althea. What happened?"

"I'm not sure, exactly," I said, reaching for the tea-pot. "Old age, maybe. I'm getting crotchety."

The ringing of the phone made us both jump. Grace spilled tea on her crossword puzzle.

"Althea, are you and Grace booked for Christmas Eve?" asked Delilah Cantwell, her resonant alto voice booming across the kitchen through the phone. "If not, I have a last-minute gig for you both. It pays pretty well, too. St. Timmons Episcopal Church is doing their usual Christmas Eve midnight service with their regular choir and a small chamber orchestra, only we're down one violin and a cello because of the flu that's going around. Could you two possibly fill in at the last minute? You don't mind playing violin rather than viola, do you, Althea? We'd be so grateful!" she rushed on.

"Wait. I'll ask Grace, but I think we can do it." Grace, who'd heard every word, nodded her assent. This was just what the doctor ordered to pull Grace out of her funk, and we could certainly use the money. "Okay, count us in. What's the dress?"

"Concert black. The usual," Delilah said. "There's a rehearsal first at 7:00 p.m. tomorrow night and then a buffet supper provided by the church committee before the service. We start playing as the congregation comes in at half-past eleven. The actual service only lasts about an hour, and we play everybody out with Christmas carols. Don't bother bringing music stands. We have plenty. Have I forgotten anything?"

"Only one thing. Where's St. Timmons?" I said.

"Ah, yes. There's that," she said. "St. Timmons is very near you, where Kirkland intersects with Bellevue." She proceeded to give me detailed directions. I dimly recalled having driven by it a number of times on my way to go shopping in downtown Bellevue.

"Don't worry. We'll find it," I assured her. "See you tomorrow night at seven." Which to us musicians always means at least fifteen minutes or so before the actual time of the rehearsal.

"We have a gig, Grace!" I said. "The nice folks at St. Timmons are going to feed us between the rehearsal and the performance, and I bet it'll be something delicious. Episcopalians usually serve excellent food, sometimes even wine with dinner."

Grace, still in a blue funk from her snubbing at the symphony, shot me a look that said, "Just shoot me, or better still, shoot my friend here," but I remained undaunted.

"And they're paying us. It doesn't get much better than that," I said.

Grace shrugged and pulled her faded pink robe a little tighter. I made a fresh pot of tea and soon had a batch of French toast on the table, along with scrambled eggs and some sliced oranges. Conrad arrived while I was scrambling the eggs. He proceeded to riffle through the Sunday *Seattle Times* for the Arts and Leisure section before he settled in at the kitchen table for breakfast.

"Thank you again for the beautiful symphony concert, Conrad," I said. "It was a wonderful performance. I thought they did awfully well with the Ninth in particular."

I looked over at Grace and signaled with my chin that she should say something as well. "It was a lovely evening. Really, it was," she said. "I'm only sorry for the way I behaved. I've never done anything like that before, and believe me, I never will again. Please forgive me," she said.

"Oh, hush up, Gracie," Conrad said. "That pathetic rag you're wearing is penance enough, don't you think? Is this your version of sackcloth and ashes? Stop being so silly. I would have insisted on taking you both backstage anyway, Emile or no Emile. Well, not dressed like this, of course, but you ladies looked good enough to eat last night."

"Thank you, Conrad," I said. "Say thank you to the nice man, Grace."

"Thank you," she said, mumbling into the collar of her robe.

"I still like to show my face to my colleagues whenever I'm there," Conrad said, reaching for a piece of toast, "and I figured that you two would help bolster my lagging reputation as a ladies' man. It always tickled me to have my fellow musicians coming backstage to say hello when I performed. Don't you like to know who's out there when you're onstage?" he asked, taking a bite while looking directly at both of us.

The silence was deafening. I always found performing before colleagues unnerving, and by Grace's involuntary shudder, I could see that she felt the same way. Annabelle had been the one exception to my backstage "no visitors until the concert's over" rule, however, because she was always so eager to say something nice and put me at ease. Other colleagues in Los Angeles weren't generally so kind, as I recall. A famous woman violist who was otherwise charming had said to a mutual friend after a recital, "Don't feel too bad, dear. It'll go better next time." And then there were the dreaded phrases that, when offered after a performance, meant there wasn't much good to be said, such as, "Well, you've certainly done it again," or, "I can honestly say that no one plays Bach the way you do."

Dennis could be a brutal critic, taking out his own frustrations with the music business by finding fault with other string players' interpretation, overall tone quality, or phrasing. I came to dread attending concerts or recitals with him. The more I admired a colleague's playing, the more he felt obliged to denigrate it. Eventually, he became relentless in his criticism of my own playing as well, and toward the end of our marriage I absolutely loathed performing with him. Perhaps it explains why I felt drawn to teaching as opposed to reestablishing myself as a performer when I moved to Seattle. I'm demanding of my students, but I try to be kind and encouraging. I know firsthand how destructive harsh criticism can be, and have shaped my teaching methods by balancing necessary critiques and instruction with healthy doses of well-earned praise. Ironically, Dennis himself has always reacted positively to praise by saying, "It's nice to be appreciated," with a rather self-satisfied air. It never seems to occur to him that others might feel the same way. Dennis and Marvin Pratt certainly had that particular character flaw in common, I realized. I wondered if Marv's vicious criticism at our party had triggered my subconscious resentment toward Dennis and the many years of arrogant, judgmental sniping I'd endured during the course of our marriage.

I was snapped out of my brief reverie when I heard Grace invite Conrad to the midnight Christmas Eve service at St. Timmons. Conrad assured her he wasn't even slightly interested. He said he hoped to get to bed earlier than two or three in the morning, thank you, and declined.

"Well then, you'll be up bright and early to see what Santa brought, won't you?" I said. "No opening of presents until we get up, though. Promise?" I gave him a stern look.

"Is Santa bringing me something? I had no idea," he said seriously. "In that case, I'll take the dogs for a walk first thing and allow you ladies to sleep in."

"You're a prince among men, Conrad," I said. Grace managed to smile weakly across the table at him.

"Look, Grace, I know your feelings were hurt last night, but I saw the once-over that Emile Girard gave you backstage. Take it from me … he saw you and then some! I'm a man. I know that look." Conrad wagged his finger at her. "He's in the middle of a nasty divorce. He doesn't know if he's coming or going at the moment. He's shy to boot. Timing is everything, Grace."

"Please don't patronize me, Conrad," she said. "Emile Girard looked right through me. I didn't exist as far as he was concerned. He remembered Althea … or pretended to, and he was obviously delighted to see you, but I didn't register with him in the slightest. I could have been wallpaper. *Old* wallpaper." With that, she pushed away from the table and left the kitchen.

"Oh, dear! I've really stepped in it, haven't I?" Conrad asked me. "And here I was only trying to help. Honestly, Thea, I saw the look in Emile's eyes when he saw Grace, and believe me, it wasn't apathy. It was more like a lion eyeing a lamb chop."

"You know the old saying, 'A woman scorned—'" I said. "Grace has been many things in her life, but never ignored. And to be brutally honest, Grace and I are at that age when every man we meet seems to be looking for someone much younger than he is."

"Have you seen yourselves lately?" Conrad asked. "You two have nothing to worry about."

"Easy for you to say. You're a man. It's different for men. I'm sorry, but I thought Emile was rude." I dug into my French toast, cutting it up into tiny pieces, imagining Emile Girard wriggling helplessly beneath my knife and fork. I don't like it when people hurt someone I care about, especially Grace. "No wonder his wife left him," I said. "He's a boor."

Conrad reached across the table and put his hand firmly on my arm, stopping me in mid-slice. "No, Althea, he's not. For your information, he's the one who left the marriage, and not through any fault of his own. Zita was cheating on him very publicly, and he eventually found out. Everyone else knew long before he did, but no one wanted to tell him."

"That certainly must have been humiliating," I said, regretting my rush to judgment.

"It was, I'm sure," Conrad said. "Give him a break, Althea. You've been divorced for what? Three or four years now? Are you completely over it yet?"

I felt my cheeks burning. Conrad was right, of course. It's so easy to second-guess someone else's motivations, but at times, one can be completely wrong. Like now.

"I've always liked Emile, and I respect him, too," Conrad said. "He's one of the good guys. He was caught off-guard last night—that's all."

"I'm sorry for jumping to conclusions, Conrad," I said. "Of course, you're right. I guess I took his behavior personally on Grace's behalf. I hadn't taken into account what Emile's circumstances might be, and God knows I'm not one to talk. I haven't been able to strike up a relationship with another man or even go out on a date since Dennis left me."

"I know, Thea," Conrad said. "I shouldn't have brought it up like that, either. Some wounds run deeper than others. I imagine it can take a long time to learn to trust yourself and your own judgment after a long marriage blows up in your face." Conrad looked at me intently.

"You've never been married, have you?" I asked him, but I was pretty sure I already knew the answer. I'd never known him to date, either. He looked at me and shook his shaggy head. Conrad was a loner from way back. "May I ask you a personal question then? Have you ever been in love?"

"A few times. Long ago," he said. "The ladies in question got tired of waiting for me to make the first move and eventually married someone else. I've often wondered what might have happened if I'd spoken up when I should have. As I told Grace, timing is every-thing." I remembered the narcissus flowers that had ap-peared anonymously at Annabelle's bedside and how Conrad had lowered his voice when he spoke to Annabelle on the night of the party. It seemed probable that Annabelle Pratt was one of the "ladies in question."

"I'm sorry about that, Conrad," I said. "You'd have made someone a wonderful partner. I hope you know how much Grace and I love having you here with us. You're a perfect houseguest in my humble opinion. And of course, the animals all love you."

"That means a lot to me, Althea. This is the first Christmas I've shared with anyone remotely like family since Betsy married Marvin Pratt. Be careful, though, or I'll turn into *The Man Who Came to Dinner*, only it'll be *The Man Who Came to Tea*." He laughed that lovely, grumbling laugh of his, and I patted his hand.

"Stay as long as you like, Conrad," I said. "It's been great for us, too."

"Oh, I wouldn't exactly say that," he said. "It sure seems as if I ruined Grace's evening by bringing her backstage, but she asked me to—"

"She'll get over it," I said. "You know Grace. She's resilient. Perhaps a little manic, a touch histrionic, but resilient. You can always count on Grace to throw herself into a few projects whenever she's upset. Trust me. By lunchtime, she'll have written 'thank you' notes to you, the limo driver, and some stranger who held the door for her at the grocery store last week. Then she'll bake something with a lot of chocolate in it, and by dinnertime, she'll be all better. I've never known Grace to be so emotional, though."

"She's a soprano," he said.

"Do you really think that's it?" I said.

"Yup," he said.

We finished our meal in companionable silence.

Chapter 22

I HEADED OVER to the hospital after breakfast, stopping at our local florist on the way. The place was full of holiday plants, and the glass cases held every possible combination of red, white, and green bouquets and flower arrangements. The plant stands throughout the small store were stocked with the usual red and pink poinsettias and even some flamboyant hot-house orchids, but what caught my attention was a miniature evergreen decorated as a perfect little Christmas tree. It had tiny satin bows and the smallest pale glass ornaments I'd ever seen. Glittery artificial snow had been carefully applied to the tips of each branch, creating an effect both feminine and wintery, an ideal tree for a woodland sprite or a lovely addition to Annabelle's windowsill at the hospital. The florist rang it up and packed it in a cardboard box full of crushed tissue paper to prevent it from tipping in the car on the way to the hospital. I carried it up to the ninth floor, proud of myself for having found the perfect thing.

Annabelle wasn't in her room. Actually, the entire bed had been wheeled out, and Annabelle with it. The day nurse informed me that she'd been taken down to X-ray and wouldn't be back for quite a while. There were more cards standing open among the plants on the windowsill. I noticed that some were "get well" cards, some were holiday greeting cards, and yet others were sympathy cards. These last, however, were lumped in a pile under a small ivy plant, whereas the "get well" and holiday cards were openly displayed. News of Marv's death had obviously gotten back to LA and would soon be known to musicians all over the country, thanks to the Local 47 Professional Musician's Association's monthly newspaper and the Recording Musician's Association's e-mail service. Of course, there were also the Hollywood musicians' answering services, a direct line of information and juicy gossip to every musician in LA. I moved a drab, cream-colored poinsettia plant behind the amaryllis and the narcissus blossoms to make room for the fairy-tale Christmas tree I'd brought in, and stood back to admire the effect.

Marvella Sykes, Annabelle's roommate, was sitting up in bed, looking at a magazine, but she called to me as I backed up closer and closer to the foot of her bed. "Well, Hello there!" she said. "What a beautiful little Christmas tree! You must be Althea, Annabelle's daughter. I'm Marvella Sykes," she said, extending a small brown hand. "She's told me all about you, honey. She's so proud of you!"

I gave her an uncomfortable little smile, the kind an overly modest daughter might give upon hearing such praise.

"You don't look at all like her, 'cept you're petite like she is, but my babies don't resemble me much either," Marvella Sykes said. "They look just like their daddy. I always tell people I had 'em for a friend." She giggled. I walked over to her bedside and took her slight, papery hand in my own. She gave me a warm, toothy smile. "Don't worry. I'm not contagious. It's the diverticulitis that's put me in this bed. And it's painful as anything, but you can't catch it! They tell me I'll be headin' home tomorrow, maybe even later today, but I'm gonna miss your mama."

"I'm sure she'll miss you too, Ms. Sykes," I said.

"We've had such good conversations, her and me. I don't mind tellin' you that I don't much like that other lady, though."

"Which other lady?" I asked her.

"Oh, you know," she said. "The other one 'bout my age. Very refined. Your mama's friend from way back, Baby somebody."

"Has she been here often?" I asked.

"She's been here every day. Usually comes first thing in the morning," Marvella said. "Between you and me, I think she makes your mama nervous. That funny-looking beige poinsettia plant's from her. It's kinda ugly, but she prob'ly meant well. Anyway, she brought this here for your mama," Marvella said, holding up the *Architectural Digest* magazine she'd been reading. "Of course, your poor mama can't turn a page or do much of anything, so she had one of the orderlies give it to me. What kinda gift is that for a person with two broken arms?"

Marvella had a point. It was a rather insensitive present, but "Baby somebody" had, as she said, probably meant well.

"Rosalda Alvarez, our day nurse, and me both got to be the witnesses for your mama's will, too," Marvella said. "I never did anything like that before, but I felt honored to be asked," Marvella said.

"Her will?" I said. "My mother's had her will rewritten since she's been in here?"

I don't know why I was surprised, but I was. I guess I'd just assumed that she and Marv had taken care of all that together long before this. Now, of course, Annabelle was facing her own mortality, so it was natural that she'd want certain things taken care of. Still, this seemed strangely impromptu.

"Did she have an attorney here?" I asked.

"Yes, she did, a big, good-lookin' man he was too, but I didn't catch his name. He was here a coupla times this week, and then we all signed papers yesterday."

I wondered if Annabelle planned to tell me about this.

"Your mama seemed mighty relieved to have it done with," Marvella said. "I'm gonna have mine done too as soon as I get outta here. Not that I have that much to leave. But there's a few little things, and I'd like to see them go to the right people. You know how it is. Some people gonna 'preciate the things you've loved and kept nice all your life, and some folks gonna heave 'em out soon as you're cold." Marvella was clearly a pragmatist.

"I'm sure you're right," I said. "Making a proper will is a smart thing to do. Thank you for being such a good friend to my mother, Ms. Sykes."

"Oh, you can call me Marvella," she said.

"I've tiptoed past your bed a few times," I said, "but you were either sleeping or visiting with your family or watching television. I should have stopped and introduced myself, but I didn't want to intrude. I do intend to come back tomorrow, though, so I hope to see you then. If you're allowed to go home earlier, though, before I get back, I hope you have a very good Christmas!"

"You too, honey. You too," she said as I waved good-bye. "I'll tell your mama that you were here when they bring her back up. She'll be glad to know you came, even if you didn't get to see her. She's always tellin' me how glad she is havin' you around."

Annabelle's friend Babe is probably still here in town, I thought as I drove away from the hospital and back to Blanchard House. I wondered why I hadn't run into her yet. It occurred to me that I should probably have offered to invite Annabelle's friend from out of town to a nice home-cooked dinner long before this. It would have been a nice gesture, but my heart wasn't in it. *After all*, I told myself, *I still have to deal with Grace's hurt feelings, sight-read a midnight mass on violin, and wonder which of my friends is a murderer.* It was all a bit much.

Chapter 23

AMY LINDAL, OUR young friend and recently engaged violist, called late Sunday afternoon just after I'd
returned from the hospital and asked if she could come
and play her audition material for us. She'd been preparing her Seattle Symphony excepts, the Bartok Viola
Concerto, and solo Bach Prelude for months now, and
she wanted as much professional feedback as possible
before the actual audition, which was rapidly approach-
ing. I told her to come right over. It had been exactly a
week since Marv's death, and I was more than ready to
immerse myself in work. Music is the one thing that ab-
sorbs me completely, and coaching Amy would be a welcome distraction from worrying about who'd killed our
party guest.

An old burnt-orange Volvo station wagon pulled into
the Blanchard House parking lot just as daylight was beginning to fade. I couldn't help thinking that precisely a
week before at dusk no less, this same gravel lot was

filling up with cars, and Grace and I were happily anticipating a successful tea party. The best-laid plans of mice,
men, and musicians had certainly gone awry last week at
this time.

Amy hopped out, wearing heavy gloves, a torn green
army jacket over a heavy cable sweater, and a multi-
colored Norwegian knitted hat pulled down over her
blonde braids. She grabbed her viola out of the backseat
and was immediately surrounded and almost knocked to
the ground by my enthusiastic, tail-wagging dogs as soon
as I opened the door. *Everyone loves Amy*, I thought.

"Hey, Althea!" Amy gave me a warm hug with her
free hand. "Thanks for agreeing to do this. Where's
Grace? I'd like her to hear me play too. Do you think
she'd be up for it?"

"I don't know," I said, "but I'll ask her. Meanwhile,
why don't you go upstairs to the ballroom and unpack?
There's a stand in there already." Bert and Winnie followed her upstairs, tails wagging madly in the hopes of
another round of head patting, no doubt. I like to think
that they love the sound of good viola playing as much as
I do, but who knows? They may just like the way certain
people smell. Aren't we all a bit like that when you come
to think of it?

Grace was in the kitchen, making her famous chocolate banana bread. Whenever she needs to cheer herself
up, Grace bakes something delicious. Can I pick a
housemate or what?

"Amy Lindal is here with her viola and wants to run through her audition material for us. Can you break away from baking for a while?" I asked her.

"I guess so. Let me just pop these babies into the oven, and I'll be right there," she said, indicating two glass pans that she'd just filled with batter.

We spent the next two hours listening to Amy play through some of the most treacherous orchestral viola excerpts on the audition list, as well as Prelude #2 from the Bach Cello Suites and the Bartok Viola Concerto, while enjoying the aroma of fresh chocolate banana bread. Between running down to the kitchen to check on the baking, Grace and I occasionally pointed things out or made suggestions about tempos, but we were in over-all agreement about her interpretations of the selections. Amy was extremely well-prepared, and she was definitely a mature artist with a warm, beautiful viola sound.

As to whether she stood a chance of winning a seat in the viola section of the Seattle Symphony, it was anybody's guess. There are always so many factors involved in an audition, and the competition is stiff these days. Thirty or forty years ago the viola wasn't generally considered a solo instrument, so competent violinists could often switch over to viola, and in the year or so it took them to master the alto clef and develop a slightly heavier bow arm and slow their vibrato, they could win orchestra positions. Now, however, you could hurl a rock in any major American city and hit a darned fine violist who's been studying the repertoire since grammar school and is prepared to play anything an orchestra committee can throw on the stand.

"Amy, my darling, you're in luck," Grace said as Amy packed up her viola. "It just so happens that Althea and I are preparing a wonderful dinner, complete with fresh-from-the-oven chocolate banana bread for dessert. We hope you'll join us. I'm making chicken breasts smothered in mushrooms and onions in a white wine sauce, served on a bed of sauteed spinach, and Althea makes a Caesar salad that's *killer*."

"I sincerely hope you like garlic," I said.

"I adore it! Tor's working at the theater tonight, so I was just going to go home and open a can of sardines," Amy said. "If you're sure you don't mind, I'd love to stay."

"Great!" I said, as she gathered her music. "You've met Conrad Bailey already, haven't you? Scraggly beard, woolen shirt, fabulous pianist? He's been staying with us since the accident, so he'll be at dinner too."

"I've only met him once, the night of the tea, but I liked him. He's a real character, isn't he? That reminds me," she said. "You know, that cute Detective Demetrious was over at our house this week, asking a million questions, mostly about you, Althea."

"About me? What about me?" I asked.

"Well, he wanted to know about your relationship with the Pratts, about you and Grace and your music teaching, and he even asked about you and your ex-husband," Amy said.

"He's probably digging around for a motive," I said. "What about me and Dennis could he have possibly wanted to know?"

"Well—" she said, "he asked if *in my opinion*, you were still in love with your ex."

"What did you say?" I asked.

"I asked him what bearing that could possibly have on the case," Amy said. "He said, and I quote, 'None.' So there you are, Althea. I think he likes you."

"Please!" I said. "He's sizing me up as the likeliest suspect. You'll be bailing me out of jail soon if Demetrious has his way."

"Nah. He's got the hots for you, Althea," Amy said. "I don't believe he thought very highly of Tor and me, though. We offered him some lutefisk, and he made an awful face."

"Don't take it personally, Amy," Grace said. "I make the very same face every time I even allow myself to think about lutefisk, and I think you and Tor are swell."

"I think you have to be born with the lutefisk-loving gene or be raised on lutefisk from babyhood to actually get it down the old gullet," I said. "That seems a cruel and unusual thing to do to children, though, putting mashed up lutefisk in those little baby food jars and tricking innocent toddlers into believing it's edible."

"I don't know," Amy said. "I've always liked it. Then again, I could live on sardines and herring and mackerel. It's very healthy, you know, all that cold water fish oil and stuff."

"I'm willing to die a bit sooner then, I'm afraid," Grace said. "I do take a few salmon oil capsules every day, though."

"You're so brave," I said. "Can we get back to Detective Demetrious for a second? What else did you tell him, Amy?"

"I didn't tell him much of anything because I don't really know anything," she said. "Tor told him that he was glad Marv was already dead because it would save him the trouble of killing him!"

"I'll bet that went over big," Grace said.

"The detective just laughed," Amy said. "Apparently, lots of people said exactly the same thing when he interviewed them. I hate to admit this, but I can still hear Marv Pratt's voice in my head every time I pick up the viola, slapping me down by reminding me that I'm not Yuri Bashmet."

"That wasn't exactly a confidence builder," I said.

"That's one reason I've been running around town this week trying to play for people whose experience I respect," Amy said.

"We're flattered to be considered, Amy, but you have no reason to feel the least bit insecure," I said. "You play just beautifully. You're a first-class violist. Surely, you're aware of that yourself, no matter what anyone might say."

"It's hard, though, when someone plants that seed of doubt, isn't it?" Grace said. "Marvin Pratt had a lot of nerve, commenting on your playing when he'd never even heard you perform!"

"Well, that's not quite true," Amy said, biting her lower lip. "You know I went to college in LA, right? Well, he heard me play a student recital when I was an undergrad many years ago. Marv was still a big shot in Los Angeles then, and I made the mistake of inviting the Pratts. He was on the faculty then, remember? Who knew they'd actually show up?"

"Honey, they showed up for everything," Grace said. "Marv would have attended the opening of a can of spaghetti."

"I was only nineteen," Amy said, "and it probably wasn't my best performance, but that was a long time ago. I'm twenty-eight now, and I've been studying seriously and practicing like a maniac for years. But he's always put down my playing very publicly since then. It's been costing me recording work ever since I moved back up here, and even my sub work with the opera and the ballet has fallen off. That's why it's so important that I play well for this audition, even if I don't get the job. I have a reputation to salvage. I'm sorry to say this, but I've despised Marvin Pratt for years. I'm glad he's dead!"

"Me too! Let's eat," said Conrad as he entered the kitchen. "Mm, it smells wonderful in here!" He went to slice himself a piece of chocolate banana bread that was still cooling on the wire rack, but Grace threw herself in front of the loaf.

"No, no! That's for dessert," she said. "First, we're going to have a marvelous dinner. It'll be ready in a few minutes. Here," she said, handing him a glass of chilled white burgundy instead.

"I'm glad to see you're back to your old self," Conrad said.

"Me too," said Grace. So was I.

"There was a call for you while you were out, Althea," Conrad said after glasses of wine were poured for everyone. "I wasn't going to answer it, but I thought it might be you calling from the hospital, so I did."

"Oh, who was it?" I asked.

"That detective guy," he said. "I asked if he wanted to leave a message. He said no."

"I think he's already delivered his message," Grace said drily. "I believe our Detective Demetrious has the hots for Althea," she said, raising an eyebrow over her wineglass as she sipped.

"No, really?" Conrad said. "I'm shocked," he added, rolling his eyes.

"Cut it out, you guys. I think he has me pegged for a murderess. You know, emotionally unbalanced music teacher poisons obnoxious guest at tea party to defend honor of sainted ex-husband. Something along those lines," I said.

"You're such a cynic," Grace said.

"I prefer to think of myself as a realist," I said, "and anyway, I'm pretty sure that Detective Demetrious is already mentally fitting me for a striped prison shirt with a long, hyphenated number on it, so knock it off."

Amy and Grace barely suppressed their giggles, and I pretended to be annoyed. Actually, I was just the tiniest bit warmed by the thought that Harry Demetrious was interested in me in any way whatsoever.

"Seriously," I asked as I began assembling the makings for my Caesar salad, "do you think he has a likely suspect in mind at this point? Besides me, I mean." I wanted to add, "He really is good-looking, isn't he?" but I didn't.

"I tend to believe that he's leaning toward Annabelle," Conrad said. "The police always look carefully at the victim's nearest and dearest. Generally, they're right to do so, but not in this case. Annabelle's a cream puff. She'd never harm anyone at all, especially Marv."

"True," Grace said. "If she didn't kill him long before now, she probably loved the guy."

"Maybe it was an accident," Amy said. "I mean, what if she was planning on poisoning herself and Marv took the poison accidentally? That's silly, though. Why would she want to do that?"

I realized with a start that I could think of several reasons why she might want to end her own life, first and foremost to save her precious Marv from watching her suffer the gradual deterioration brought about by her leukemia, but I wasn't about to say so. Besides, that just didn't fit with the Annabelle I knew and admired. Annabelle had a lot in common with me and with Grace. She was no quitter either.

"Well, your new swain wants to come over to interview me and Grace tomorrow at some point, so we'll put in a good word for you, Thea," Conrad said. "I will personally assure him that, had you wanted to kill Marv Pratt, you would have done it in a far more amusing way than mere poison. It would have been an act of creative genius."

"Gee, thanks," I said.

"You know, you're absolutely right, Conrad," Grace said as she unwrapped the chicken breasts. "Our Althea would have devised some brilliant scheme that would have guaranteed severe mental anguish and eventual insanity. She'd have set him on a treasure hunt for an elusive violin, an impossible quest for a missing Strad or some such thing that would inevitably result in pathological obsession and irreversible madness. Marv would have killed himself just to get some relief."

"It's nice to see that those who know me best have such confidence in my innocence," I said. "I wouldn't just murder someone. No, I'd torture him first. Thanks a lot."

I'd like to be able to say that I was appalled by my friends' characterization of me, but I knew they were probably right. *Grace had a pretty interesting idea there,* I thought to myself. I was actually surprised that I hadn't come up with it first.

The rest of the evening was spent eating and drinking and ripping apart the reputations of the many conductors under whom we'd each played, a pastime that classical musicians enjoy as much as sex, and a sport in which Conrad Bailey excelled. After all, he'd been playing professionally for over fifty years, and so he'd known most of the greats and plenty of the not-so-greats. He could do wickedly spot-on impersonations of all the famous conductors, and he did, much to our delight. We laughed ourselves silly while we devoured everything on our plates, another thing at which musicians excel.

When the last morsel of food was gone, Grace and I walked Amy out to her car while Bert and Winnie made their final pit stop of the evening in their favorite place, the Doggie Heaven ravine. A sudden blast of icy wind howling through the pines made me shiver, reminding me again of what had happened here only a week before, and I reassured myself that Grace and I would always be protected as long as Winnie and Bert were around. The dogs came running as soon as I whistled to them, looking like nothing more than dark shadows moving swiftly past us, illuminated briefly by the headlights of Amy's old Volvo, and then disappearing quickly inside the open doorway of Blanchard House, heading for their cedar-filled doggie beds. Bert in particular likes to get his beauty sleep.

Conrad had already cleaned up most of the dinner things and loaded the dishwasher. I tackled the rest while Grace dragged herself up the stairs and went to bed. I was still wide awake when the phone rang.

"Well, I'd hate to get on your bad side, Ms. Stewart." It was Demetrious.

"What are you talking about?" I said. "You bought me a latte and a muffin. That put you up a good five points. Or are you going to spoil it now by telling me something disagreeable?"

"That depends on what you consider disagreeable," he said. "Maybe poor old Oliver Siddon should have plied you with coffee and muffins. Things might have worked out better for him."

"Has something happened to Oliver? Oh, my God!" I knew the horrible truth the second Demetrious said his name. I hadn't been looking at a mashed squirrel in the middle of the street after all, but Oliver's hideously squished toupee.

Chapter 24

"I HATE TO have to ask you this, Ms. Stewart, but where were you last night?" Demetrious asked.

"I hate to have to tell you, believe me," I said. "Grace, Conrad, and I were together at the Seattle Symphony concert, Benaroya Hall, third-row center, and then backstage at intermission among eighty or so of our beloved colleagues. We have more witnesses to our whereabouts before, during, and after the performance than you could interview in a week."

"Oh, really?" he said. "And why is that?"

"Well," I said, "if you must know, the late Oliver Siddon made a point of coming over to our row and referring to Grace and me as 'party girls' and 'wild things.' The entire block of orchestra seating at the front of the hall heard him. They thought we were a couple of aging hookers."

"A couple of *really good-looking*, aging hookers," he said, correcting me.

"Did anyone ever tell you that you have a way with words?" I asked.

"Not recently," he said.

"Well, don't hold your breath," I said. "So tell me what exactly happened to Oliver, detective. I hope it isn't what I think happened."

"I don't know," he said. "What do you think happened?"

"I think he stepped out in front of oncoming traffic at the entrance to Benaroya Hall and was squashed like a bug on a windshield. Am I wrong?"

"Only in part, although you do have a way with words yourself, Ms. Stewart. It seems that he may very well have been shoved. At least that's what the bus driver thinks and what she told the detectives at the scene. She said it looked as if he were propelled out into the street, head and shoulders first, quite fast, with an expression of shock on his face. Quite a large crowd had been standing there waiting for a walk sign, and before the driver could apply her brakes the man came lurching off the curb with his arms flailing."

"That poor bus driver must be a wreck," I said. "What time did all this happen?"

"At around 9:40. The bus driver was very sure of the time, because Metro tries to keep their bus routes on a strict schedule. Don't you ever watch the news?"

"Not if I can help it," I said.

"Well, if you had, you'd have known by now."

"Have you interviewed the other pedestrians that were waiting on the curb with him, or am I the only suspect?" I asked.

"Not me, no," Demetrious said. "The accident, if that's what it was, occurred in Seattle, so it's not in our jurisdiction. I did get to read the report this evening, though. Apparently, a lot of the crowd on the sidewalk at the intersection was comprised of homeless people, some drunk, some on drugs, and some just plain crazy. I'm sure you'd be up on the correct psychological term for it, but we police types just call street people who wander around talking to themselves 'crazies.'"

"They're probably schizophrenics," I said. "Paranoid schizophrenics. Do you think one of them might have given Oliver a shove?"

"Could be," he said. "My money was on you, though. I mean, you didn't much like Marvin Pratt, and look what happened to him. You weren't a big fan of poor Oliver Siddon either, and now he's dead too. Of course, you might have wanted to kill him, but you have a rock-solid alibi, so there goes that theory. It's a shame and a disappointment for the law enforcement community. I was going to question you over drinks and dinner."

"Are you going to let a little thing like an alibi stop you?" I said. "Perhaps I have an evil accomplice. Did you ever think of that?"

"Yup, I did," he said. "Unfortunately, all your accomplices seem to have been lolling around with you backstage at the time of the murder. Annabelle might have been a suspect before, but she's been a little tied up these days, what with the broken arms and all. Now it hardly seems that any information you can give me is worth the price of a fancy dinner, does it?"

"How fancy?" I asked.

"Pretty fancy," he said. "Good bottle of wine, too. Let's not forget about that."

"And they say crime doesn't pay. Ha!" I hung up on him. It felt good.

As I got myself ready for bed, I made yet another mental list of possible murder suspects in the Marvin Pratt case, but it wasn't reassuring. Almost everyone on the list was also in my "friend" category. All of these people, myself included, may have wished at one time or another that Marv would just hurry up and drop dead— and Oliver too—but I couldn't imagine any one of them going that extra step to make it happen. Even sweet little Amy and her fiancée, Tor, had reason to despise Marv Pratt and want him out of the way, but that wasn't enough to convince me that either of them could be a cold-blooded killer.

Someone definitely was, though, and now it looked as if Oliver Siddon may have become the next victim. What did Oliver know? Why did I think that these two deaths might be connected? Somehow, I was sure that they were. It seemed that Demetrious thought so too. Poisoning was one thing, deadly but fairly passive.

Pushing someone under a bus, though, that was completely hands-on, as it were. Doing it in public in a location as busy as downtown Seattle was nothing short of desperate. If both of these murders had been committed by the same person, things were becoming infinitely more dangerous. What was the common thread? Violins? Annabelle now owned a whole room full of priceless violins, and someone had just upped the ante. At least Oliver was no longer a suspect, but that's a terrible way to be exonerated, isn't it?

As I pulled my flannel nightgown over my head and climbed into bed, I tried to push thoughts of Oliver's sad, crushed toupee out of my head, but they wouldn't budge. It certainly appeared more and more likely that the murderer was someone I knew. At least it wasn't Grace or Conrad or me. Winnie and Bert looked innocent, too, snoring on their little doggie beds. *Lydia always looks guilty*, I thought, *but that's just the way cats are*. I closed my eyes and tried to picture myself on a hot, sunny beach, lying next to a tanned and fit Demetrious, but as I drifted off to sleep, my last thoughts were of Oliver Siddon and the terror he must have experienced as he felt himself being shoved forward into the path of a moving bus.

Chapter 25

THERE'S NOTHING LIKE hearing your cell phone jangling madly in the Byzantine depths of your purse while you're driving in heavy traffic. One is immediately jolted by the noise of that repetitious, fairly obnoxious, calypso ringtone that seemed so clever when you selected it. You may be able to feel the buzzing against the side of your wallet, too, but no matter how quickly you try to dump the contents of your oversized bag onto the seat next to you, the phone will invariably stop its melodious siren song just as you get your hand around it. That's more or less what occurred as my car inched along 116th Street the following morning on my way back to Blanchard House from the supermarket. Grocery shopping on Christmas Eve isn't the smartest move in the world, but we were out of dairy products and fresh vegetables. Grace had been doing a lot of the food shopping lately, and it was my turn to suck it up and fight the crowds.

Everyone knows you shouldn't try to use a cell phone while you are driving, but curiosity got the better of me. I glanced quickly at the screen to check out who'd just tried to reach me and saw a now-familiar number. Okay, so my pulse raced a bit when I realized it was Harry Demetrious, Kirkland PD. Big deal. Any contact with the police gives me a mild case of paranoia along with an inevitable adrenaline rush. Still, I suspected he wasn't about to arrest me or even give me a speeding ticket, so I pulled over and pushed the "call back" button.

"Harry Demetrious here," he said. "Where are you? I have something to show you."

"Excuse me? I'm driving. I mean, I just pulled over." *I'm a good girl. I am*, I thought to myself, quoting Eliza Doolittle. "Where are you?"

"Right outside your house, as it happens, but your car's gone," he said.

"Well, yes, and that would be because I'm currently in it, pulled over on 116th Street, talking to you," I said. "I'll be home in less than three minutes, if you'd care to wait for me. You can help unload the groceries. What have you got to show me anyway?"

"You'll see, Ms. Stewart. You'll see." And with that, he rang off. All I could think of was that old line, "If you show me yours, I'll show you mine." Somehow, though, I didn't think that's where we were headed at the moment. Sure enough, the unmarked gray Taurus was parked in the graveled lot in front of Blanchard House, and Harry Demetrious was standing near the hood of his car, checking his cell phone.

"Where's your buddy, the charming Sergeant Zeigler, by the way?" I asked Demetrious as I got out of my little Honda, balancing several overloaded canvas shopping bags in the process. "He seems to have disappeared lately. Why is that? Am I considered so much less dangerous these days that you no longer require backup?" Why couldn't I bring myself to say a polite hello like a normal person? Detective Demetrious just smiled slowly and grabbed for one of the heavier grocery bags with one hand while he held out a bulging manila envelope with the other.

"You may want to take this inside to open," he said, "and you may need to be sitting down." He hoisted all of the grocery bags while I took the proffered envelope and headed to the kitchen table, the detective hot on my heels. Winnie and Bert were tagging along too, so I gave them each a biscuit. Loyalty should always be rewarded is my motto. I spilled the contents of the envelope onto the table, realizing that what fell out was a robin's egg blue Tiffany box. Inside that was another box, black velvet, long and slim. My fingers shook as I pried the lid open.

"Oh!" was all I could say before my resident devil kicked in. The half-inch wide bracelet inside spelled out the word *Bellissima* in tiny diamonds on filigreed white gold or possibly platinum. *Most Beautiful One* in Italian.

I looked up at Demetrious with a trembling chin and my best wide-eyed lash flutter. I put my hand over my throat and drew in my breath audibly.

"I had no idea you felt this way about me, detective," I said. "Oh, my God! This is the most beautiful gift I've ever received, and here I just got you a paperback book! Wait until I tell my mother. She'll be so excited! Thank you. Thank you. I'll wear it forever!"

Demetrious went white, I swear. The thing about a really good put-on is that you have to keep it going just a wee bit longer than one might expect. The victim needs time to think to himself, "She's just kidding, right?" and then you have to make him squirm just a tad longer. It's an art form.

I took the bracelet out of the box. I tried it on. I held it up to the light. All the while, he was saying things like, "Well, I—" or "You see, it's not—" I jumped up and kissed him heartily on the cheek for good measure, seemingly oblivious to his discomfort. You see, this is why I've been asked to leave almost every school I've ever attended. Opportunities as ripe as this one are just too hard to resist.

"I hate to have to say this, Ms. Stewart. I mean, it's very beautiful on you, but it's not ... not for you." He practically choked on the words.

I allowed my breath to catch and then looked up very slowly at him in mock dismay. I bit my lower lip and dropped my eyes.

"You bought it for someone else?" I faked a stammer. "Oh, I ... I'm so sorry. I just thought, well ... I'm sure she'll love it. How embarrassing—" Then I let my lower lip quiver a bit. I've always wished that I could blush on command. It would have come in handy right about now; however, I've never been able to work up a nice, bright flush without actual shame involved, and when it comes to things like this, I'm quite shameless. At this point, Harry Demetrious looked positively agonized.

I couldn't resist giving him a very evil grin with an eyebrow twitch for good measure. Finally, the man roared.

"I think I may have to strangle you, Ms. Stewart," he managed between bursts of laughter. "How could you? I almost believed you."

"Almost?" I said. "Almost? You went pale. It was a thing of beauty, detective. I shall remember it always. Oh, and I did get you a book for Christmas. That part was absolutely true."

"Stop it. I ... I can't breathe," he said. "Haven't you toyed with me enough?" He wheezed, wiping a tear from his eye. "You knew whose this was all along, didn't you? You may look angelic, but underneath that pretty little exterior beats a wicked, wicked heart."

Demetrious removed the bracelet gingerly from my wrist and put it securely back in its velvet box. It really did look pretty swell on me. Of course, a dazzler like that would have enhanced the forearm of a gorilla, so I tried not to get too excited over the compliment.

"Well, this is what we retrieved from Tiffany's with that jeweler's receipt in Marv's wallet," Demetrious said. "They didn't want to surrender such an expensive little bauble, either, until we showed them our badges and the coroner's report."

"I'll bet they knew Marvin Pratt very well," I said.

"As you suspected, he had Tiffany's design this as a custom order for his wife's Christmas gift," he said. "He was supposed to pick it up sometime before Christmas Eve, but he never got around to it. I promised the staff that I'd personally deliver it to Mrs. Pratt in the hospital. The manager of Tiffany's was actually pretty broken up when he learned that Marvin Pratt had died in a car accident."

"Wouldn't you be ... in his shoes?" I said. "Only imagine what Marv spent there annually. He was probably the source of Christmas bonuses for the entire staff. And let's not forget Annabelle's birthday, Valentine's Day, their anniversary. Poor Marv! He used to call her his *Bellissima*. Annabelle is, you must admit, a most beautiful woman, even with a black eye."

"If you say so," Demetrious said. "Hard to tell when she's all banged up like that. Honestly, I thought that thing looked pretty good on you too, though. Not the black eye. The bracelet. It's kind of a shame there weren't two of these babies," he said, wagging the box in my face.

"You can always go back to Tiffany's and have them make me one," I said. "I'll bet they still have the wax mold for the original. The second one should be a snap." Demetrious ignored me and put the Tiffany box back in the manila envelope.

"I can see that it's coal for you this year, young lady," he said. "I'll bet there's been coal in your stocking for a whole bunch of years. Am I right?" he asked.

"Unfortunately, yes, but these little flights of fancy always seem worth it at the time," I said. *You truly have no idea*, I thought. If even a small portion of my odious past transgressions had been recorded on Santa's list, that jolly old elf would have been justified in backing up a good-sized coal truck onto my front lawn.

"You'll have to give this bracelet to Annabelle, detective, and soon. Marv would have wanted her to have it in time for Christmas."

"*We'll* have to give it to her, you and I," he said. "I'm not going up there alone to deliver something like this. You're going with me. Please, Ms. Stewart. You know it would be better coming from you." Demetrious looked pleadingly at me with his blue-gray eyes and those incredible dimples, and I thought to myself that I might enjoy doing a lot of things for him if he asked nicely. Bring on the dump truck, Santa.

"I hope you don't mind, but I have to put these perishables away while we talk," I said, shoving butter pecan ice cream into the freezer. "What about Christmas morning? Grace and I are playing a midnight service at a church tonight. But if you get to Blanchard House by around nine or ten tomorrow morning we can all have a rousing breakfast, and then you and I can hit the hospital together."

"I'm afraid Christmas morning is out," he said.

Of course, I thought. He probably has a beautiful wife and many dimpled children. They'll be spending the day together opening presents and having a big Christmas dinner. What was I thinking, anyway? Men this good are all taken. Oh, well, it was a pleasant dream while it lasted.

"I was thinking about this afternoon," he said. "What would it take to bribe you into coming with me? How about a festive lunch?" His eyes twinkled. "Besides, we have a few more things to talk about."

"Such as?" I asked, now all business. *Save the twinkling eye bit for your wife, buster*, I thought.

"Such as your visit to Marilyn Litzky," he said. "Your friend called me last night with 'the rest of the story,' as it were. She said you talked her into getting her business dealings with Marvin Pratt out in the open, for which I and the Kirkland Police Department thank you. Are you some kind of mother confessor, Ms. Stewart?"

he asked as he watched me stuff lettuces and dairy products into the stainless steel fridge. Was he checking out
my backside? *Shame on you, Mr. Married Detective*, I
thought.

"People do tend to tell me things," I said, "and not
always things I enjoy hearing, either. It's a curse, and it's
been going on since grade school. By the time I graduated from the Conservatory, I knew every little thing
about everybody, because they all felt compelled to share
their most unpleasant secrets with me."

"Lonely people obviously trust you," Demetrious
said, his eyes so focused on mine that I had to turn away
and stare at the wallpaper. "Of course, they don't know
you like I do," he said.

"Thanks for that glowing character analysis, detective," I said. "No, really, it's uncanny how many people
have confided in me. All those unsolicited confessions
used to unnerve me, but I've learned a few things over
the years," I said, turning back to him. "The trick is to
keep whatever you hear to yourself and to develop a fa-
mously bad memory. How about you, Detective? Any
nasty little secrets you'd like me to take with me to my
grave?"

"You know, that's a strange but extremely apt way
of putting it," Demetrious said. "Have you ever thought
that someone who knows too many secrets, even one
secret too many, might be in real danger? If you know
something that has any relevance at all to either of these

cases, Ms. Stewart, even if you don't think they're somehow connected or even important, I'd wish you'd share it
with me. Someone you probably know has killed twice
already. Why wouldn't that person kill again if he or she
felt threatened? Even the cleverest murderers have been
known to say too much and then regret it."

Demetrious was right, I knew, but I was having a
hard time imagining Conrad, Andrew, or even Marilyn at
her most desperate as a killer. Conrad, of course, still felt
tremendous animosity toward Marvin Pratt because of
his sister, but he'd always been up-front about letting his
negative feelings show. Marilyn was clearly determined
to get her husband's violin back for him, but, if she and
her mother could be believed, she'd already made a satis-
factory deal with Marvin Pratt to accomplish just that.
Suddenly, it occurred to me that Andrew Litzky knew
nothing about his wife's machinations. Here was a man
obsessed with the loss of his violin, possibly to the det-
riment of his marriage. How far would an extremely
driven musician go to get back the instrument that he felt
was rightfully his, or to punish the man who was responsible for taking it in the first place? No, that just didn't
feel like the Andrew I'd known all these years. The
question I had to ask myself was whether or not my instincts could be trusted.

I could easily have imagined Oliver Siddon, on the
other hand, pushing his own grandmother off a cliff to
get at those priceless instruments, but that's not the way

the story played out, was it? He'd certainly never been a confidante of mine, and Oliver wasn't even on the premises the night of the murder. At least, no one had seen him there. Could he instead have conspired with someone who was at the tea itself?

Harry Demetrious, meanwhile, was watching me carefully for my reaction to his suggestion. It made me extremely uncomfortable. How much did he suspect about my friends and their secrets? Did he expect me to break their confidences in a moment of fear?

"There is something you might want to check into," I said. "It slipped my mind, but it could be important. Conrad mentioned that Oliver Siddon was known to leave the Symphony concerts at intermission and head for a bar across the street. I don't know which one, but perhaps someone there knows something."

"There are a couple of bars near Benaroya," he said, "and a number of restaurants which are also popular watering holes. I'm sure the Seattle PD will be checking around to see who, if anyone, knew Oliver Siddon. If he was a regular, someone will recognize him."

"So where are you taking me, detective? I hope it's someplace with hefty portions, because I'm starving."

I didn't add that I thought we might need all of our strength just to deal with Annabelle's reaction to the bracelet. I fully expected that her husband's final gift to her would precipitate an emotional crisis. Would she finally accept Marv's death, and how would it affect her frame of mind? I was anxiously anticipating what lay ahead, but I thought a good lunch might help. It certainly couldn't hurt.

"I was thinking of someplace on the water," Demetrious said. "How's about I drive us over toward Lake Washington, and we'll see what we can do at lunchtime on Christmas Eve with no reservations and a badge."

"Isn't that cheating?" I asked.

"Nah. Only if we don't pay the bill and refuse to tip," he said. "I intend to do both, and I always tip lavishly. I'm also delighted to learn that you're not one of those dainty eaters, Ms. Stewart. I like a woman with a healthy appetite."

I found myself reimagining his wife, a regular chowhound, probably overweight with a well-developed jaw. Strangely, it didn't make me feel any better.

"Great. We'll be friends for life," I said. "Wait! Winnie and Bert need to go out for a few minutes. Hold that thought, detective." I called over my shoulder as I made my way to the front door and released the hounds. Both dogs bounded outside toward the wooded ravine next to the house. We could hear them rustling around through the bushes and wet leaves, doing their doggie thing. After a few minutes, I whistled for them to come back, and they came running right in for their treats.

"Done!" I said.

"Do you expect everyone to respond when you whistle like that?" Demetrious asked.

"Only truly clever and obedient creatures, detective." I said.

"Ah ... well, hop in, madam." He held open the door of his gray Taurus. "You are now officially my prisoner. We feed our prisoners well in Kirkland, fortunately for you, Ms. Stewart. By the way, where are your friends, Ms. Sullivan and Mr. Bailey? I'd hoped to speak with them later this afternoon."

I knew they'd be less than thrilled by the prospect, especially because he hadn't offered to take them out for lunch as part of the deal. *Food can go a long way toward making one socially acceptable*, I thought. Demetrious turned on the engine and headed for the waterfront.

"I have no idea where Grace and Conrad went," I said. "I'd have thought that they'd be waiting eagerly by the front door just hoping for a glimpse of you, ready to bare their souls. People can be so difficult, don't you agree? They go on living their lives without consulting us or begging our permission before they wander off. In this case, though, I'm sure they'll turn up soon. Please call me Althea, by the way. Buying me a nice lunch does convey certain privileges."

"Really? Must it be a 'nice' lunch? What else does it get me? Besides putting us on a first-name basis?" he said. He flashed a dimpled smile.

"Well, for one thing, you can call upon me to pro-vide all sorts of terribly arcane information, musicologi-cally speaking," I said. "I might even be willing to share the inside scoop on the lives of famous composers, which is more intriguing than one might expect."

"Oh, goodie!" he said.

"Don't be such a smarty-pants, Mr. Hotshot Detective. Do you know much about Rachmaninoff, for instance?" I asked him. "And by the way, shouldn't you have insisted on me calling you Harry by now?"

"Yes, I should have, although it's highly unprofes-sional. I was just getting around to it when you distracted me with decomposing composers. Call me Harry. Now what's so intriguing about Rachmaninoff?"

"Well, for one thing, if you really want to know, he was a necrophiliac," I said. "He used to haunt the morgues and funeral parlors of Paris every evening after dark. His buddies, other famous composers like Debussy and Ravel, used to go searching for him amidst the corpses, hoping to find him and pull him off the dead bodies before the local constabulary got their hands on him. When this guy suggested stopping off after work for 'a few cold ones,' he wasn't kidding." I looked away from him, watching the wind-blown pedestrians hurrying along the lakefront.

He guffawed. "Are you pulling my leg again?" he asked.

I assured him that I wasn't.

"No wonder my mother warned me about musicians," he said. "You know, Ms. Stewart … I mean Althea, you may be my all-time favorite murder suspect, and I've known more than a few memorable ones in my time."

"Flatterer!" I said as Demetrious turned into the parking lot of Fiorente, formerly Clancy's Bistro, formerly the Foghorn. "It's my insouciance, isn't it? Great choice of restaurant, by the way. Italian. Yum!" I rubbed my hands together gleefully.

"Your enthusiasm is worth the price of lunch, you know that?" he said.

"I should hope so!" I said. "I pride myself on being an excellent eater, so you'd better have plenty of money."

"Don't you worry," he said. "I do. They call me 'Moneybags Demetrious' all over town. Hadn't you heard?"

Demetrious not only got a prime parking spot, but the maître 'd knew him by name, thus ensuring us a table for two overlooking Lake Washington, no badge necessary. I decided not to worry myself wondering how many ladies he'd taken here before me. Okay, the truth was that I was a little curious, but not enough to ruin the moment. We both ordered Caesar salads and scampi and sat back to enjoy the view.

"Now tell me about the will," he said, casually flicking his napkin onto his lap.

"The will?" I looked at him blankly, momentarily disconcerted. How could he already know that Annabelle had just made a new will?

"Yeah, Marvin Pratt's will," he said. "Do you happen to know who his beneficiary is?"

"Oh." I took a deep breath. "Well, I don't know for sure, but I'd assume that Annabelle will inherit everything. As far as I know, Marvin Pratt had no children, and as for other possible beneficiaries, we won't know until the will is read, correct?"

"You tell me," he said.

"I've heard a strong rumor that Marv was planning on leaving his entire violin collection to the Seattle Symphony," I said. "I also heard that Horst Beckman, a well-known violin dealer in Chicago, was prepared to appraise and authenticate the entire collection. You could call him and find out. Of course, since so many instruments were acquired during Marv's marriage to Annabelle and they were living in California at the time, which is a community property state, she'd have to agree to such an endowment as well. Am I right about that?"

"I'm not an attorney, but that sounds about right. We should ask her about it after lunch."

"You know, detective ... I mean Harry, you have a unique way of ruining a good meal. I have no intention of mentioning it to her after lunch. I suppose you'd like to tell her about Oliver winding up on the bumper of a Metro bus, too, wouldn't you?"

"Well, she might be able to shed some light on what Oliver Siddon was up to," Demetrious said. "He did call the police station and insist that he and the Pratts were bosom buddies, don't forget, and he did go to visit her just before winding up dead as a doornail outside Symphony Hall. We also know he called you asking about the Pratts' accident and what would happen to their instruments. I'd say she has a unique perspective on this entire affair."

"Don't you dare mention what happened to Oliver Siddon, detective," I said, pointing a finger at him. "I'm warning you."

"You're warning me?" he said.

"You heard me," I said. "As Annabelle's friend and make-believe daughter, I absolutely forbid you to bring up yet another morbid topic in front of her right now. She's barely hanging on. Can't you see that?" *And by the way, Detective Demetrious, what's going on in your life on Christmas morning?* I know. I know. None of my business. It was just a random thought.

"Why do you think I invited you along, Ms. Stewart? Just to watch you devour my Christmas bonus? Which I'm perfectly willing to do by the way, so if you finish up all your vegetables, you may have dessert."

"No thanks. I'm not a dessert kind of girl," I said.

"Neither am I," he said. "Not the girl thing. The dessert thing."

"I got that," I said. "So do we have a deal?"

"Maybe," he said.

The food arrived, and conversation took a backseat to the joys of the table. The pasta was al dente. The salad was just right, and every shrimp was succulent and garlicky. Even the bread was warm and crusty. A glass of cold pinot grigio would have been perfect, but it was too early in the day for wine, so we made do with iced teas. For the moment, I could pretend that I was here on a romantic lunch date with a handsome man for no other reason than pure pleasure. I tried to push any thoughts of a tubby wife and sprawling family out of my mind, but it wasn't easy.

I learned something rather soul-stirring about Harry Demetrious over lunch, though. Here was a man who enjoyed food as much as I did, and that's saying something. We may have been heading into an emotional firestorm at the hospital, but at least we had enough garlic on our breath to frighten off any vampires we might encounter along the way, as well as pleasant memories of a deeply satisfying lunch.

Chapter 26

ANNABELLE WAS NAPPING when we arrived. She seemed even paler than she'd been the day before, if that were possible. Her black eye still retained its egg-plant color but with a yellow ring spreading around it. Her hair had been neatly combed and arranged on the pillow by some kind nurse. Sure enough, Marvella Sykes had been released from the hospital, and her bed had been freshly made up, one half of the room cleared of any sign of its former occupant.

"Should we wake her?" Demetrious whispered to me from the foot of the bed as he watched Annabelle gently snoring.

"No, let's just spend the day standing here and hope she opens her eyes," I said. "Are you kidding? Of course we have to wake her." I bent over the bed and gently touched Annabelle's cheek with the back of my hand. She opened her good eye drowsily.

"Oh! Althea, darling!" Annabelle said. Her normal voice was returning little by little, and now it resembled a gentle purr. "I was just dreaming about you and Dennis playing the Handel-Halvorsen *Passacaglia*. You two always played the hell out of that piece. My roommate, Marvella, said you'd been here yesterday and brought me this marvelous little tree. I'm sorry I missed you yesterday. They were x-raying me. It took forever. Oh, you're here too," she said as she spotted Demetrious standing off to the side. "I certainly wasn't dreaming about you! What can I do for you, detective?"

"Actually, ma'am, there's something I'd like to do for you. We brought you something," he said, taking the Tiffany box from the manila envelope. "Here!" He held out the box to her as if she might actually be able to throw off her plaster casts and reach for it.

Annabelle just looked at him as if he were completely stupid.

"I can't even scratch my own nose with these casts on my arms. What is that, detective? Althea, can you open that for me?" she asked, craning her neck slightly forward to get a better look at what he held in his hand.

I took the package from Demetrious and slid the black velvet box out of its Tiffany wrapper. I opened the lid, carefully turning it toward Annabelle so that she would be the first person in the room to glimpse the bracelet in all its shimmering glory.

"*Bellissima!*" she gasped. "It says *Bellissima!* Oh, my dear Lord! It's from Marv, my dear, darling Marv, isn't it? Only my husband has ever called me that, his *Bellissima*. It's so perfect, so absolutely divine! Wherever did you get it?"

The silence in the room seemed to go on and on. I sure wasn't going to be the one to break it. Finally, Demetrious spoke up.

"Your husband had a receipt from Tiffany's in his wallet the night he died in the accident. We retrieved this for you yesterday. I'm so sorry, ma'am."

Annabelle visibly crumpled. All of her postponed grief appeared to hit her at once. I laid the bracelet gently in her lap, since there was no way for her to wear it over the casts that imprisoned both of her arms. She closed her eyes and slowly allowed her head to fall forward, letting the tears flow freely down her pale cheeks. When she spoke again, it was in a quiet, composed voice.

"Thank you, detective. He's gone, really and truly gone, isn't he? My beloved Marv, my own precious piece of humanity."

"He loved you right until the very end, Annabelle. It was always you, only you," I said.

"No," she said softly, choking back tears. "It wasn't. I'd like to think so, but it's not true. He adored his first wife, too. You can't imagine what Betsy's death did to him, Althea."

"But he left her," I blurted out before I had time to catch myself.

"Only because she forced him to!" Annabelle said. "Betsy insisted that he leave. She was brave and loving and strong, all the things I'm not. She knew he'd never get through her illness and her dying if he had to stay there and watch her waste away. She understood him completely. Betsy was the only person besides me in whom Marv ever confided. Marv trusted that his secrets would always be safe with her, and he was right." Annabelle gazed around the room at nothing in particular. "He'd never have survived seeing me like this, either, but I've been much too cowardly to send him away. I've always been a coward, a selfish coward."

"No, you certainly are not!" I said. "You've always been the first one to stand up for others, for what's fair, Annabelle."

"Not in my personal life, believe me. Marv may have had his phobias, but I was always the one who was truly afraid," she said. "Marv, at least, had a good reason."

"What reason? What happened to him?" I heard Demetrious say, pulling me back from my flashback to a small, gold-framed picture of Betsy Bailey on the wall of Marv's study.

"I promised him I'd never tell a soul while he was alive, but he's gone now, isn't he?" Annabelle looked at the stack of sympathy cards on the windowsill and sighed. "His secrets probably don't matter anymore. My poor Marv. Everyone thought he was a callous, uncaring man. There was that side of him, of course. He could be jealous and critical and at times even ruthless, but he was so wounded in early childhood that I couldn't help but feel protective of him. It's a horrific story, detective. He wouldn't want it known. Promise me you won't repeat this to anyone, either of you."

We promised.

Annabelle took a deep, painful breath. "Well, when he was not quite four years old," she began, "Marv's mother went into labor alone. They lived in a tenement in New York City somewhere. Marv never even knew where exactly, but he remembered that night for the rest of his life. His father was working the docks, you see, and couldn't get home for days at a time. When his mother started screaming in agony, Marv ran down the hall for help. Some neighbor women came in, but there was no money for a doctor, so they tried to deliver the baby themselves. It may have been a breech birth or some other complication, but the baby wouldn't come out no matter what they did. One of these women finally took a knife and tried to cut his mother open to get the baby out. That's when he hid in a cupboard. When the screaming eventually stopped and the women left, they put the bloody sheet over the body and left her and the dead infant in the bed for her husband to find and bury.

"Everyone forgot about her terrified child. Poor little Marv stayed in that cupboard all the next day, afraid to move. He was alone with his dead mother and the half-delivered baby until his father came home and discovered the bodies. The poor man went crazy with grief. Marv was sure his father was going to kill him next, and so he remained in the dark, afraid to move. The police were called when the neighbors heard someone breaking up the apartment. They found the child curled up inside the cupboard, wet and cold but absolutely silent.

"Marv didn't speak again, not a word, until he was almost seven. His maternal grandparents came and took him to live with them in Brooklyn. One day, his grandfather came home with a little violin for Marv to play, not a toy but a real half-sized violin. His grandmother managed to scrape together enough money for lessons, and somehow, the child regained his voice through music. Still, the damage was done. Do you know that my husband never agreed to see a doctor or dentist in his whole life? Never. He's had a terrible throat problem for years, but he'd never see anyone about it. Wouldn't even take cough medicine. We almost didn't get married because you had to take a blood test back then with a huge needle, and he dreaded it. I can't believe what it took to get him to go through with it. I finally told him that he'd done it once for Betsy, so he could do it for me, and he did."

"Attagirl, Annabelle!" I said. "Brava!"

"You have no idea how delicate the situation was," she said. "Marv was deathly afraid of having children, of putting any woman he loved through the ordeal of childbirth. He always blamed himself for his mother's death, you see, as if a four-year-old could have done anything about it, but there you are. It wasn't rational, but it haunted him. Betsy couldn't have children, they learned early on in the marriage, and he always told me that he'd been relieved. Marv was happy and at peace for the first time in his life when they found each other. He'd never been in love before, although I know there were many women in his past before he met Betsy.

"When Betsy realized that she was dying, she did the bravest thing imaginable. She bought him a beautiful new car, packed up all of his things, and sent him away. Marv never stopped loving Betsy, and I've always admired her. I've never had that kind of courage. Marv has been my whole world. I could never bear the thought of losing him," she said and sobbed.

"You never did, Annabelle. You never did," I said. I wiped her tears with a tissue. Then I wiped mine.

She looked up at me with red-rimmed eyes. "Althea, please do something for me. Take the bracelet home with you. Keep it for me. I can't wear it now, and it might get lost in the hospital ... or worse. If anything happens to me, please wear it. It would make me so glad, thinking of you wearing it, my sweet, sweet girl. Believe me, Marv would have wanted you to have it too. It's my fault that you two never got to really know each other the way you should have."

"Annabelle, what are you saying?" I said. "You've always been wonderful to me."

"And thank you, detective," she went on in a hoarse whisper. "I know I've been uncooperative and even rude to you. I'm so sorry. You didn't deserve that. I couldn't bring myself to face the truth—that's all. You may not believe me, but you two have given me the best Christmas gift of all. I know now that my husband truly loved me, right up until the moment that he died, and that's all I've ever wanted. I wanted Marv to love me as much as I loved him." She turned her head away and closed her eyes, utterly exhausted.

I kissed Annabelle on the forehead.

"I love you, Annabelle," I said.

"I love you too, Althea. Merry Christmas, my darling girl," she whispered into the pillow.

It was a good thing that Demetrious was driving. I cried like a baby all the way home.

Chapter 27

"HELP! DON'T LET me step on Leopold!" Grace shrieked as she came down the stairs a few hours later, her arms full of wrapped packages, a fluffy gray cat weaving between her ankles. Grace was clearly Leopold's new person. If she was going downstairs, so was he. Now it was simply a question of how they'd get down those stairs, either one step at a time or in a rolling, tangled heap. I rushed halfway up the stairs and grabbed the chubby gray ball of fur from directly beneath Grace's raised left foot. Leopold's whole demeanor registered shock and annoyance. I'm not unusually perceptive about cats and their moods, but his rigidly stiffened legs and outstretched claws gave away his innermost feelings concerning my snatch-and-grab routine.

"It's okay, buddy," I said. "Just relax, and Auntie Thea will put you over here on this nice, cozy ottoman. See? Just pretend you're on the *Concorde* and preparing for a smooth landing." Leopold gave me a nasty look, hissed loudly, and darted for Grace as soon his feet hit the upholstery.

"Oh, well, you can't please everybody," I said, "but if you're putting out presents, Grace, then so am I!" I hurried upstairs to my room and began dragging shopping bags full of professionally wrapped gifts out of my closet. Winnie and Bert came up behind me and cautiously sniffed at the bags and the wrappings.

"Don't touch these," I told them. "I mean it. Not until tomorrow morning, anyway. Yes, of course there's something for you in here. You're the very best dogs in the whole world, and Santa would never forget you!" It took a few minutes' worth of belly rubs to convince them that they were indeed cherished and adored.

After a respectable period of rolling around on the floor, we all trooped back downstairs to the tree, where Grace was artistically arranging her packages. I got down on my hands and knees and joined her, placing each gift carefully so as not to crush the bows and gift tags.

"Honey, you look terrible," Grace said, looking me up and down for the first time since I'd gotten home from the hospital.

"Thanks," I said.

"No, really. Have you been crying?" Grace put an arm around me. Sometimes it's great to have a best friend.

"Yup. I'm pretty sure Annabelle's dying, Grace. It's not just her injuries from the accident, either. She's sick, really, really sick, and now I can see that she's not going to get better." I sniffed and wiped away a tear on my sleeve.

"You love her, don't you?" Grace asked.

"Yes, I suppose I do," I said more to myself than Grace. "I didn't keep up with our friendship the way I should have. We used to be close, Annabelle and I, and then the Pratts left LA and moved up here, and we never got it back together. I should have called her more once I moved to Kirkland, but I didn't. I'm not even sure why."

"Althea, don't torture yourself. Friendship is a two-way street. She could have called you, too. I think Marv got in the way for both of you," Grace said.

"It didn't seem to get in the way of her lifelong friendship with Babe," I said. "Have I told you about Babe?"

Grace shook her head. "Who's *Babe*?" she asked.

"Well, apparently, she and Annabelle were friends at Juilliard." I filled Grace in on the Babe angle.

"She must be a pretty terrific friend!" Grace said.

"The weird thing is I don't get the impression that Annabelle's all that happy about her being here," I said. I recalled what Annabelle's hospital roommate, Marvella Sykes, had told me as well.

"You usually have excellent instincts about these things," Grace said.

"Do you have any deep, dark secrets you're keeping from me?" I asked. "One day, years from now, will I find out that you have a two-headed twin or that you're really a Hungarian princess who was stolen by gypsies or something?"

"I think you're relatively safe on that score," Grace said. "My life's pretty much an open book. Oh, except for my wild affair with JFK."

My mouth dropped open, but Grace wiggled her eyebrows and laughed.

"Just kidding," she said. "Don't look at me like that. I wasn't old enough at that point for anything but a diaper change, but I couldn't resist trying the idea on for size. Doesn't it seem like everyone who's anyone had an affair with him at some time or other? I hate feeling left out. What about you, Althea? Any shocking revelations? Tabloid fodder?"

"Well, perhaps," I said. "I've had my moments of unforgivable stupidity, Grace. Let's just say I would never chance running for congress or allow myself to be vetted for a cabinet position. I stay awake at night, going over and over the worst of my transgressions when I don't have more important things, such as credit card bills, to worry about. It's like counting sheep, only I count snarling wolves."

Grace laughed. "Honey, you'd feel bad about stepping on an ant. What did you do, inadvertently take an extra after-dinner mint from a restaurant?"

"Never you mind. As far as I'm concerned, discretion is the *only* part of valor. Maybe I shouldn't be so surprised that Annabelle has an old friend from her past that I've never even heard of. I actually have a few old friends you've never met, either. After all, you and I only began our friendship as adults. There's a lot that can happen to a person during her teens and early twenties."

"Althea, can you imagine the life Annabelle and her friend Babe shared in New York? It must have been the most exhilarating time, two talented young women giving concerts all over, having an apartment on Riverside Drive of all places! And the men! Can't you just picture it, Annabelle at her most gorgeous, long hair, fabulous gowns, and playing violin the way she did?"

"I wish I'd known her then," I said. "It makes me wonder what Babe was like in those days, too."

"Probably equally stunning and talented," Grace said.

"Can I tell you the truth?" I said. "I'm just the tiniest bit jealous of Babe and her years of friendship with Annabelle. It's silly, of course. I don't even know the woman. Still, I feel as if I've missed out on so much, you know?"

"There's an old Yiddish saying, Althea: You can't dance at two weddings with one behind. You've been living your life with your own generation, your own peers, and Annabelle's been living hers. You weren't even born then! At least you've had a chance to get to know Annabelle better now as adults. If there's any upside to this whole mess, perhaps this is it," Grace said, smiling at me.

"Maybe. You know, Annabelle said the strangest thing this afternoon. She said that it was her fault that Marv and I never got to really know each other. He and I never, ever liked each other. You know that. It had nothing to do with Annabelle. Why should she feel responsible? It makes me sad, knowing that she thinks she's somehow to blame," I said.

"Sick, dying people sometimes say strange things," Grace said. "My Uncle Howard believed he was a Russian spy at the very end. He claimed he'd stolen the plans for an atomic bomb. My poor Aunt Lillian was terribly upset. Uncle Howard had been a children's clothing salesman all his life and a treasurer of the Rotary Club. Go figure."

Grace stood up and adjusted a few ornaments on the tree. I just sat there like a lump.

"Did I mention that Detective Demetrious came back here after he dropped you off and spent a good hour grilling Conrad and me?" she said. "While you were out walking dogs, we were getting the third degree."

"What did he ask you?" I said.

"Oh, the usual. How long had we known the deceased, how long had we wished him dead, and why you left your husband." Grace straightened her skirt and gave me her best deadpan expression.

"Well, what did you tell him?" I asked.

"I told him that I'd known Marv a long time and that I'd always thought he was a creep."

"Not about that! What did you tell him about me?"

"Oh, that," Grace said, slowly examining her finger-nails one by one, sighing over each cuticle until I was ready to strangle her. "As nearly as I can remember, I told him that your husband came to the realization that he'd never been worthy of you and therefore had found it incumbent upon him to slink back into the primordial ooze from whence he'd originally emerged. Something like that, although I can't recall word for word exactly how it went."

"Dear God! What must he think of me now?" I bit my own knuckle.

"It almost doesn't matter, does it?" Grace said. "The important part is that he's thinking about you at all. I kind of like him. Really, I do, and he suits you, Thea. You both have really big dimples." Trust Grace to zero in on what really matters, having matching dimples for goodness sakes.

"Yeah, like that counts for anything," I said. "Did he know that your ex-husband Rolfe was the Pratts' tax accountant?"

"No, he didn't, and I neglected to mention it. One thing I can honestly say in Rolfe's favor is that he never divulged any information about his clients. He was as silent as the grave when it came to his practice," Grace said. *Or about complimenting his wife,* I thought to myself.

"How about Demetrious's interview with Conrad?" I asked. "What did they talk about? Any idea?"

"Nope. The two of them were shut up in the sunroom for quite a while. But I couldn't hear a thing, and believe me, I tried. Then Demetrious left, and Conrad went up for a nap. By the way, isn't it hilarious that this house has a 'sunroom' when we barely ever get to see the sun?" she said.

"Wait until May, Grace," I said. "You'll be so glad you moved up here. We have perfect weather from May until almost October every year. It's dry. It's sunny, and everything blooms like mad. You'll see."

"Yeah, sure," she said. "And I'm Marie of Romania."

Well, it's the truth. There's a reason rhododendrons are our state flower. We have the most glorious late springs and summers imaginable. She'd just have to wait and be surprised.

"I hate to leave you sitting here, Thea, but I have to go practice the cello so I'm in shape for the rehearsal tonight. How about you? Are you going to be all right for this thing?"

"You know me, Grace," I said. "I always come around once I get an instrument under my chin. It'll be fine, I promise you." We stood there pretending to ad-

mire the tastefully decorated tree and the presents beneath it.

"We're both going to be fine, Althea," she said. I felt
for the slim velvet box currently resting in the pocket of
my sweater coat. Right. Fine. It sounded good, but we
both knew they were just hollow words. Things were a
mess any way you looked at them. Let's see. We had a
dying friend and two unsolved murders, and we, along
with most of our colleagues, were still considered suspects. Was it any wonder that I wasn't in the mood for
Christmas? Oh, I felt like decking something all right,
but not the halls.

Chapter 28

THE PARKING LOT at St. Timmons Episcopal Church was well-lit but empty when Grace and I drove in. Quickly plummeting temperatures ensured that the shallow puddles of rainwater, shimmering here and there on the uneven asphalt, would be frozen solid by the time we emerged after midnight services. The wind had picked up already, whipping our long velvet coats and dresses around our ankles. We got our instruments out of the backseat of Grace's BMW, hugged them close to our bodies, and made our way as decorously as we could manage across the windy parking lot and toward the church.

"Remember when we used to wear stilettos every day?" Grace yelled to me as we tried to walk and run to the church portico. "How did we ever do it? And I was carrying a cello case, no less! I tell you this whole Pacific Northwest lifestyle has made me see the light. I haven't owned a pair of flats since I was twelve years old. But here I am in ballerina slippers, and my feet are so happy!"

Grace was indeed wearing flats, but hers were the latest offering from the fabled Nordstrom shoe department, covered in black jet beads, and they were absolutely adorable. With her black high-waisted Georgian gown, she looked like someone straight from the pages of a Jane Austen novel. In fact, we both did, having opted to wear similar dresses that had once been used for string quartet performances at other people's weddings. The gowns were demure but sexy, like something one might find on the cover of a Georgette Heyer regency romance. The moderately low-cut necklines were extremely flattering without revealing too much. Grace was wearing a black velvet ribbon and a tiny gold locket at the throat. I was wearing an enormous red-and-blue-striped scarf, more of a Dr. Seuss *Cat in the Hat* approach to fashion. It may not have been as romantic, but it was a heck of a lot warmer than a ribbon.

"I think ballerina flats look great with period gowns," I said. "Very authentic. After suffering in those miserable high-heeled sandals I wore Saturday night to the concert I've learned my lesson. You won't be able to get me into a real pair of stiletto heels again for at least six months. It takes my feet that long to recover." We finally made it to the covered walkway.

"Oh, great!" Grace said, pulling at the handles of the heavy chapel doors. "The door's locked, and it's freezing out here. That's what comes of always being early. What do we do now? Wait in the car? I don't feel like dragging this heavy cello case across that windy parking lot again, but I swear I'm heading right back to the car and turning on the heater if someone doesn't show up in the next minute and a half!"

"Saint Augustine said, 'The reward of patience is patience,'" I told her.

"And that's why no one liked him much!" she snapped back at me, hair blowing across her face. "Eww! I've got hair in my mouth. Get me outta here!"

"You made it!" James Cantwell, our friendly choir director and Delilah's husband, hollered to us cheerily as he ran up to the door with keys jangling. "Sorry it wasn't open for you. Wait a sec, and I'll get the lights." He fumbled momentarily with the lock, pulled open the massive doors, hit a few wall switches, and the chapel's interior lit up to reveal a masterpiece of neo-Gothic design. Soaring ceilings, a graceful pulpit garlanded in simple greenery, carved stone pillars, stained glass windows, and dark wooden pews with wine red velvet cushions almost made up for the still, ice-cold air inside the massive building. The poor baby Jesus figurine lying there in the manger on the altar looked like he was liable to freeze to death in those skimpy ceramic swaddling clothes. I thought about putting my coat over him but soon realized that I'd be needing that coat more than he would.

"Please tell me there's going to be heat in here for the rehearsal," Grace said. She groaned loudly as she wrapped her velvet coat firmly around her torso, hugging herself. "It's almost impossible to play a stringed instrument when it's this cold. The fingers won't move."

"Oh, don't worry. By the time we do the service, it should be fine," James Cantwell said, waving a hand nonchalantly.

"Fine for him," Grace muttered *sotto voce* as James loped toward the altar. "He directs a choir. He doesn't have to do anything but flap his wrists and make exaggerated faces at the singers. Plus, the choir gets to wear robes over their clothes. That's a whole extra layer!"

"And the actual performance is more than five hours from now," I said. "We could freeze to death by then."

"Look, Thea, I can see my breath." Grace exhaled a few times into the frosty air to make her point.

"Hi, girls!" called Delilah Cantwell, lumbering up the aisle with a pile of black music folders balanced precariously in front of her. Her Junoesque body was wrapped in a heavy woolen sweater, black trousers, and a bulky cape thrown over all of it, and fur boots completed the outfit. Apparently, she'd played here before. "Here's the music. It's easy. You'll be sitting up there in the choir loft," she said, pointing to the balcony at the back of the church with her chin, almost dropping the entire pile of folders. "It's already set up with stands and chairs. Thank you again for agreeing to play on such short notice." She plopped the heavy stack of music noisily in a nearby pew, reached into her gigantic shoulder bag, and handed us two envelopes with our names on it, obviously containing the checks for tonight's work. *Those checks might never make it to the bank*, I thought. If it got any colder in this church, we might have to burn them for warmth.

"Have you noticed that it's freezing in here?" Grace asked her, visibly shaking by now.

"Oh, don't worry," Delilah said. "When the church fills up, it'll get warmer."

"How much warmer? The siege of Moscow was toastier than this!" I said under my frozen breath as Delilah wandered off to put music on the stands. "Honestly, Grace, I'm shivering so hard that my teeth are chattering."

"Yeah, me too. We won't need vibrato tonight. We'll just shiver and shake in time to the music," she said, rubbing her arms. I was beginning to reassess my opinion of the Cantwell's overall fitness to become adoptive parents. Could an infant survive for long living with two abominable snow-people?

Soon, other musicians carrying various instrument cases sauntered in, all of them dressed for a North Pole excursion. Grace and I followed the heavily bundled crowd up the circular stairs to the choir loft and unpacked our instruments. We left our coats and gloves on as we thumbed through the music on our stands. Nothing much to worry about there, we quickly surmised. We'd played it all before many times—Corelli, Bach, Gounod, Mozart, and some lovely old English carols.

Three more violinists, two violists, and a cellist, all unknown to either of us, unpacked and took their seats. The woodwinds and brass players were filling the chairs on the other side of the choir loft. A large church organ separated the string section from the rest of the orchestra, but the organist, whom I assumed would conduct us, hadn't arrived as yet. I'd seated myself in the last violin chair, and Grace had also assumed the last cello position. We were just subs after all, and thus we deferred to those who did this job on a regular basis. Our romantic and way-too-skimpy clothing made it patently obvious that we were the only neophytes hired for the orchestra this Christmas Eve. Everyone else was sensibly garbed in heavy wool and furs. We introduced ourselves around, attempted to get our fingers moving with a few scales, and then sat shaking in the cold as we waited for the organist to appear.

"Hi, Althea." Someone tapped me on the shoulder, and I turned to look up into the face of Emile Girard. "Isn't this a coincidence?" he said, smiling at me with the first trace of genuine warmth I'd felt all evening. "Imagine! We haven't seen each other in over twenty years, and here we are running into each other twice in two days! And this is your friend Grace, isn't it?" he asked, turning to Grace and extending his hand. "Hello! Remember me from last night?"

"Yes, of course," Grace replied sweetly, turning in her chair to take his hand. "Hello." Grace wasn't exactly making brilliant small talk, but as she looked up at Emile Girard with her enormous sea-green eyes, I realized that it didn't matter one bit. I held my breath as they continued to stare at one another, neither one moving or saying a word. Grace's hand was still encased in his as the organist rushed in, pushing past Emile and his double bass, hurriedly handing out programs for the service. Our conductor was indeed the organist, a tall, thin, nervous fellow in his mid-thirties who introduced himself as "Greg."

"Welcome to St. Timmons," Emile whispered to Grace and me, "or as I like to call it, the Sacred Meat Locker. If you need a place to hang a side of beef, this is it! Searching for the Lamb of God? He's hanging in the back, too, poor thing. You'd think they'd turn up the heat earlier in the day, wouldn't you? No one ever thinks of making it comfortable for the musicians. It's like this every year. I'm wearing long johns underneath. Too bad they don't make long black ski parkas for church musicians!" he said and chuckled. Those were the most words I'd ever heard out of Emile Girard in all the years I'd known him, and here he was endeavoring to crack jokes. I gave him points for trying. Had he also perhaps spent a sleepless night thinking back on what he might have done or said differently when we had all met backstage on Saturday night? *Do men actually do this too?* I wondered.

"So what are you doing here?" I said. "Slumming, aren't you? This isn't exactly a Seattle Symphony kind of job."

"Hey, I do the midnight service at St. Timmons every year," Emile said. "It's better than being home alone on Christmas Eve, and they usually have a terrific spread between the rehearsal and the service, over in the social hall. Of course, the buffet here may be frozen solid, too, if they don't turn up the heat soon. Remember, ladies, if they call you to play here next Christmas Eve, wear layers!"

Grace, meanwhile, had turned back to her music. She sat up straight, and proceeded to ignore Emile Girard for the rest of the rehearsal. From where I sat, I could see him staring at Grace's back for the next two hours. He sought her out on the break, though, leading her down the stairs and away from the rest of the musicians. They seemed to be talking quietly by themselves in a far corner of the vestibule, but I couldn't make out a word of what was being said. Grace, I noticed, was behaving in an unusually aloof manner. Not Emile. The more she pulled back, the more he pursued. It was fascinating to watch. They made a gorgeous couple, though, I had to admit, Grace with her dramatic Gaelic beauty and Emile with those dark, brooding good looks.

Contrary to Emile's comment about the terrific meal provided by the church ladies, he didn't seem the least bit interested in heading toward the buffet when we broke for dinner. Grace was also ignoring the lovely supper that was spread out in the social hall. Not me. I can smell a first-class lasagna from a mile away, and sure enough, there was a great one waiting for the musicians, and plenty of it. There were also green beans, salads, rolls, and all sorts of cakes and Christmas cookies. A huge coffee urn was set up on its own table, with white china cups and saucers laid out all around it. Even if I hadn't intended to drink the coffee, I probably would have taken a cup of it just for the pleasure of holding something warm in my icy hands. The coffee turned out to be surprisingly good, though.

We could hear the choir practicing in the chapel as we ate, and they sounded well-rehearsed and quite lovely. The other musicians were friendly enough, most of them being freelancers from Seattle along with a few who taught music in the local school district. Grace and Emile were talking. Dinner was delicious. The music was going to be appropriately moving, and the heat was gradually coming on. All in all, things were looking up at St. Timmons.

Promptly at 11:30 our small orchestra began playing the opening notes of the Corelli "Christmas Concerto."

Candles had been lit throughout the chapel. There was the nostalgia-inducing smell of fresh fir and incense permeating the hall. We could hear the sounds of wooden pews creaking and the soft shuffle of footsteps as the congregation found their seats. What can I say? The sermon was witty and heartwarming. James Cantwell's choir, which sang from behind the carved railings on both sides of the altar, sounded divine. Delilah delivered her rich mezzo soprano solo with confidence. Every so often, I glanced over at Grace, but she was staring at the music on her stand as if she'd never seen notes before.

We played Bach during the communion, and then the choir sang *a cappella*, which gave the orchestra a few minutes to just sit back and enjoy the beauty of the service. I took this opportunity to tiptoe to the loft's railing and glance down at the seated congregation. I almost dropped my violin. There in the center aisle, two worshipers in, was a woman in an apple-green suit, a large-framed woman with a thick head of white hair. Could this be a coincidence, or was I losing my mind? Was the woman I'd been so sure I had recognized at Benaroya Hall here at St. Timmons as well? I decided to rush downstairs as soon as the service ended to find out.

As luck would have it, the organist insisted on leading our small band through at least a dozen Christmas carols at the end of the midnight service. I could barely remain in my chair through the last strains of "What

Child Is This" before I raced down the steep, circular stairs only to discover that the church was empty. The woman in green had already gone, along with everyone else. *Perhaps it's my mind playing tricks on me*, I thought. It wouldn't be the first time that stress has been known to cause hallucinations, and what with the untimely death of Marvin Pratt, Annabelle's terminal illness, Grace's emotional meltdown of the night before, the realization that Detective Harry Demetrious was most likely a happily married man, and having fought off frostbite for five hours straight, I was plenty stressed.

I trudged back upstairs in time to see Grace and Emile decorously shaking hands and wishing each other a "Merry Christmas" before he maneuvered his bass down those steep stairs. It looked tricky, but he managed. Well, at least things were going better in that department. Grace Sullivan and Emile Girard seemed to have salvaged some sort of friendship out of the wreckage of their previous meeting.

Grace and I wished our fellow musicians happy holidays, packed up our cases, and headed out to the car. Sure enough, the parking lot was now frozen over, and it made for treacherous walking with our instruments. Thin sheets of ice crackled under our feet as we gingerly made our way across the nearly empty lot. Emile Girard was still there, carefully placing his huge double bass and his metal stool inside his van. He waved good-bye to us as he climbed behind the wheel and waited to make sure that we were okay before he drove off. It must have been almost two in the morning by now, and it had been a long day, followed by a longer, colder night. We finally managed to load up the BMW, get in, and start the car. While we waited for the engine to warm up enough to make turning on the heater worthwhile, Grace looked straight ahead, her hands tightly gripping the steering wheel.

"Thea," she almost whispered, "please don't laugh at me. Something happened tonight in that church between Emile and me. I can't even talk about it, so please don't ask me to." She took a few deep breaths and then continued, "I'm not really sure yet, but I think I might be in love."

Chapter 29

GRACE DROVE US home through the icy streets of Kirkland, her gloved hands maintaining a death grip on the steering wheel. Even as the public displays of Christmas garlands and colored lights swayed from overhead streetlamps, looking as if they might come crashing down with the next mighty gust of wind and land on the BMW's hood, she stared unblinkingly straight ahead. I did my best not to say a word, which wasn't easy.

We pulled into the parking lot of Blanchard House at around 2:30 in the morning. It was all I could do to get my violin out of the backseat and open the front door because I was so cold and tired. A heavenly blanket of warm air inside our hallway caressed us as we stepped inside. Conrad had built a fire in the living room fireplace before he had gone up to bed, and the remnants of it were now just glowing embers behind the glass fireplace doors. I put a few more logs on and stirred the coals to rekindle the flames. Grace hung up our coats and poured small glasses of sherry for each of us.

"Okay. I'm ready to talk now, I think," she said, curling herself up among the sofa cushions and wrapping a woolen throw around her shoulders.

"I don't know what to say," I said. "You two looked pretty intense, standing there talking together over in the corner all night. You didn't even have supper."

"No, we didn't," Grace said. "There was so much to say, and it felt as if we had to cram our entire lifetimes into that hour and a half. Did you know that Emile's been married for seventeen years, Thea, and that he's separated? Or that he has two teenaged children who refuse to speak to him?" Grace looked pale and slightly stunned, as if she were seeing into the future or hearing the voice of some long-dead relative at a séance.

"Conrad told me some of Emile's history, yes. I take it Emile told you a great deal about himself tonight," I said.

"Everything he could manage, and I told him my whole life story as well. I never intended to, but I did. At first, I tried to keep my end of the conversation very measured, very controlled, but as he talked, I felt my heart opening up to him. Oh, God, Thea, I'm not sure how it all happened, but he's asked me to wait for him until he gets his divorce."

"Really?" I said. "Isn't that a bit premature? What did you say, Grace?"

"I don't remember. I only know that I want this man. I want to be with this man more than I've ever wanted anyone or anything in my entire life. Am I crazy to feel this way after we've only just met?" she asked, looking at me for an answer I didn't have.

All the psychology books I've read reiterate that "love at first sight" says more about a person's need to be "in love" than about authentic feelings, so I was wary and said nothing.

"You know me, Althea," Grace said. "I'm the most pragmatic person alive, but I can't stop thinking about Emile Girard. I have the strongest feeling that we belong together, that we've always known each other. I knew how I felt the moment I laid eyes on him, and he says he knew it too. He told me that he was stunned when he saw me backstage and that he didn't want to feel anything at all because he wasn't ready for another relationship, but he felt it down to his core. And the strangest thing of all is that I believe him." She tilted back her head and downed her small glass of sherry in one gulp. "Now I'm going to get looped and try to fall asleep. I don't think I'll have much luck, though, do you?"

For once, I didn't know what to say, so I sat there watching her, sipping my sherry. She looked beautiful and strangely lost in the firelight. A big part of me wanted more than anything for Grace to have her Christmas miracle, a handsome Prince Charming and a "love at first sight" romance. Didn't she of all people deserve happiness? From what Conrad had said about Emile, he did, too. All I could see at the moment, however, was my best friend shivering on the couch, and not from the cold but from a wild sort of vulnerability that had momentarily stripped her of all her defenses.

Please don't let this turn out badly, I thought. A clear vision of Grace and Emile standing together in the vestibule of the church suddenly filled my mind. I felt intuitively that they were meant to be together. A glow seemed to surround the two of them, an intense energy that emanated from them as they gazed at each other for the first time in the choir loft. How beautifully matched in appearance and gentility they seemed, and I allowed myself to be temporarily reassured that everything would be okay.

Grace's idea of getting looped was another thimble-sized glass of sherry. I joined her. Exhaustion overcame us rather quickly after that, and we both headed upstairs to our respective rooms. I could barely get my flannel nightgown over my head fast enough before I threw myself under the comforter and drifted into a deep sleep. The next thing I knew, it was Christmas morning.

***

Pancakes! The smell of them wafted deliciously up the stairs and filled the house. Conrad was manning the stove and had coffee going, too. Grace was already floating around downstairs in her slippers and a plush bathrobe, a welcome change from the torn pink rag she'd been wearing several mornings before. Winnie and Bert had already been out for their walk with Conrad. Grace had fed Leopold and Lydia. There was nothing left for me to do but grab a plate of pancakes and a hot cup of coffee and enjoy Christmas morning.

I was on my second bite when the phone rang. It was Annabelle.

"Althea, darling, merry, merry Christmas! Are you planning to come to the hospital today?" I assured her that I was. "Wonderful! Could I ask you to come in the afternoon, say around one o'clock? Babe said she's planning to come sometime after two, and much as I'd like to see you both together, I think I need to talk to you first, if that's all right with you. Rosalda, my wonderful day nurse, is kind enough to dial and hold the phone up for me, so I can't talk long. Will that be possible for you, do you think?"

"Absolutely, Annabelle," I said. "I'm dying to see you too, and to finally meet Babe. How are you feeling? And by the way, merry Christmas to you, too!"

"I've got to go now, darling. Rosalda has to get back to her rounds. See you this afternoon," she said, and I heard a female voice say something in a lilting Filipino accent before the line went dead.

Eventually, all the current residents of Blanchard House, both human and almost human, ambled into the living room, and we seated ourselves comfortably around the tree. Grace passed out presents, and we took turns opening them. Conrad seemed genuinely interested in the books about Whidbey but gave the rubber duckie to Winnie for a chew toy.

"We can share," he said graciously.

Winnie seemed delighted. Bert lay patiently among the discarded wrapping papers and bows, occasionally wagging his tail and scattering paper scraps as we patted his head. Grace had bought Conrad some soft leather slippers and a digitally remastered set of CDs featuring Glenn Gould performing Bach. Who wouldn't love that?

Grace made a show of being delighted with the large cache of books she received from me, piling them all around her on the floor and reading the jackets out loud. She'd bought books for me as well, lots of American history and biographies. She'd remembered what a Revolutionary War and Civil War buff I've always been, and her selections were well-balanced between the two. There was also a brand new copy of *Love's Executioner* by Irwin Yalom, my very favorite book of case studies in existential psychotherapy. Grace must have noticed that the cover was falling off my old, dog-eared one. The ladies of Blanchard House might not have to turn on the television set until late spring at this rate. Our late nights were spoken for.

Or course, the most enthusiastic gift recipients were the furry ones. The cats dragged off their catnip mice in two seconds flat, and the dogs could hardly decide which squeaky toys to tackle first. Henrietta, the rubber chicken with a hideous squawk and a painted-on purple bikini, proved to be the most popular. The squeaky terry cloth pig was a close second, however, so everyone went away happy. Did I mention the special homemade biscuits for the dogs or the feathers on fishing lines for the cats? It's always a pleasure to buy toys for animals. They really throw themselves into the sheer fun of everything. Conrad in particular seemed to get a kick out of watching them chew and sniff themselves silly. I was so glad that he was here with us this holiday season. It all felt just right, the way Christmas is supposed to feel, heartwarming.

Under the tree, there was still one unclaimed present, and I realized with a pang that it was the Michael Jecks medieval mystery I'd purchased for Harry Demetrious. I decided to retrieve the wrapped book before anyone else noticed it or commented on it and dropped it into my shoulder bag in the hall. *If I ever run into the detective again*, I thought, *I can casually hand it to him as a "thank you" for bringing the diamond bracelet to Annabelle and for the splendid lunch at Fiorente. If not, I can always donate it to the Veterans Hospital.*

I thought of Harry Demetrious again as I cleaned up the breakfast things and straightened up the living room. What was he doing now? Had he given his wife something special this year, perhaps a long, bulky sweater to cover up her size-twenty-four thighs? *Stop, right there, missy*, I told myself firmly. *You're being catty and horrible.* I did, however, allow myself to wonder if Marv Pratt's bracelet might have inspired Demetrious to give his chunky bride a special piece of jewelry this year. Was he, perhaps at this very moment, taking his many children out to ride their shiny new Christmas bikes up and down their tree-lined street? Perhaps they were all going to church first before they partook of a juicy, standing rib roast with the in-laws. Oh, I was busily torturing myself in countless ways, imagining the happy little Demetrious family enjoying their perfect Christmas as I cleaned the greasy, cast-iron griddle and emptied the coffee grounds. All the while, I pictured Harry Demetrious grinning his amazing, hundred-watt, dimpled smile, and my heart sank. Oh, well. I was a big girl, and I'd get over it. At least my best friend, Grace, seemed headed in the right direction romantically, or was she just being set up to be pushed off another emotional cliff? I was more worried about her than I cared to admit.

Chapter 30

IT WAS OVERCAST and still decidedly frigid outside, so I pulled on my cashmere turtleneck sweater, a long Stewart tartan wool skirt, and dressy black boots for my visit to the hospital. It was Christmas Day after all, and because I hoped to look more festive than I felt for Annabelle's sake, I also threw my tartan shawl over the sweater and anchored it with a large thistle pin, the emblem of the Stewart clan. *Maybe all that red plaid will cheer Annabelle up*, I thought.

Christmas Muzak was playing in the hospital elevators as I made my way to Annabelle's room on the ninth floor. The high heels of my boots clacked on the linoleum with every step I took, announcing my arrival the minute I stepped off the elevator.

The ubiquitous, hospital-green curtain between the two halves of Annabelle's room had been drawn back, flooding the entire space with light from the large picture window. She still had the room all to herself, and she was sitting up and watching some small blackbirds hopping around on the sill outside.

"Blackbirds," Annabelle said. "They're very smart, you know. My mother always said blackbirds were bad luck, but I didn't believe her. Maybe she was right."

"Baloney!" I said, kissing her forehead. "These are our native, red-winged blackbirds, a completely different story. I think they're attracted to the glittery ornaments on your little tree, but they can't figure out how to get at them through the glass. Birds don't understand the concept of glass very well. Okay, here's a little something for you from Santa. I'll have to unwrap these for you, though. Is that okay?" I asked, digging a pile of beautifully wrapped little packages out of my shoulder bag.

"Do I have a choice?" she said. "*I* certainly can't do it! What have you brought me, Althea? You know how much I love presents, especially at Christmas!" The slim, square shape of the packages instantly gave away the contents, but I enjoyed playing along with her.

First, I unwrapped the Recorded Books CD, a famous movie star reading the latest Anne Tyler best seller. Then I moved on to the digitally remastered Leonid Kogan recording of the Brahms Violin Concerto, the latest recording by the Ahn Trio, and a CD of Giuliano Carmignola performing Vivaldi Violin Concertos with the Venice Baroque Orchestra. Finally, I pulled my personal CD player out of my shoulder bag and plugged it in by the side of Annabelle's bed.

"You can ask the nurse or one of the orderlies to help you get the headphones on. I'm sure they'll be happy to help you operate it," I said.

"Of course they will," she said. "Everyone here has been nothing but kind and helpful, especially Rosalda. These are absolutely marvelous CDs, Althea! I'm so glad you brought the Carmignola recordings. Marv never appreciated his playing, all that bravura and those scorchingly fast *vivaces*, but I adore it! No one understands Vivaldi like a true Venetian, I think, and no one has ever understood me the way you have. Thank you for being in my life, Althea."

"My pleasure," I said.

"Now sit down," Annabelle said. "There's something I absolutely have to get off my chest before Babe arrives. I'm sorry to use you as a sounding board, but there's no one else I can talk to about this."

"I'm honored, Annabelle," I said. "Flattered, actually."

"Don't be silly," Annabelle said. "You really are the closest thing to a daughter I've ever had, so let me be honest, Althea, and ask you something. I'm not even sure how to begin." Annabelle looked off to the left at nothing in particular, gave a deep sigh, and continued, "Have you ever had the awful feeling that you've outgrown a longstanding friendship? This is one of the most difficult things I've ever had to admit, but there it is. You know, I've always cherished my memories of studying music at

Juilliard, living in Manhattan when New York was really elegant, and concertizing with my friend Babe."

"It must have been so amazing to be young in New York then with that energy all around you and the beginning of your career," I said.

"I suppose it was," Annabelle said, "but perhaps I built these experiences up in my mind as being more meaningful than they actually were. They've been all jumbled together, these memories of my youth, as part of a magical time in my life. We were both so young, so carefree, and doing what we loved best. Babe was a big part of all those exciting adventures." Annabelle looked into her lap for a long time before she continued, "These last few days, though, with Babe here, with her coming to the hospital every day, have turned out to be so exhausting, so horribly strained. It's not at all as I imagined it would be when we finally saw each other. I just have the gnawing feeling that whatever connection we once might have had is gone, and I feel just terrible about it. I don't know if she feels it too. I hope not. I mean, she's come all this way and gone to all this trouble and expense just to see me and be with me. I would hate to think that she's as disappointed as I am, or perhaps worse, believes that things have continued on in the same way between us."

"I must say I'm more than a bit sorry to hear that, Annabelle," I said. "You two have been close pals for over forty years."

"Fifty-four," she corrected me. "I've been lying here, doing the math, and it's been fifty-four years since Babe and I met. That's what makes it all so dreadful. Have I been deceiving myself for that long, or did we once have something special that time has eroded until we've become practically strangers?"

"Honestly, Annabelle, I've had quite a number of friends myself who've drifted away, and sadly, I'll probably never see them again. Still, I don't know if all friendships are meant to last forever or if they're merely part of our different life stages."

"So you understand what I'm talking about here," Annabelle said.

"Of course I do," I said. "On the other hand, there's the 'best friend' category, which is entirely different. Grace and I have shared a close, sisterly bond almost from the first moment we met, and we keep learning that it's renewed by the most mundane things. We enjoy so many of the same interests, our music, teaching, reading, cooking, throwing parties, teapot collecting, and now that we're living together, it's even more apparent why we've always been such good friends. We see the world in a similar way. We have similar values. More to the point, we really like each other and make each other laugh."

"Then there are the really dear old friends you only talk to once or twice a year but you can just pick up with them over the phone right where you left off," Annabelle said. "It's uncanny, but there you are."

I'd found that to be true, too. There are people from whom you can move thousands of miles away, and yet one phone call brings you together as if you've just gone into the other room for a cup of coffee and come right back.

"Althea, that's the kind of friendship you and I have," she said. "I've always understood that, too, and counted on it. Even when circumstances kept us from being together, I always felt secure in your regard. I hope you know that I've appreciated every effort you've made over the years to keep in contact, including enduring that dreadful lunch with Marv."

"I'm glad," I said.

"Here's the thing, Althea. I'm not so sure I feel that same way about Babe. It occurs to me that in all the time we've known each other, it's really been a very superficial kind of knowing. I've tried over and over to disclose intimate thoughts and feelings to her, my hopes, my fears, little things about my relationship with Marv that I believed only another woman of a similar age could appreciate, but she never seemed to want to hear about any of them. She'd always manage to change the subject."

"Perhaps she envied the closeness of your relationship to your husband," I said. "People are funny that way."

"No," Annabelle said, "I don't think it's that. Babe and her husband have been married longer than Marv and I have. Maybe not as happily, but who knows? No, the thing that ultimately hurts most is that it feels is if she's purposely kept back so much of herself from me."

Annabelle asked for a sip of water, so I held the sippy cup with the flexi-strawfor her.

"Babe may complain about her husband at times and make nasty jokes at his expense, which I don't really approve of, but not one intimate detail about her inner life has ever escaped her lips," Annabelle said. "She goes on and on about money or the lack of it all the time, but I'm sure she's always known I'd help her out financially, and I have. Am I wrong to want a deeper emotional connection? Is it me? Am I just a needy old gal who been trying to use her oldest friend to unload about her own petty problems? Have I presumed too much? Tell me, Althea. I really need to know."

I was frankly surprised. All I could think about was how kind and generous and sensitive Annabelle had always been to me and to everyone around her. If there was a reticent nature at the core of her friend's emotional makeup, I could hardly believe it had much to do with Annabelle's level of sensitivity or interest in others.

"You're certainly no emotional vampire, if that's what you mean," I said. "In fact, I've always worried that you kept too much bottled up inside yourself and took better care of everyone else than you did of yourself."

"I wonder if Babe thought that I wouldn't care, or that she couldn't trust me with her secrets." Annabelle was obsessing at this point, and I felt I had to stop her.

"Annabelle, my dear friend, you have always been a rock. A rock. And I have never, ever heard a mean bit of gossip from you about anyone. With all your suspicions about Marilyn Litzky and Marv, you still couldn't find it in yourself to bring those suspicions to the attention of Detective Demetrious."

"It was none of his business," she said.

"Maybe not," I said, "but I was actually relieved that you allowed yourself to get them off your chest to me so I could look into them and prove them to be unfounded. I don't know if you've ever considered this, but perhaps there's something in Babe herself that prevents her from trusting others." I poured myself a small paper cup of water and drank.

"Go on," Annabelle said. "I'm very interested."

"I'm not a psychologist or anything, but everything I've read says that keeping one's feelings to oneself while listening to the doubts and vulnerabilities of others puts one firmly in the power seat. Think about it. Therapists work hard not to reveal their innermost feelings or personal problems and doubts to their patients. It's their way of holding a certain position in the relationship. In the case of therapy, it's done to help the patient feel secure. It's supposed to stop the therapeutic relationship from developing into something which makes the patient feel like the caretaker of the therapist. Inequality is meant to be maintained in order to facilitate the work. In friendship, though, emotional withholding can be a way of establishing moral superiority."

"Yes, you're right!" Annabelle said. "That's just it. That's what I'm feeling from Babe. It's not just distance. It's moral superiority."

Annabelle glanced over at the blackbirds still pecking away at the glass, an exercise in futility if there ever was one.

"I've been just like those birds, trying to get at something that isn't there, Babe's acceptance. I'm sorry she ever came ... to tell you the truth. Things were so much nicer just as they were. I always hoped to sustain the illusion of having a close, chummy relationship with someone from my past. I liked writing intimate letters to a friend on good stationery and hearing a familiar voice on the telephone at the end of a tiring day. It made me feel anchored and safe having a touchstone, an old pal who supposedly knew me so well. I know now that it's time to cut myself loose and face the reality of years and distance. People change. I've changed—that's for sure. It's just that it's all been too much to deal with, and everything's happened too quickly," she said, looking down again into her lap.

"If you're feeling this way," I said, "perhaps your friend is too. I still think it says a lot about her loyalty to you that she's come all this way to be with you during such a difficult time."

"I know, Althea. That's one reason why I'm feeling so guilty. I don't honestly know that I'd have done the same for her if the situation had been reversed. I'd have probably done what I always do—send flowers and throw money at the problem. Would I have left Marv the way she left her husband to fly across the country at Christmas time for an indefinite stay? Probably not. Every day with Marv was precious to me. I put him before everything and everyone else, and he did that for me, too. Maybe it was wrong, but that's what we've always done."

"I don't think for one minute that you two were wrong to put your marriage first," I said. "I've always wished for someone who could love me like that, Annabelle. I really do. I don't think I've ever felt cherished, even though I've loved deeply and at times rather foolishly. I've always been the one who loved the other person a little bit more. That's not such a good thing."

"Maybe not, but that's who you are. You can't help that, can you? There's more to this whole episode with Babe, Althea, and I don't think you're going to be very happy with me when you find out what it is."

What could Annabelle's relationship with Babe possibly have to do with me? I couldn't imagine.

"Babe helped me out of a terrible situation many years ago, helped me in a way that no one else in this world would have or could have," Annabelle said. "I owe her an enormous debt, and though I've spent the better part of fifty years trying to make it up to her, I don't know if I ever can. I don't know quite how to handle the whole thing, Althea. I don't know what to say without hurting her feelings ... or if I should say anything at all. That's one reason I wanted you here, to talk the situation over with me. I trust your judgment about people. As for this great secret of ours, well, I wanted to discuss it with you in front of Babe. She should be here any minute now. Could you help me sip some more water? All this talking has made me so thirsty, and my voice is going."

I refilled the cup of water and guided the flexi-straw to Annabelle's parched lips.

"Leopold is having a ball at Blanchard House by the way," I said as she sucked at the straw a few times. "He and Lydia have been sitting side by side on the window-sill in Grace's room, looking out at the birds that live in the big cedar tree outside her window. It's kitty television, I swear."

"You have no idea how grateful I am to you and Grace for taking my sweet little cat and giving him a good home," Annabelle whispered hoarsely.

"It's just temporary, you know. As soon as you're better, he'll be coming home to you. We're not planning on stealing Leopold forever, much as Grace adores him."

"Thea, can't you see that I'm never coming home again, at least not for very long? You know it, and I know it. Every day I'm a little weaker, and it has nothing to do with the accident. Acute leukemia seems to be winning this round. That's why it means so much to me that my baby Leopold is going to be loved and cared for. Grace is an angel. Oh, and look, it's Babe!"

I turned quickly toward the door and froze. In walked the same large, white-haired woman I'd seen twice before this week, once at Benaroya Hall and once at St. Timmons Episcopal Church. There, not three feet away from me, stood my former mother-in-law, Ruth Littleton. Babe Ruth!

Chapter 31

"RUTH!" WAS ALL that I could manage.

"Althea, how are you? You look surprised to see me. I thought Annabelle had told you by now that I was in town," she said, brushing by me on her way to Annabelle's bedside.

Ruth Littleton wasn't wearing her green suit today but had opted for a boxy brown tweed jacket and dark woolen dress slacks that made her look smart but mannish. She shrugged off her heavy, camelhair overcoat and dropped it casually on the back of a chair. Her magnificent mane of white hair was brushed back dramatically, and she wore large pearl earrings. Ruth Littleton looked slightly older than the last time I'd seen her, which was over four years ago now, but she was still extremely handsome.

"It's been rather a while since we've seen each other, Althea. I must say you look absolutely hideous in that outfit, though," she said. "Red doesn't become you in the least, you know. I'm sure I've told you that before. Oh, well. It's not as though you're famous for your sense of style, though, is it? As I've always said, my son married someone more like me, rather plain, but very intelligent and with a solid talent. You don't look as dreadful as I thought you would, though, considering. Being single must agree with you. I've often thought it would agree with me, too, but after all these years, I guess I'm stuck with Stanley," she said.

If I'd had any doubts that it was my former mother-in-law standing there in front of me, they were instantly dispelled. All I could think of was that Annabelle had once compared me to Ruth Littleton and found us to be somehow alike. Did she actually believe that Ruth was kind? Of course, she also thought that Marv was a catch and a half. Annabelle was loyal, I'll say that for her, but the mind reeled at such obvious delusions. Me ... like Ruth? Shoot me now!

"How is Stan?" I asked her, straining to be polite.

"Oh, he's as annoying as usual," she said. "He wasn't happy about me to coming all this way by myself and leaving him alone at Christmas time, but he'll get over it. It's actually been quite pleasant going wherever I want without having to account to anyone else for a change. I went to hear the Seattle Symphony play the other night. Annabelle gave me her tickets. She and Marv have box seats in the mezzanine. Such comfortable seats, and the acoustics were perfect! I was truly surprised to learn that a second-rate city like Seattle has such a first-class concert venue. Before that, I heard a simply wonderful young pianist, Andre Kepner, in his Town Hall debut. I've had a lovely week."

Of course it had been Ruth Littleton at the symphony on Saturday night. I was sure she'd been to midnight services at St. Timmons as well, being a staunch Episcopalian. She certainly didn't seem to be allowing her friend's terrible accident and life-threatening leukemia to spoil her good time.

"Besides," Ruth went on quickly, "Annabelle and I have been best friends since Juilliard, and I wasn't about to let her languish in some wretched hospital all by herself. I suspected that you might be here too, but it's not quite the same as having a dear old friend that you can count on by one's side, is it?"

"You knew I lived up here now?" I asked. "I had no idea that you and Annabelle even knew each other. No one ever told me that you were friends, never mind former roommates, or that you'd performed together in New York once upon a time."

"It's a long story, Althea," Annabelle said. "I told Babe that you were up here, of course. I've told her all about you, how you were kind enough to invite Marv and me to your home for a lovely tea party and how much you've always meant to me. Babe and I have been confidantes for years. Of course, Marv only knew of her as Ruth Maddox, her maiden name. We haven't actually seen each other in person in over forty years. As I said, it's a long story, darling."

"Annabelle has a lot to tell you," Ruth said.

"Why don't you both sit down and get comfortable," Annabelle said, "and Babe and I will try to fill you in. Of course, it's 'Ruth' to you, but I'll never get used to calling her that."

I grabbed for the metal visitor's chair, while Ruth Littleton settled her large frame into the softer armchair next to the bed.

"Goodness, I don't know where to begin!" Annabelle looked at us both and sighed. "Let's see. It's all so long ago. I've never shared this story with anyone, Althea, and I never thought I would. Babe and I have kept a secret between us, and of course Stanley, all of our adult lives, but things change. You need to know the truth finally, and I need to tell it."

"Are you sure about this, Annabelle? I think this is very ill-advised," Ruth said.

"I'm sure," Annabelle said. "I wish I'd done it a long time ago." She took a few weak breaths and proceeded. "I began my studies at Juilliard at age sixteen. I was much too young to be on my own really, and I was terribly lonely. But then Babe and I were matched up to play the Beethoven Spring Sonata together for a recital at the beginning of my second year, and we found that we worked very well together. You know what a wonderful accompanist she is. There are lots of fine pianists, but being a good accompanist is a completely different and very rare skill."

All I could think was that Annabelle was being overly generous with her praise in this case. Ruth had proven to be a rather insensitive accompanist every time we'd ever attempted to play together, but to be fair, perhaps she'd played better when she was younger. I realized that by the time I'd married Dennis, she must have been seriously out of practice after so many years away from New York. She'd never mentioned that she'd graduated from Juilliard, either. I'd always believed that she'd majored in education.

Annabelle continued her narrative, "Well, we hit it off, and the next thing you know, we'd rented a lovely apartment together on Riverside Drive. My parents actually rented it for us. They were well-off, and they traveled most of the year. But they could always be counted on to throw money at anything that kept me out of their hair, a habit I seem to have inherited, by the way, so Babe and I could afford to live in something a lot nicer than the usual student apartment. I can still picture our lovely flat. Can't you, Babe? It was a big, elegant place with high ceilings and an incredible view, Althea, with enough room for a nine-foot Steinway grand piano. We played so much wonderful music there. Babe became the sister I never had."

"I'm only three years older than Annabelle, you know," Ruth said, "but I was always the sensible one, rather like you, Althea. She was the stunning beauty, and I was her foil. In fact, I've always thought that you and Grace Sullivan were just the same. Grace is the clearly the beauty, and you're the plain older sister. Do you ever see Grace anymore?" Ruth asked sweetly.

"Yes, I do," I said. "In fact, we just bought a house together."

"Oh? Are you two lesbians?" Ruth asked, looking at me as if she'd never really seen me before. "I shouldn't be surprised, of course. It's considered very chic to be gay nowadays. You must be the dyke, of course, and Grace would naturally be the femme. I should have known. You were always a little too independent to be truly feminine, I used to tell Stanley. Is that why Dennis left you, Althea?"

"No, Ruth, it isn't why Dennis left me. In fact, I still have no idea why Dennis left me, but perhaps his current wife, the woman I suspect he was seeing all along while still married to me, could fill you in on that. And no, I am not a lesbian, nor is Grace. We're just housemates who've started a music school together." *Not that it's any business of yours*, I thought. This wasn't going to be a fun afternoon. Time spent with Ruth was always a trial, as I recalled.

"Where was I?" Annabelle said to no one in particular. "Oh, yes. So I graduated from Juilliard when I was only twenty. We gave a few recitals together at Alice Tully Hall, Carnegie Hall, the usual, and we garnered excellent reviews for all of them. We weren't really making a living, though, no matter how glowing the reviews were. Babe, meanwhile, went back to Michigan to visit her family one summer and met Stanley. He was quite a bit older than she was, and he was already the headmaster of a boys' school. Stanley was smitten and proposed within the month, and Babe moved up to Lansing. I was suddenly alone in New York."

"I couldn't very well refuse him, could I?" Ruth said. "Stanley was quite dashing in those days, Althea," Ruth said, "and how many offers was I likely to get? Men were always falling all over Annabelle. As long as she was around, no one ever really noticed me."

"You're being ridiculous again," Annabelle said.. "There were quite a few very nice men who asked you out for dinners and concerts when we lived in New York, and you know it."

"Nothing like the hordes that were pursuing you, though, were they?" Ruth said. "You were always the one people noticed and admired. Anyway, Stanley heard me playing the piano at my cousin's birthday party and was instantly taken with me. I've never understood it, because I was certainly nothing special to look at, more like you, Althea, but there you are. Every pot has its lid."

I wanted to smack her.

"Stanley and I found that we both enjoyed tennis and golf and a good book, so it wasn't a total mystery why we got on, I suppose," Ruth said. "That was probably the

last time I ever played the piano in public, though, because Stanley was insanely jealous and demanded that I
stop performing the minute we became engaged. It was a
shame really. I'd been such a fine pianist, and it had been
my life's ambition to perform, but there you are. Stanley
was adamant. We were married the following spring, and
I settled for becoming an English teacher in a local
school."

Normally, my heart would have been aching from
such a story, but if Ruth Littleton was looking for com-
passion from me, she'd be waiting a long, long time. I
mean, Hitler hoped for a career as an artist, too, didn't
he?

"So Babe moved up to Michigan to marry Stanley
Littleton. I was her maid of honor, and it was a beautiful,
beautiful wedding at his family's home. I wore that peri-
winkle blue silk dress with the fitted skirt, remember?"
Annabelle asked, looking at Ruth.

"Who could forget, Annabelle?" Ruth said. "I can
still picture you in it perfectly. Stanley couldn't take his
eyes off you."

"My dear, you are so wrong," Annabelle said.
"Stanley only had eyes for you that day. Water please,
Althea."

I brought her sippy cup over and held the straw
while she drank. Ruth, meanwhile, stood up and
whacked the glass window with her palm, scattering the
birds. "Shoo, shoo!" she said sternly.

"Anyway," Annabelle continued as Ruth reseated herself, "I decided then and there to go to Los Angeles and make my way in the Hollywood studio orchestras. One of the first people I met in Hollywood was Marv. Talk about handsome! He took my breath away, and could he play the fiddle! Of course, he was a concert-master at one of the major studios as well as a few local orchestras, and he was playing with a famous string quartet then too. I was 'gaga' over him from the first time I saw him. Violinists actually had to audition for him just to get a job in the studio orchestras."

"That was still going on when I first got to town," I said. "It was pretty nerve-wracking playing for concert-masters and first-chair violists just to get hired for the smallest thing."

"Then you know exactly what I'm talking about," Annabelle said. "I will always remember going to Marv's apartment in the Hollywood Hills one afternoon and playing the first movement of the Sibelius Violin Concerto, parts of the Brahms Concerto, and the Bach Chaconne. My legs were shaking. I was that nervous around him, but I played fairly well. The next thing I knew, I was getting calls to play on major motion pic-tures and on all sorts of record dates. Marv sat me right up on the front desk of every session with him. He took me to lunch at the best places, Ollie Hammond's, the Brown Derby, you name it. He sent roses and tulips and lilacs, huge bunches of them. He bought me a diamond watch! Who could have resisted? Eventually, we became lovers, and it was sublime. I'd never been with a man before, and you know how it is with your first love. You feel as though you'll die if it doesn't last."

"Things were different in our day, Althea," Ruth Littleton said. "We generally married the first man we slept with. Truly nice girls usually married the man first, though," she added, casting a sly glance at Annabelle. "Of course, women today are so modern, and by the time you married Dennis, I'm sure you'd slept with oodles of men and perhaps even other women. But it was different back when we were young."

"I've never been all that *modern*," I said, "and I'm not that nice, either, so don't push me." I was tempted to stand up and leave the room right then and there. But I felt sure that there was a point to Annabelle's story, and I intended to find out where it was leading.

"Just about six months after our affair began," Annabelle said, ignoring Ruth's insinuations and my growing annoyance, "I discovered that I was pregnant. The very same day that I got the news from my doctor, I opened the *Los Angeles Times* and read the obituary of a former debutante, Betsy Bailey Pratt, and learned that at the time of her death she had still been Marv's wife."

"I'll never understand how you could have been so naïve," Ruth said.

"Annabelle has always been far too trusting," I said, giving Ruth a look that should have killed her but unfortunately didn't.

"My world fell apart in that moment, Althea," Annabelle said. "The realization that I'd been having an affair with a married man, a man whose beautiful and very current young wife was dying of cancer while we were falling in love, shocked and infuriated me."

I could imagine it clearly. It was the worst kind of betrayal.

"I didn't know what to do," Annabelle said. "I was angry and ashamed but most of all, terrified. When I confronted Marv about Betsy, he admitted that he'd only been separated when we got together. He was ashamed of himself, of his inability to deal with suffering of any kind. He told me then about his childhood trauma, about his fear of death, illness, and most importantly, his decision never to have children. His fear of childbirth was overwhelming, and here I was, unbeknownst to him, about to have his baby!"

"What a horrible situation for any woman," I said, "especially forty or fifty years ago."

"He begged me to forgive him," Annabelle said. "What could I do? I didn't want to lose Marv. I was quite literally mad about him. Abortion in those days was unavailable to the average woman, and for me personally, it was out of the question. If it happened to me today, I'd keep the baby and tell everyone to go to hell, but I was young, afraid of public censure, afraid of disgracing my parents, and most of all, I was afraid of losing Marv. He'd told me that he loved me, and I knew that in spite of everything, I loved him too."

"Annabelle called me in a panic," Ruth said. "I told her to take the train to Lansing, and she arrived four days later. Stanley wanted children, the more the merrier, and he agreed that we should adopt Annabelle's baby. I hadn't been able to conceive, and in fact, we never did manage to have any other children, as you know."

Thank God, I thought.

"Stanley was thrilled with the prospect of a child, any child," Ruth said. "Annabelle lived with us until the baby was born, a perfect baby boy, and then went east to stay with her parents for six months longer. We didn't tell anyone that the baby wasn't ours, not even our families. Dennis doesn't know, because that's the way Annabelle wanted it, and frankly, so did we."

The floor seemed to be rising up and hitting me in the face. I grabbed for the arms of the metal chair to keep my balance.

"Are you telling me that Dennis is Annabelle and Marv's son?" I could barely get the words out.

"In a matter of speaking, yes," Ruth said. "Of course, Stanley and I have always considered Dennis our child, and to this day, he has no idea that we aren't his birth parents."

I thought of all the times that Dennis had talked about how isolated and "different" he had felt around his parents, his sense of "otherness."

"Why didn't you eventually tell him when he was an adult?" I said. "It might have made a big difference in his life if he'd known who his parents were. He might have felt whole at last."

"Oh, no, Althea! We couldn't have done that." Annabelle said, sounding horrified by the suggestion. "I made Babe and Stanley promise never to tell anyone, especially Marv and Dennis. I was afraid that the only man I ever loved would leave me because I was pregnant just as he'd left Betsy when she was dying, so I told him I had to go home and spend some time with my parents because they'd been missing me. Ha! They didn't even know I was at their house because they were wintering in the Bahamas!"

I grabbed a tissue and wiped away a tear that was sliding down Annabelle's cheek.

"I went back to Los Angeles a year later," she said, continuing her story, "and learned that Marv had been waiting and pining for me. He asked me to marry him, and I said yes on the spot. We went to the courthouse a few days later and had a quiet ceremony. As time went on, I just couldn't face telling him the truth. It was over and done with, don't you see? Our son was being raised across the country as part of a loving family. Stanley and Babe had no other children, and they doted on Dennis.

He went to the private school where Stanley was head-master. He attended the best colleges. I should have anticipated that he'd be attracted to music, but it never occurred to me that he'd follow directly in his real mother and father's footsteps and wind up playing the violin in Hollywood!"

"Stanley and I are his *real* mother and father, Annabelle," Ruth said, lips pursed. "Heaven knows we both tried to dissuade him from becoming a violinist, but he was so determined. We sent him to Oberlin, and then Dennis did graduate work at Indiana. He wanted to audition for Juilliard, but Stanley and I dissuaded him from going there. We worried that he might have made the connection between Annabelle and me if he'd run into professors who'd known us both years before. Stanley and I assumed he'd go on to symphony work or maybe teach at a good college or conservatory. But then he went to LA to perform with his string quartet, and he met you, Althea. That's when things started to unravel for poor Dennis."

"Poor Dennis?" I said. "Poor Dennis? Excuse me, Ruth, but I treated Dennis like a king! We had a beautiful home in Malibu. We both worked a lot. Our duo was going well, and Dennis seemed genuinely happy. My God, he played tennis three or four times a week, ran on the beach every day, and fished and sailed whenever he felt like it. We entertained so much it felt as if I were running a four-star a restaurant out of our home."

I could feel the steam rising as I recalled the lifestyle I'd knocked myself out to maintain for Dennis Littleton's pleasure.

"Then why did he feel he had to leave you, Althea?" Ruth asked, looking me up and down, making no attempt to hide her distaste.

"Dennis was a fool," Annabelle said. "A fool and a drunk. There, I've said it. He took after my father. Blood always shows, doesn't it? It certainly did in this case. Dennis is my son too, remember, and I was always grateful that he'd had an excellent woman like Althea looking after him. You weren't there, Babe, and I was. I saw firsthand how she catered to him, how she put his needs before hers all the time. He didn't even begin to appreciate her. He's become a spoiled, narcissistic drunk."

"Annabelle! How can you say such horrid things about your own child?" Ruth said.

"Because they're true," Annabelle said. "I've been a coward all my life. I certainly denied my son. I allowed you and Stanley to raise my only child because I was afraid of telling Marv the truth. I've even been too afraid to tell Dennis that I'm his mother. I'm sick of myself. Well, the time for lying is over. Althea, you've always been more than a friend and colleague to me. I want you to know that. You've been my daughter-in-law all these years, and I've always considered you my real daughter."

"Oh, Annabelle!" I said. "It all makes so much sense now. I should have guessed. That picture of Marv on your dresser looked so familiar. I couldn't think who he reminded me of, but of course, there's a strong resemblance to Dennis. How could I not have seen it?"

"Actually, Dennis looks exactly like my father, who was handsome beyond description, and he drinks like him, too," Annabelle said. "Perhaps if I'd warned Dennis about our family history of alcoholism, things would have turned out differently. I've always blamed myself for that," she said softly.

"You couldn't have changed what happened," I said.

"I don't know, and maybe I'll never know," Annabelle said. "But I'll always wonder."

"He certainly didn't get it from us," Ruth said. "Stanley's never had a drink in his life."

Annabelle and I ignored her. "Why do you think I didn't want you to use our security keypad, Althea?" Annabelle said. "You'd have known right away that the numbers you were punching in spelled out the date of Dennis's birthday. It was my silly way of remembering our only child. I felt a strange satisfaction knowing that Marv had unwittingly memorized his son's birthday and had to punch it in every time he left the house or entered it. Over the years, I insisted on using that number for every account and password, as if that would make up for abandoning our son. Oh, God, Althea, I've made so many bad decisions, one right after another!"

"No, you haven't, Annabelle," I said. "It's perfectly understandable, knowing how uptight and judgmental

society has been until fairly recently about having children out of wedlock. You didn't terminate the preg-
nancy. You didn't give him up to strangers. You gave
Dennis to your best friend, someone you trusted, and
made sure he had the best of everything. It's not too late
to tell Dennis, either. He should know that he has *two*
mothers who love him, and that he had a famous, talented father. It would clear up so much for him, and I
think he'd be grateful for the truth. I know that if I were
in his place, I would be," I told her.

"What do you know about what children want or
need?" Ruth said. "You couldn't even be bothered to
have any of your own, and suddenly, you're an expert on
mother and child relations." *She's right*, I thought. I
couldn't know what Dennis would want, and I realized
that I'd never known. Even after years of marriage, he
had remained closed off from me about the things that
really mattered to him. Maybe he did get something from
Ruth after all, his inability or unwillingness to share his
feelings.

"The very worst thing," Annabelle said, looking directly at me, "is that Marv is dead, and he'll never even
know that he had a son. I didn't truly understand until the
night of your party just how jealous Marv had become of
Dennis. Every time I'd praised our son over the years,
I'd alienated his father from him even more. I probably
destroyed my own son's career because I was oblivious
to my husband's ridiculous insecurity. Do you really

think that Marv would have treated his own child the way that he treated Dennis had he known the truth? He'd have given him the world! Marv never knew that you were his daughter-in-law, either. I'm sure he would have grown to love you just as much as I do if he'd had the chance. I know he would have, but I never gave you two the opportunity to get close. I've done so much damage to the two men I loved the most, Althea, and to you too." Annabelle was sobbing now, and I was dabbing at her eyes with a tissue. As I glanced over at Ruth, I saw her sitting stiffly in her chair. Her face was set in a stern mask of disapproval.

"I don't think it would be wise to upset Dennis at this point, Annabelle," Ruth said firmly. "He's perfectly happy believing that he's a Littleton. Do you really think he'd be grateful to learn at this point in his life that he's a bastard?"

Annabelle's head jerked backward as if she'd been physically struck. "Is that what you really think, *Ruth*? That my son, *our* son, is a *bastard*?"

Ruth stood up slowly, smoothed down her slacks, and said, "Of course not, Annabelle. I was just thinking of how this might appear to Dennis. He's always trusted that he belonged to a family he could be proud of. I don't think it would be in his best interest to lose that belief in exchange for some lurid history."

"Why should he lose anything?" I said. "Wouldn't he gain a lot more, knowing that his parents were two outstanding musicians, well-respected artists who loved each other? He could finally get to know his real mother and find out about his family history and even his medical history. Although I'm sure it would be strange for him at first, I believe it could be very healing for Dennis and Annabelle."

"And what about me and Stanley, *our* family?" Ruth said. "Dennis is our only child. He's all we have. It could tear our family apart."

"But you're all adults now, Ruth," I said. "I'm sure Dennis would be grateful to you for raising him. He loves you very much, you know," I added.

"And I'd like to keep it that way," Ruth said. "What if he's furious at us for not telling him the truth for so long?"

"You could always blame it on me," Annabelle said. "Tell Dennis that I insisted that you keep his adoption a secret. I'll explain it to him. The thought of telling Dennis that Marv and I are his real parents has always terrified me, but I think I really need to see my son before I die ... and beg his forgiveness."

"I think it's an idiotic scheme!" Ruth said. "Besides, he'll know soon enough when he comes into his inheritance and he gets Marv's instrument collection, and it will soften the blow of it all."

"The *blow*?" Annabelle suddenly looked furious. "What blow? That his father was a brilliant concertmaster? That his mother gave him to her best friend and

her husband to raise and sent money to pay for his education at the finest schools in the country? Where did he
think his fabulous violin came from, and all those beautiful French and English bows that I sent for him over the
years? Did he really believe that you and Stanley
scrimped and saved for them? I've been ashamed all my
life of what I did, but I never stopped loving and protecting and supporting my son. Now that I think about it,
I supported you and Stanley pretty well, too!"

"Annabelle, you're upsetting yourself," Ruth said.
"This conversation isn't good for you. You should be
trying to get better. You need your rest. Althea, you
should be leaving now too, and stop sticking your nose in
where it doesn't belong. You're not married to Dennis
anymore, thank heaven. He's moved on with his life. I'm
going back to my hotel now, Annabelle. I'll see you tomorrow. Good-bye, Althea. Merry Christmas." With
that, Ruth grabbed her coat from the back of her chair
and stomped out of the room.

Annabelle and I just looked at each other. "You
know, we've never had cross words before today, not in
our whole lives," she said, shaking her head.

"Perhaps it's because you never crossed her," I said.

"That was the most frigid 'merry Christmas' I've
ever heard. It sounds as if she's a bit ticked off,"
Annabelle said.

"It sounds as if she's been used to getting her own
way about everything with you because she believed you

were in no position to object," I said. "Ruth got to have your only child plus a sizeable chunk of financial support. By the way, how did you keep Marv from finding out about the money you sent?"

"My trust fund," she said. "It's huge!"

"Well it certainly worked out well for Ruth," I said. "She figured you'd do anything for Dennis and to keep your past a secret, and she was right. You did."

"Not anymore, Althea, although she doesn't know it just yet. I've had a lot of time to think, lying here in this miserable bed, fully aware that the end of my time here is coming very quickly. You know, Marv and I had been going back and forth about his violin collection. He wanted to give the whole thing to the Seattle Symphony as a posthumous gift from both of us. I kept putting him off. It seemed to me that our son should have the pick of those marvelous instruments, especially having become a fine violinist himself. Of course, I wasn't brave enough to tell Marv about Dennis, and I'll never forgive myself for that. But I thought I could change my husband's mind about the bequest or at least stall him until I died. I knew it would be a while before he could get all the instruments appraised and catalogued. I'd left a letter for Marv with our attorney only to be read after my death, telling him about our son. I trusted my husband to do the right thing by Dennis in the end, you see. Marv wasn't a monster, Althea, just a flawed human being."

"That's the way I always felt about Dennis, Annabelle," I said. "He wasn't perfect. But he was mine, and I loved him."

"I know, Althea. I know. That's what helped me make up my mind in the end. I've rewritten my will. I'm sure that Marv has left everything to me, as he truly had no one else in this world, and we'd always planned to leave everything to each other. We never got around to rewriting our wills to bequeath the violin collection while Marv was alive. I've had to change my will, since I originally intended to leave most of my estate to Marv, with a good deal of money and my personal violins and bows going to Dennis. Babe would have been the execu-trix, which she knows because I told her about my plans a long time ago. She also would have come into quite a bit of money from my family trust," Annabelle said. "Marv's death changed everything, though. I'm sure that Babe still expects me to leave Dennis the entire instru-ment collection as well as our houses and all of our as-sets, which are considerable, except what I would have left her, that is. As of several days ago, though, I changed my mind."

"I don't think you should discuss this with me or anyone, Annabelle," I said. "It's none of my business what you do with your possessions or your money."

"Well, that's where you're wrong," she said. "You see, I've thought long and hard about who could benefit the most from all the money, the properties, and the instruments that Marv and I spent our lives collecting. Would Dennis really benefit from unlimited funds, or would he simply use them to drink himself to death? Oh, don't worry. I'm leaving him a few very special violins, a gorgeous Strad and a famous Guarnerius that I hope he'll never be tempted to sell, and our beautiful house here and the one in Palm Desert to do with as he sees fit. He might decide to move there with his new wife and live in it once he sees it."

It wouldn't hurt him a bit to start over in a new place and give up his LA drinking buddies, I thought. *Perhaps those incredible instruments will inspire him to play again.*

"I want Dennis to be able to walk around our place in the California desert," Annabelle said. "It's an architectural gem we had built in the sixties full of wonderful art and first-edition books, and maybe it would help him understand on some level who his parents were. At least, that's my hope."

"What about the violin collection?" I asked.

"The remainder of the 'Marvin and Annabelle Pratt Collection' will be given to the Seattle Symphony, just as my husband would have wanted. That is, minus a certain Testore violin that I'm bequeathing to Andrew Litzky, along with a lovely Tourte bow that I know he'll adore. I've been thinking about what Marilyn Litzky was trying to do for her husband. It's no different than what you or I would have tried to do for ours if we were in her place. I'll never learn to like her because I distrust a certain type of perkiness in a grown woman, but I do, on another level, admire her."

"What about Ruth?" I said.

"What about her?" Annabelle said. "She and Stanley have gotten plenty of money from me over the years. I've been too stupid and too ashamed to admit to myself that those two have been bleeding me for more and more money as time went on, but all that's over now. I've made you my executrix, Althea. I'm sure Babe will be furious, but I really don't care anymore."

"Are you sure about this, Annabelle? I feel strange taking anything that should come to Dennis. After all, you're his mother. I'm just an ex-daughter-in-law," I said.

"Not to me, Althea. You're the one person besides Marv who ever really treated me as a friend. Plenty of people in LA fawned all over me because they wanted to get close to Marv and be part of his inner circle of first-call studio musicians. Not you. It was different with you. And I could see how much you loved my son and took care of him long after anyone else would have."

"Oh, Annabelle! Everyone loves you, and they always have, not just because of Marv or the work situation. You have to believe that. I would never lie to you about something so important."

"I'm also leaving you every bit of jewelry I own," Annabelle said. "It will look superb on you, and, if there's anything remotely resembling an afterlife, I will look down on you and feel happy, knowing that you're wearing something special from Marv and me. Don't you listen to Ruth, either. You're far from plain, Althea. You're adorable. Look at those dimples! Anyone who really knows you can see that you're beautiful inside and out. Now go, my darling, and enjoy your Christmas."

I was too stunned to object. I kissed Annabelle on the brow and somehow made my way down the corridor, blinded by my own tears, into the elevator, and outside to the parking garage. My head was swimming, and my nose was running; however, my mind was suddenly clear for the first time since the accident.

I got into my car, locked the door, and called Demetrious. His phone went right to voice mail, so I left a message. "Detective, this is Althea Stewart. I know this is Christmas, and I'm sure you're busy with your family, but I have to see you. I'm pretty sure I know who killed Marvin Pratt. The thing is I'm afraid that Annabelle's in danger, and I very well may be too."

Chapter 32

GRACE AND CONRAD left a note saying that they were going out to a movie. Of course. What else do people do on Christmas Day after the presents have been ripped open? Blanchard House was dark and empty at 4:30 in the afternoon, except for the animals and me. The Christmas lights were on a photoelectric cell, and they wouldn't go on until the daylight completely faded. Conrad's car was gone, so I parked next to Grace's BMW and hurried to unlock the front door and let the dogs out. Winnie and Bert were all wagging tails and big doggie smiles as they headed for the small ravine next to the house. I watched them run around doggie heaven, disappearing off and on among the holly bushes along the muddy streambed for a few minutes as I waited in the parking area for Harry Demetrius to drive over. The wind was picking up, and I was thoroughly chilled; however, I dreaded going inside that enormous, empty house more than enduring the cold.

Ten minutes later, to my great relief, a dark gray sedan pulled into the near darkness of the graveled lot. By now, my nerves were frayed. What if my suspicions were totally off base? My gut told me that they weren't, though. *Listen to your intuition*, I reminded myself. I hurriedly walked over to the car, expecting to see Harry Demetrious pop out.

"Hello, Althea. May I come in?" Ruth Littleton said as she shrugged herself out from behind the wheel of her gray rental car. "I feel just awful about our little set-to at the hospital this afternoon. I don't know what you must think of me. Annabelle's illness, Marv's death, it's been so stressful for all of us. Here," she said, holding out a small box of French bonbons in her leather-gloved hand. "These are for you, dear. Please take them along with my apologies for anything hurtful I may have said. You know that Stanley and I have always considered you to be a member of our family, even after the divorce."

I made no move to take the chocolates, backing away slightly as Ruth Littleton moved ever closer.

"Why don't we go inside, Althea? It's getting chilly out here, and I'm not as young as I used to be. A nice cup of tea would be lovely." Ruth Littleton at her full height was, even at her age, a good four or five inches taller than I was, and she must have outweighed me by at least sixty pounds. She'd been a strong tennis player and golfer all of her life, and it still showed.

"Really, Ruth, I can't go in yet. I'm waiting for someone. Thank you for the candy, though. It's very thoughtful of you. And don't you worry about this afternoon. I've forgotten all about it already," I told her, smiling slightly, trying to appear calm but watching obliquely over her shoulder for Demetrious's car to arrive. Where was he? What could be keeping him?

"Althea, you can't fool me. I know how clever you are, you and your psychology fixation. You always remember everything anyone says, and unfortunately, I said a few things this afternoon that I regret saying very much. I know you'll figure it all out sooner or later, if you haven't already, and I can't risk that." Ruth Littleton pulled a pearl-handled revolver from her pocket and pointed it at my stomach. "Open the door, Althea. It's teatime, and I really think you should have a chocolate or two with your tea. Now move!"

"Really, Ruth. Don't you think you're being a bit hasty here?" I said. My voice cracked slightly, and I hoped that Ruth wouldn't notice. I didn't want to give her the satisfaction of knowing that I was absolutely terrified. "I have no idea what you're talking about."

I backed up a little and tried to move away from the door. Ruth Littleton took another step forward and kept her gun pointed directly at me.

"Oh, please, Althea. What do you take me for? Do I look like a fool to you? Oliver Siddon made the very same mistake, and look at what happened to him. That idiot thought he could blackmail me, *me* of all people! Of course, he made it so easy for me, leaving Benaroya Hall during intermission and waiting politely on a crowded curb with all the other little lemmings."

"My God! You didn't!" I felt myself trembling all over now.

"Of course I did," Ruth said. Her voice was low and calm, almost a purr. *She's enjoying this*, I thought.

"The perfect opportunity presented itself, and I never hesitated for an instant," she said. "I enjoyed it. I'd wanted to do it for years. He's always been an obnoxious little twit. I've known him forever. Oliver Siddon's father was our butcher back in Michigan. I'll bet you didn't know that, did you, Miss Smarty-pants?"

It was all falling into place, the allusions Oliver Siddon had made to people we had in common, Annabelle's reference to Oliver and Babe growing up together in the Midwest, the "friend" he noticed at Benaroya Hall on the night of the concert. If only I'd paid attention to my intuition and tried to connect the dots long before this. I might have saved poor Oliver's life. I could still picture his crushed toupee lying in the middle of that busy street and felt a pang of regret. He'd never been a favorite of mine, but I certainly never wanted him to end up in a body bag.

"Clever little Oliver," Ruth said, "whose real name is Otto Schmidt—can you even imagine?—went away to Europe and came back with a fancy new handle and that phony accent and all those ridiculous mannerisms. He hoped that everyone would forget about where he'd come from, so I played along. I called him up out of the blue a few years ago. He was thrilled to hear from me. I flattered him and cultivated our 'old friendship' as soon as I knew Marvin and Annabelle were coming up to Seattle. He kept me informed of every move those two made. He just loved to gossip."

"But why did you kill him?" I asked, playing for time, hoping that Demetrious would be along any minute. What was taking him so long?

"Oh, he was a sly old thing, little Oliver," Ruth said. "As soon as he told me about the possibility of a trust, about Marv's priceless instruments going to the symphony, I knew I had to act ... and act quickly. He recognized me at a Town Hall piano recital and came scurrying over. He asked if I'd been invited to your tea party, being your former mother-in-law and all. It gave me an idea about how to get Marv out of the way, but Oliver put two and two together the minute he found out about the so-called accident."

Ruth waved the gun under my nose as she told her story. I hoped she had the safety on.

"He got it into that silly, bewigged head of his that Dennis was really Marv's son, not Stanley's, and that I must be Dennis's birth mother," Ruth said, "What a revolting concept! He insisted on meeting for lunch, all the while insinuating that I'd somehow killed Marv to ensure that the violin collection came to Dennis. He wanted a piece of the inheritance in exchange for his silence. Naturally, I had other ideas. If Annabelle hadn't offered me her symphony tickets, it could have gotten a lot messier, believe me." Ruth's unpleasant smile never reached her eyes. They were unimaginably cold.

"Enough chitchat, Althea," she said, giving me a rough shove. "Let's get inside and have that lovely tea. I don't know about you, but I'm parched."

My lips and mouth were certainly dry, but as I turned reluctantly toward the door, I managed one pathetic, nervous whistle. Out of the bushes rushed two enthusiastic dogs, both of them racing toward the front door, ready for dog dinner. Bert managed to run smack into Ruth Littleton at full speed, hitting her just behind the knees. The box of chocolates fell from Ruth's left hand, scattering candy on the frozen gravel. As she tried to regain her balance, I quickly stomped on her instep with the sharp high heel of my boot while I shoved her backward, almost crushing poor little Winnie under Ruth Littleton's generous frame as my former mother-in-law fell awkwardly to the ground. The gun slid from her gloved hand as Harry Demetrious finally pulled up, his headlights illuminating the scene. Just then the front porch of Blanchard House began to sparkle with twinkling white Christmas lights as the timer clicked on.

"Hold it right there!" Demetrious yelled, rushing from his vehicle, kicking the gun well away from Ruth as he ran and then standing directly over her, his own gun pointed at her head. After he grabbed Ruth Littleton by the wrist, he pulled her to her feet and pushed her over onto the hood of his gray Taurus. After he handcuffed her, recited her Miranda rights, and placed her in the car, he called for backup. He then used his shirttail to pick up the gun and dropped it into the plastic bag he'd fished out of his glove compartment.

Meanwhile, Winnie and Bert were anxiously milling around and sniffing the gravel.

"Don't eat those chocolates, you two!" I said in the firmest voice I could muster. "Leave them! They're bad for dogs." *These aren't that great for people, either*, I thought, carefully picking up each deadly piece and putting them back in their box. I got down on my hands and knees and felt around carefully in the semidarkness to make sure I had them all.

"My hero," I said, handing over the box of poisoned chocolates as I wobbled over to Demetrious. My adrenaline was receding, and my legs, so steady until now, began to shake uncontrollably. Or it might have been those deep blue eyes staring down at me as he put out an arm to steady me. Certainly, I looked up at Demetrious with gratitude but also with an unexpected wave of sexual desire. It was primitive, and I'd deny it if anyone asked me later, but at that moment, I'd have given myself to him then and there.

"Are you okay?" Demetrious asked. "You look a little pale."

"I'm fine now," I said. "You saved me."

"Your dogs saved you," he said. "I watched them knock the old lady over as I drove up."

"Don't ruin the moment," I said.

"Sorry," he said.

"I also think you should run those chocolates through the lab," I said. "You'll probably find them laced with the same poison that killed Marv Pratt."

I managed to open the front door of Blanchard House and let Winnie and Bert in. "What wonderful, clumsy dogs," I whispered into their ears as I knelt down and ran my fingers through their coats and rubbed my nose into their fur. "You are the best, most obedient, perfect dogs in the whole world, and you'll be getting the best belly rubs of your entire lives tonight, I promise." They seemed happy to hear it.

"Are you all right, Ms. Stewart?" Sergeant Matt Zeigler asked as he and another officer pulled up in a Kirkland Police cruiser a few minutes later. "Do you need to go to the hospital or talk to someone?"

I shook my head.

"You look a little shaky," Demetrious said. "Can I get you something?"

"I could use a whiskey," I said. "Maybe two. And hold the chocolate."

"I thought women like chocolate," he said.

"I used to," I said.

Chapter 33

"WHAT'S GOING ON?" Grace said, dropping her shoulder bag on a kitchen chair. "There are so many police cruisers in our driveway that we could hardly get into the house!" She and Conrad had just returned home from their afternoon at the movies. I was just taking the kettle off the stove and pouring boiling water into Grace's favorite teapot.

"What the hell happened here?" Conrad demanded. "Thea, are you okay?"

"Just a little shaken up, Conrad," I said. "And just the slightest bit tipsy. Grace, would you be kind enough to feed the animals their dinner? It's after five, and I'm sure they're hungry. Bert and Winnie saved my life tonight, so maybe they should get some turkey sausage too. They love turkey sausage."

"What do you mean they saved your life?" Grace said, coming over to me and putting a hand on my shoulder. "Saved it how? From what?"

"I'll tell you all about it right after the animals get their dinner and I pull myself together," I said. "So how was the movie?"

"Who cares? It was just a movie," Grace said, opening a can of cat food with a snap. "It sounds like the real drama happened right here."

"It was a pirate movie," Conrad said. "I've always liked pirates."

"Me too," I said as I attempted to pour tea for everyone. Conrad couldn't seem to take his eyes off the hot liquid splashing into the cups and the saucers too. Finally, he took the teapot out of my hands and motioned for me to sit. I obeyed.

I looked down and noticed that my hands had almost stopped shaking. The two shot glasses of whiskey I'd knocked back were working their magic. Conrad put out some of the fresh scones that Grace had made before they'd gone to the matinee. The dogs were happily chomping away at their kibble and turkey sausage. Lydia and Leopold seemed to be enjoying their smelly cat food as well. I was feeling woozy but cheerful.

"Okay," said Grace, seating herself at the table and leaning toward me. "Tell us everything. First of all, did you figure out who's responsible for the murder? Or murders—"

I tried to keep from giggling, but it was no use. God, I'm such a cheap drunk.

"It's such a cliché that I can't believe it myself," I said. "Didn't I always tell you that my mother-in-law was a killer?"

"You're kidding, right?" Grace said. "Ruth Littleton? What has she got to do with anything? I thought she lived in Michigan. What's she doing here?"

"She's Annabelle's old friend 'Babe,' if you can believe it. Babe Ruth! I still can't believe I didn't put that together. She killed Marv the night of our party, and she came here late this afternoon to kill me!" I said.

"No way!" Grace said. "How could it have been Ruth? She always liked me."

"Ha! She thought we were lesbians," I said.

Grace looked into my face this way and that. "Are you drunk?" she asked.

"I thought that much was obvious," I said. "Do you want to hear this or not?"

"You have no idea how much," she said.

"Well, then," I said. "I'm doing my best."

Conrad just sat there, quietly observing me, not touching his steaming tea. I took a deep breath before I began the story.

"Today, I learned that my ex-husband, Dennis, is the son of Annabelle and Marv Pratt," I said.

I could hear Grace's sharp intake of breath and saw Conrad's shocked expression. Here was a story he'd obviously never heard before and never even vaguely suspected. The room fell silent as the tale unfolded. No one interrupted until I'd finished explaining the entire history of Dennis Littleton's birth and adoption.

"But how did you figure out that Ruth killed Marvin Pratt?" Grace asked.

"Detective Demetrious said something yesterday that kept running through my head. He said that even the cleverest murderers sometimes say something that they later regret. Today at the hospital Ruth Littleton made just such a mistake, and the more I thought about it the surer I was that she'd never meant to say it and that she'd undoubtedly realize it herself sooner or later."

"What did she say?" Conrad asked.

"First, she mentioned that she'd been to the Symphony Saturday night, and I knew that much was true, because I saw her there. I wasn't absolutely certain that it was Ruth at the time, but it was her all right. In fact, I'm sure it was Ruth at St. Timmons Episcopal Church on Christmas Eve. She must have been staying at a hotel on the eastside, probably in Bellevue. She'd never have missed the Christmas Eve service because she'd been raised a strict Episcopalian."

"You never mentioned seeing her to me," Grace said.

"I wasn't sure it was her," I said. "Anyway, Ruth also mentioned that she'd attended Andre Kepner's Town Hall debut. Then I remembered reading the review of that piano recital in the Arts and Leisure section of the paper—only it happened two weeks ago. Annabelle distinctly told me that Ruth had come to Seattle to be with her after learning of the accident, but I knew for certain that the Kepner recital had taken place at least a week before our party. The reviewer was very witty, you see, and I'd enjoyed reading about it so much that I'd cut it out of the paper and saved it. I still have the article somewhere on my desk."

"That's funny," said Conrad. "I almost drove in from Whidbey Island to hear that very recital."

"It's a small world," I said.

"That's so weird," Grace said. "So she was the friend Annabelle told you about. You might have figured things out sooner if she'd called her friend 'Ruth' rather than 'Babe.' Babe Ruth. What a stupid nickname."

"I don't think Annabelle wanted anybody to figure things out," I said, "especially Marv, so she'd always called Ruth 'Babe.'"

"I hope they have a good softball team at the women's federal penitentiary," Grace said.

"Not me," I said. "I hope she rots. And no, it's not my highest self, but I've been drinking."

"Completely understandable," Conrad said.

"So that's it?" Grace said. "You guessed just from that?"

"Not exactly," I said. I explained about Dennis's birthday being the numeric code for everything the Pratts' owned. "I'd been wracking my brains, trying to figure out how Marv could have been poisoned.

Suddenly, I knew. I remembered that Marv and Annabelle had touch-pad, keyless entry panels installed on all their cars. Annabelle was forever locking herself out of the car when they lived in Beverly Hills, and Marv would have to come rescue her time and time again from the Saks parking lot or from her hairdresser's. He finally decided to make it impossible for her to lock herself out anymore."

"Oh, my God!" Grace said. "Anyone who knew the code could get in and out of the Pratts' house or their cars at will. Ruth must have known about the security code, and certainly her son's birth date wasn't something she'd easily forget."

"Right," I said. "Annabelle had confided in Ruth Littleton for years. She'd told her best friend everything, even about their plans to come to the Christmas Tea at Blanchard House. Oliver Siddon confirmed it, so Ruth knew exactly when and where the Pratts would be that night."

"Ruth must have been well aware that Marv was a compulsive eater," Grace said. "All Ruth Littleton had to do was place a few poisoned chocolate bonbons on the console of Marv's car while our party was in progress, and Marv would eventually eat them. It's really pretty diabolical."

"And all of Annabelle's friends know that she's allergic to chocolate," I said, "so Ruth could be fairly confident that as long as the poison was concealed in chocolates, no one in that car but Marv was going to touch them."

"Perhaps Ruth planned it so the blame would fall on us, Althea," Grace said. "It would look as though someone poisoned Marv at our tea."

"Someone did," I said.

"What about motive?" Conrad asked.

"Oh, she had that in spades. Or violins," I said. I explained about the planned bequest of the violin collection and Marilyn Litzky's unsuccessful quest to regain Andrew's lost instrument.

"Wow!" Grace said. "No wonder Andrew was upset. Good-bye Testore."

"Exactly," I said. "At any rate, Marv Pratt had no heirs other than Annabelle. Once Annabelle confided in Ruth that she was seriously ill, Ruth knew that she had to act right away. Annabelle had been assuring Ruth all along that she'd be leaving almost everything she had to Dennis with Ruth as beneficiary."

"Annabelle is seriously ill?" Conrad asked, sitting up straight and looking me directly in the eyes. "With what?"

I took a deep breath. "Acute leukemia," I said. "Annabelle didn't want anyone to find out, especially Marv, but she told Ruth. And me."

Conrad looked away and shook his head.

"That's what you meant the other night, wasn't it?" Grace said.

"Yeah," I said. "I think you're going to be taking care of Leopold from now on, Grace. Annabelle is just too sick to cope anymore."

"I don't mind at all. I love that little cat," Grace said, "but I feel awful about Annabelle."

"May I have some more tea please?" I asked. "My throat is so dry."

Grace poured me a cup across the table and sat back down, chin cupped in her hands.

"What about Oliver Siddon? Was Ruth responsible for that too?" Conrad asked. "I never liked the guy, but that's a hell of a way to go. From violin dealer to roadkill."

I once more pictured Oliver's shaggy toupee lying on the dark street like a dead animal and shuddered.

"You mean Otto Schmidt?" I said. "That's his real name it turns out. Oh, yeah, Ruth took care of Oliver too. He'd guessed some of the story, you see, but he'd gotten it wrong. He thought Ruth had actually given birth to Marv's illegitimate son all those years ago and had been hiding the secret from everyone, including Annabelle. He was off on the wrong track about that, but he'd still put two and two together and came up with Ruth for the murder of Marvin Pratt. He'd been trying to blackmail her."

"That was a pretty foolish thing to attempt, especially since he believed she'd already committed murder," Grace said. "When were you sure that Ruth was the killer?"

"I wasn't completely convinced until the moment she stepped out of the car at Blanchard House. What could she possibly have come here for, I asked myself, and how did Ruth know exactly where I lived? We'd both left the hospital only a short while before, yet here she was on our doorstep with a box of chocolates and a phony apology. I knew then that she must have been here at Blanchard House before this afternoon, and I was suddenly positive that it was the night of the tea, the night she placed the poisoned chocolates in the Pratts' car. I suppose the picture first began coming into sharper focus at the hospital, though."

Conrad hadn't said much until now. He got up and put his hand gently on my shoulder. "I think you did a remarkable job of putting the pieces together, Althea," he said. "According to Detective Demetrious, the DA was convinced that Annabelle had poisoned her husband and was hoping for a murder-suicide kind of thing. Who else had access to the car and knew his habits? Quite honestly, it's usually the husband or wife they suspect first in murder cases like these."

"Annabelle would never hurt anyone," Grace said. "How could anyone believe she was guilty of murder?"

"You'd be surprised how many murders are committed by people whose friends and neighbors swear that they're the nicest folks in the world," Conrad said. "Last time Demetrious and I spoke, he told me that they were prepared to investigate Annabelle as soon as she was

well enough to stand up to questioning, but now I'm
hearing that she'll never be well enough for that. Still,
the state would have pursued the case, and her name
would always have been linked to the unsolved crime.
You saved Annabelle from all of that, Althea, and you
probably saved her life."

"Do you think Ruth meant to kill Annabelle too?"
Grace asked. "Why would she do that if she knew
Annabelle was dying? All she had to do was wait."

"That was true right up until this afternoon," I said.
"Annabelle had a change of heart, you see. She ex-
pressed her desire to see her son before she dies and to
tell him the truth about his birthparents. Ruth looked horrified and said some terrible things to Annabelle in an
attempt to talk her out of it. The thing is, Ruth couldn't
hide the contempt she felt for Annabelle, had probably
always felt, and I was suddenly able to see her for what
she was: a grasping, angry woman who would do anything to get what she wanted."

"Do you think she would have killed Annabelle just
to shut her up?" Grace asked.

"Annabelle had also made a point of saying in front
of Ruth that she considered me her real daughter," I said.
"I saw the look on Ruth's face as she assessed the possible consequences of that remark. Ruth had already
killed once. What was to stop her from murdering
Annabelle before her 'best friend' had a chance to tell
Dennis the truth or make another will, perhaps not solely

in Dennis's and her favor? I didn't realize until it was almost too late that Ruth might consider getting me out of the way to be in her best interest as well. If Winnie and Bert hadn't knocked her over, she might have succeeded."

"Here, have a glass of water to wash these down," Conrad said, handing me some aspirins and a full water glass. "You're going to feel like hell in a little while unless you do."

"I feel okay," I said, "just a little sleepy."

"Drink," he said in his no-nonsense voice.

I did.

"You must be exhausted, Althea," Grace said. "I think you should get your pajamas on and let me bring you a nice hot dinner in bed. How about some lovely roast chicken? I can have it ready in just over an hour, or are you back on the tofu and vegetables again? I never know with you. I can do a vegetarian stir-fry in twenty minutes."

"No thanks, Grace," I said. "Not unless you're willing to chew it for me, but I appreciate the offer."

My legs still felt a little wobbly, but somehow I made it upstairs to the bedroom, tugged off my clothes, and fell into bed. Lydia jumped up onto my chest and rubbed her little cat face against my chin. The last thing I remembered was feeling two cold, wet noses pressing against my outstretched hand as I whispered over and over, "What good dogs. What good, good dogs."

Chapter 34

JANUARY IS ALMOST over. My students, all twenty-four of them, gave a duo recital last week at the Kirkland Woman's Club, and it went better than expected. Annabelle is still hanging on. I go to the hospital every day, and Grace and Conrad have started coming too. It won't be long now, I'm afraid. Dennis received a letter from Annabelle's attorney explaining his parentage, but he never responded. He's become an angry, unforgiving kind of guy, but I wish he could learn to put his anger aside and think of someone beside himself for once, before it's too late.

Ruth Littleton has been charged with two counts of first-degree murder and one count of attempted murder. For someone who was worried about tearing her family apart, she's sure done a bang-up job of it all by herself.

Conrad has moved into one of our guest rooms for an indeterminate stay. I think he feels that he's protecting Grace and me, and perhaps he is. We all love him, and the animals are delighted to spend time with him every day, especially Leopold and Lydia, who nap with him in the afternoons.

Grace has seen very little of Emile Girard by mutual agreement; however, he sends her armloads of flowers, and they've been exchanging letters. He's told Conrad that he's working on getting a divorce as quickly as possible. Poor Grace seems to be standing with one foot on the dock and one in a small boat, off-balance and fragile. Still, a number of cello students have started coming to her for lessons, and she seems to be enjoying the work.

As for me, I'm just taking things as they come for the time being. I hadn't seen Harry Demetrious since he arrested my former mother-in-law at Blanchard House on Christmas Day, so I was surprised when the doorbell rang this morning and I saw him standing on the front porch of Blanchard House. Winnie and Bert rushed out to greet him, circling his ankles and sniffing his trouser legs as soon as I opened the door.

"May I come in?" he said. "I thought I should drop by and update you on the case that almost got you killed."

"Thanks," I said. "So is this an official visit?"

"Not really," Demetrious said, "but it's as good a reason as any to see you again. I was hoping, if you're not too busy right now, that you'd come out for coffee with me."

"As it happens," I said, "Conrad and Grace and I are just about to sit down to breakfast. French toast and scrambled eggs. Come join us. I know they'd love to hear about whatever the police found out, too."

"Yes, they probably would, but would I enjoy telling them as much as I'd enjoy telling just little old you?" he said.

"You haven't tasted our version of French toast," I said. "It's stuffed with cream cheese and marmalade. It'll be worth your while."

"Will you be there?" he asked.

"Yup," I said.

"You've talked me into it," he said.

"Wait, I have something for you, detective." I stepped over to the coatrack and stuck my arm up to the elbow into the cavernous reaches of my leather shoulder bag. "Here," I said, presenting him with the sadly disheveled package containing the medieval murder mystery that I'd been carrying around since Christmas. "By the way," I said, looking up into those piercing blue-gray eyes, "what took you so long?"

"I've been pretty busy, but here I am," he said. "Why? Did you miss me?"

"Don't flatter yourself," I said. "I meant what took you so long on Christmas Day after I called you and told you my suspicions about Ruth. I almost got shot out there."

"Sorry, ma'am," he drawled. "Seriously, I was volunteering at a soup kitchen on Capitol Hill just like I do every Christmas. I'd been there since early in the morning, and I was just doing cleanup when I got your call. Believe me ... I raced over to you as fast as I could."

"What about your family?" I said, my heart beating a little too fast. "Don't they miss you on Christmas Day?"

"My family?" he said. "Hmm. Well, there isn't a whole lot going on there. My folks are in their seventies. We exchange presents on Christmas Eve and have a glass of champagne. Then they go to bed. My sister, Iris, lives in Brooklyn with her deadbeat husband and two kids, so I'm kind of on my own. Anything else you want to know?"

"I guess that'll do for now," I said.

"So what's in here?" he asked, holding up the small mystery book in its frayed Christmas wrapping and shaking it several times.

"A thirty-six-inch plasma TV," I told him. "Just add water."

The End

Unstrung
Discussion Questions

1. Early in this mystery we are introduced to Althea Stewart's passion and avocation: psychology. As every amateur sleuth knows, crime—and especially any "delicious" murder—relies on means, motive, and opportunity. In what ways do motive and suspects intersect? How does Althea make use of her understanding of human nature to organize the pieces of this particular puzzle?

2. Several "minor characters" are introduced in this first Blanchard House Mystery and they act as important catalysts that move events forward. How would you identify, and describe them? How would you assess what drives them to act as they do? We all have a back-story, and as we get to know these characters we are given a glimpse into their thought processes. What pivotal actions in the story do these processes trigger?

3. Althea and her best friend Grace share many similarities in that they are gracious party organizers,

professional musicians, currently single, old friends, and recent transplants to the Seattle area. There are, however, essential differences in their respective coping strategies, general outlooks on life, temperaments, as well as character strengths and weaknesses. In some ways they complete each other, and in other ways these differences present challenges to being housemates and business partners. How does their friendship serve to provide mutual support under stressful circumstances?

4. Companion animals play an important role in Althea's life. How we relate to animals—and they to us—gives us a certain type of insight into human ethics, priorities, and sense of responsibility. Several animals in this novel are crucial to the plot in ways both overt and subtle. What insights do they provide into the essential characters of the humans who interact with them?

5. This mystery connects generations and reaches back in time as well as place. There is foreshadowing, the reinvention of several characters over the decades, and the inevitable changes in relationships which occur over time. Certain personalities evolve morally as others around them resist change or even regress. Are these arcs of personal development or stagnation apparent in the story? How is personal growth revealed in the characters? What choices are personality-driven?

6. Families and relationships. Some are inescapable and haunt us to the end of our days. What notions of responsibility and obligations, expectations, and familial encumbrances do we see in this mystery that encourage the characters to act in ways that are satisfying and/or problematic for them?

> For more information about the author go to:
> www.cynthiamorrowmysteries.com and read
> "Interview With Cynthia Morrow."

Continue reading for a preview of
the next novel in the **Blanchard House Mystery** series

Domestic Violins

Chapter 1

MY SUPERSTITIOUS SCOTTISH grandmother once told me that the dead smile one last time if it rains on the day of their burial.

The late Annabelle Gardner Pratt must have been grinning from ear to ear. Her lengthy funeral cortege splashed its way through the rain-soaked streets of Kirkland, Washington on a dark Monday morning in early March after a relatively short service at Saint Timmons Episcopal Church. My name is Althea Stewart, friend and former daughter-in-law of the deceased, and, just my luck, the person designated by Annabelle to give the eulogy. She'd left detailed instructions about the entire affair, starting with the music. This was only to be expected, since Annabelle Pratt had been a first-class violinist.

When I was initially told in no uncertain terms by Annabelle herself that I was to write an unaccompanied viola piece to perform for her funeral, I quite naturally balked. A few weeks later, struggling to accept the inevitable—that I would soon be losing my dear friend to her exhausting battle with acute leukemia—I reluctantly buckled down to focus on the task at hand and came up with a lilting adagio. I then offered to bring my viola and play it for her in the hospital, but she said no thanks— she'd rather be surprised at the funeral. That's the kind of goofy optimism that made the thought of losing Annabelle so darned hard in the first place.

She'd also requested that my best friend, colleague, and housemate Grace Sullivan sing Schubert's "Ave Maria" before the eulogy just to kick things off. Now, anyone who had ever heard Grace's thrilling, almost otherworldly soprano already knew that the entire con-gregation would undoubtedly be weeping within the first thirty seconds, and so it went. Grace, ever beautiful in her black St. John suit and black lace mantilla over long, golden-brown curls, brought the crowd to tears and racking sobs and then modestly sat back down in the front pew, leaving me to cope with a sniffling, nose-honking churchful of mourners.

Had Annabelle Pratt been buried at Forest Lawn Cemetery in Burbank, California, as she rightfully should have been, every musician in Hollywood would have turned up to see her off. She'd been a well-known and generally revered violinist who'd made her mark in the film studios for almost fifty years. Her late husband Marvin Pratt had been a less-liked, somewhat infamous concertmaster in Los Angeles before they both retired and moved up to Seattle. His murder, only a few weeks before Christmas of this last year, had shaken up all of our lives, even those of us who had unhesitatingly stuck him in the "nuisance" category.

As it was, I found myself standing there on a sopping wet Monday morning in March at Saint Timmons Episcopal, looking out at a sea of tear-stained—and, for the most part, surprisingly familiar—faces. I smoothed my long black skirt and pulled the sleeves of my black cashmere turtleneck sweater down to cover my wrists, a nervous gesture I thought I'd outgrown but obviously hadn't, while taking a measure of the crowd. There were local musicians, quite a few members of the Seattle Symphony, and freelancers and music teachers like myself and Grace who'd known Annabelle Pratt from Los Angeles. There were also dozens of friends and colleagues who'd flown in from LA, Cleveland, Boston, and New York for the funeral. I knew the entire LA musical mafia well, having been one of that select coterie of recording musicians myself until a little over three years ago when I moved up to Kirkland, a Seattle suburb, after a rather painful divorce. My ex-husband, Annabelle's son Dennis Littleton, was sitting stiffly in the first pew next to my replacement, his second wife, Simone. This was my first chance to get a good look at her, but there wasn't that much to see. Simone was a tanned and fit California blonde in her late thirties, sedately garbed in a navy-blue Donna Karan suit and large pearls. She seemed pretty enough, I thought, in an athletic sort of way. Of course, Dennis was the real looker in that couple or practically any couple: a tall, blond god with a drinking problem who used to play excellent violin. He'd left me one day with no explanation whatsoever, and then proceeded to marry Simone the day after our divorce was final. On the bright side, he was her problem now.

I don't really remember actually giving the eulogy, although I'd written it painstakingly and rehearsed it in front of my bedroom mirror for several days prior to the funeral. Now that the dreaded moment had arrived, the words themselves seemed to float out of me in a strangely disembodied fashion. I don't remember playing the viola piece either, although many of my fellow musicians assured me afterward that it went well and was extremely moving. Honestly, though, "Twinkle, Twinkle, Little Star" would have made everyone weepy after Grace got through singing it. My thoughts were, for the most part, consumed by memories of my last few weeks with Annabelle, a beautiful woman of seventy, a grande dame until the very end. I'd visited her every day in the hospital for the last three months, and we'd grown closer than ever before during that time. I fingered the magnificent half-carat diamond earrings she'd given me just before her death, the ones she usually wore, and felt her comforting presence all around me. Perhaps she'd heard her viola piece after all.

Our mutual friend Conrad Bailey, a gruff cream puff of seventy-something, was sitting up straight in the front pew, looking unusually well put together in his dark-gray suit and knitted tie, his wiry salt-and-pepper hair pulled into a smooth ponytail, quite a change from his usual plaid woolen shirt and baggy jeans. Conrad, an internationally acclaimed pianist who'd always had a thing for Annabelle, had arranged for six strong, younger men to act as pallbearers. At the end of the service I looked sharply to the left and couldn't believe what I was seeing. Six gallant gentlemen, two of them horribly familiar, stepped out of their respective pews and headed toward the flower-strewn casket at the front of the altar. One was Emile Girard, a darkly handsome bassist with the Seattle Symphony, a man who was as completely infatuated with my friend Grace as she was with him, currently separated from his unfaithful harridan of a wife and actively seeking a divorce. He and Grace hadn't run into each other since their unexpected meeting at a service in this very church on Christmas Eve. They'd experienced one of those rare "love at first sight" moments, the kind therapists warn us against. I was hoping that this time would be the exception that proves the rule. They'd mutually decided not to see anything of each other until Emile's divorce was final in order to avoid temptation. It hadn't been easy for them, but Grace had been standing firm. One look now at her stunned expression said it all. Emile's presence at Annabelle's funeral was a complete surprise to Grace, and one she wasn't completely happy about.

The other fellow—and here was where it got a bit sticky for me—was Detective Harry Demetrious, Kirkland PD, as sexy a detective as the law allowed. It was Harry Demetrious who'd been assigned to Marvin Pratt's murder case, and ever since we'd met during the investigation we'd flirted wildly, but nothing much had come of it. He'd arrived at Blanchard House one morning in late January, ostensibly to tell me about the wrap-up of the murder investigation. He'd joined Grace, Conrad, and me for breakfast and intimated that he wanted to see me again. Well, here we were in March, and I hadn't seen hide or hair of him since then. I'd awakened in a sweat more than once because of those dark-blue eyes and mischievous dimples, but by now I felt resigned to the sad truth—that our initial attraction had come to a dead end—so I was more than a little surprised by that familiar adrenaline rush as Demetrious glided silently by.

No one is expected to look his best gripping a casket. I would imagine that it's a fairly awkward business. Still, I couldn't help but notice those heavy shoulder and arm muscles rippling beneath his dark suit jacket as he easily hoisted his end of the brass bar, and I thought—in a purely objective sort of way, of course—that he looked pretty darned good. For the briefest moment I imagined him naked to the waist, a dutiful bronzed slave carrying

my palanquin through the bustling marketplaces of
Rome. I felt an immediate tug of guilt for allowing my
mind to wander so inappropriately during my friend's
funeral, but there you have it, the duality of the psyche in
all its fickle splendor. *I'm only human,* I told myself.

What the hell was Conrad thinking, anyway, inviting
these two men to act as pallbearers? Had Seattle run out
of trombonists? Harry Demetrious hadn't made himself a
favorite of Annabelle's, I'm afraid, due to his role as the
heavy during her husband's murder investigation, and
Emile Girard had, as far as I knew, never even met the
woman. They did fill the bill nicely in the brawn department, though. I'd have to give Conrad that much, and
Annabelle would probably have enjoyed knowing that
she'd had two of the best-looking men in Seattle carrying
her down the aisle. I glanced over at Conrad and
scowled, and he returned the look with a huge grin and a
theatrical wink. Men!